K

"I think we can drop the 'Mr. and Mrs.' business now," Jillian said.

"Well, actually…" Devlin gave her a lazy grin from across the hotel room. "I've been wondering if we couldn't keep that going—at least for tonight."

Jillian stared at him, and her heart began to flutter. What had she gotten herself into? *Don't ever go anywhere with a stranger.* Three-year-old kids knew better than to do what she'd done.

"Jillian. I'm not the big bad wolf."

Devlin's deep voice made her blink. His amused tone turned her panic button down a notch or two. "I didn't think you were," she replied.

She knew she was less than convincing. Devlin apparently thought so, too, because he smiled widely and shook his head.

"Yes, you did," he murmured, and his smile faded. "And maybe you're right…."

Dear Reader,

Our lead title this month hardly needs an introduction, nor does the author. Nora Roberts is a multiple *New York Times* bestseller, and *Megan's Mate* follows her extremely popular cross-line miniseries THE CALHOUN WOMEN. Megan O'Riley isn't a Calhoun by birth, but they consider her and her young son family just the same. And who better to teach her how to love again than longtime family friend Nate Fury?

Our newest cross-line miniseries is DADDY KNOWS LAST, and this month it reaches its irresistible climax right here in Intimate Moments. In *Discovered: Daddy*, bestselling author Marilyn Pappano finally lets everyone know who's the father of Faith Harper's baby. Everyone, that is, except dad-to-be Nick Russo. Seems there's something Nick doesn't remember about that night nine months ago!

The rest of the month is terrific, too, with new books by Marion Smith Collins, Elane Osborn, Vella Munn and Margaret Watson. You'll want to read them all, then come back next month for more of the best books in the business—right here at Silhouette Intimate Moments.

Enjoy!

Leslie Wainger
Senior Editor and Editorial Coordinator

Please address questions and book requests to:
Silhouette Reader Service
U.S.: 3010 Walden Ave., P.O. Box 1325, Buffalo, NY 14269
Canadian: P.O. Box 609, Fort Erie, Ont. L2A 5X3

HONEYMOON WITH A HANDSOME STRANGER

ELANE OSBORN

Published by Silhouette Books
America's Publisher of Contemporary Romance

ISBN 0-373-07748-3

HONEYMOON WITH A HANDSOME STRANGER

This edition published by arrangement with Harlequin Books S.A.

Printed in U.S.A.

Books by Elane Osborn

Silhouette Intimate Moments

Shelter in His Arms #642
Honeymoon with a Handsome Stranger #748

ELANE OSBORN

is a daydream believer whose active imagination tends to intrude on her life at the most inopportune moments. Her penchant for slipping into "alternative reality" severely hampered her work life, leading to a gamut of jobs that includes, but is not limited to: airline reservation agent, waitress, salesgirl and seamstress in the wardrobe department of a casino showroom. In writing she has discovered a career that not only does not punish flights of fancy, it demands them. Drawing on her daydreams, she has published three historical romance novels and is now using the experiences she has collected in her many and varied jobs in the "real world" to fuel contemporary stories that blend romance and suspense.

To Mom and Dad—for all the trips to the library, to the mountains and to the sea that fueled my imagination. And for your love and for your faith in me.

Prologue

"Bloody hell!"

The two words, softly spoken, echoed through the deserted room, bouncing off the polished mahogany bar.

The muted hum of Saturday afternoon traffic, punctuated with the *clang-clang* of a cable car, brought the unmistakable sounds of San Francisco into the authentic British pub interior of Ale's Well That Ends Well.

The owner stood behind the bar. In front of him, the *San Francisco Chronicle* lay open to the personal advertisement section. Impatient fingers dug through the thick hair waving onto his forehead as he frowned down at the newspaper.

The tiny ad seemed to leap out at him. *To M.D.S.C. "'The time has come,' the walrus said." Immediately, if not sooner. M.C.S.C.*

The message could only be from Colin. No one else would use that particular quote from *Alice in Wonderland* in combination with that set of initials.

He'd begun to think he'd never see these words, actually hoped he would never see them, because they meant he would have to go home.

Home.

His eyes narrowed. The only time England was home to him these days was when he was putting on his show, telling the customers about "jolly olde England" to heighten the atmosphere he'd developed in each of the eight pubs he'd set up in as many years.

Now he'd have go back and deal with the past. Immediately, if not sooner.

He glanced at his watch. Four in the afternoon. He normally read the newspaper much earlier in the day, but the first several weeks of opening a new pub were particularly hectic. Today there'd been a problem with the new brewing equipment in the morning, followed by a large lunch crowd to delay the daily ritual he'd followed for the past twelve years. It wasn't until the lull between late lunchers and the after-work rush that he'd had a chance to check the personals column.

Tightening his jaw, he stepped toward the end of the bar. He knew there was an evening flight. After a few carefully vague words of explanation to his partner, he'd throw a few things into a tote and be on his way.

Chapter 1

She couldn't believe it. This was the craziest thing she'd ever done.

No, Jillian Gibson reminded herself, this was the *only* crazy thing she'd ever done.

Adjusting the shoulder strap of her oversize leather purse, Jillian glanced at the two tickets from San Francisco to London clutched in her fingers. Her sister, Holly, speaking with her years of experience as a travel agent, had assured Jillian that she should have no trouble cashing in on her trip insurance, given the circumstances.

Something twisted in Jillian's stomach at the thought. She couldn't bear to do that. Every other part of her carefully constructed plan for today, as well as her entire future, had been destroyed. The next three weeks was all she had left. She was going to see *this* dream fulfilled, no matter how crazy or obsessive her actions might look to others.

There were just one or two details that might trip her up.

Jillian's jaw tensed as she shifted her weight from one

foot to the other in an attempt to control her rising impatience. On the other side of the counter a blond and bronzed young man was staring at his computer screen. The talking, laughing, arguing cluster of people in line behind her muffled the tapping of the ticket agent's fingers on his keyboard.

Above the persistent din rose a high-pitched, painfully polite voice. "Sir, I have already informed you two times that there are no tickets to be purchased on the next flight to London. Not at any price. Not even in first class. I don't care *how* much you are prepared to pay."

The woman's tone sent annoyance skittering up Jillian's spine and drew her glance to her left. A female ticket agent with dark auburn hair pulled tightly back into a ponytail stared over her computer monitor at the passenger standing two feet from Jillian.

"No seats available on the wing, I take it?" a deep voice asked.

After a pause in which the ticket agent registered no reaction to his attempt at levity, the man spoke again. "Well, love, I know I've already explained that I have just learned of a family emergency in London. Are you sure there isn't *something* you might do for me?"

The man's words were only slightly accented with British inflection, but it was enough to make Jillian look at him. She regretted this immediately. The moment her eyes fell on the tall, lean figure in the brown leather bomber jacket, a curious, searing pain twisted through her chest.

She'd suffered this identical reaction when she'd taken the place directly behind this man in the ticket line. His dark hair and chiseled profile had, at first glance, looked so much like Brett Turner's that for one tiny moment she'd forgotten that it would be impossible for Brett to be there.

"Mrs. Turner? Mrs. *Turner.*"

The heavily emphasized name brought Jillian's attention back to the clerk in front of her. She was *not* Mrs. Turner, she wanted to scream. However, screaming was not how she handled things, so she tightened her grip on the ticket and gave the man her full attention.

"First-class tickets *are* refundable," he informed her with a taut smile. "If Mr. Turner is not going to make the flight, I can send his ticket to our accounting office, and they will reimburse him by mail. We *never* refund cash here. I'm sorry if your travel agent told you otherwise."

Her travel agent had done no such thing. Holly had warned her that the airline would react this way, but Jillian had thought it was worth a try to ask.

Well, it didn't work, a small voice whispered. *It's time to start behaving logically. Apply for the refund, and cut your losses.*

Every muscle in Jillian's body stiffened. Cut her losses? She'd already lost everything, all the money she'd so carefully saved, her well-planned future, and worse, any faith she'd ever had in her own instincts. She was not going to give up on this chance to revisit a place she'd been in love with since the age of eight.

Her mind raced past the cautionary voice that had always been her guide. She was too close to her goal to give up now. Her hotel accommodations were prepaid and she had her BritRail pass to get her around the country. The only sticking point was the fact that Brett was to have brought the traveler's checks, and since he wasn't here, she had less than one hundred dollars in her tote to cover three weeks' worth of food, tips and taxi fare.

A credit card would be invaluable in this situation, but Granny Weston's old-fashioned values and Jillian's experiences with bank customers overburdened by credit card debt, had kept her on a cash only basis. Her single other asset, besides the extra plane ticket, was the set of wedding bands in her purse, which she had brought along with the idea of throwing them into the Thames.

The part of her that had conceived this uncharacteristically emotional gesture conceded that she might pawn them instead, but Jillian didn't think they were likely to bring too much. Perhaps she could somehow sweet-talk this fellow into refunding even *part* of Brett's first-class ticket....

"*And* if Mr. Turner is not going to be joining you," the ticket agent said pointedly, "we would like to know that now. This flight is overbooked. We could use his seat."

Jillian stared at the clerk. Sweet-talk this android? What was she thinking? Flirting was an activity totally foreign to her, having spent the past eighteen of her twenty-eight years in far more practical pursuits. So, maybe she should listen to the voice of reason, the one that had whispered all along that Brett Turner had been too good to be true, the one that now suggested she should just turn in both tickets and abandon this insane idea completely.

It wasn't as if a visit to England were going to suddenly change her life, after all. That had been done completely and irrevocably several hours earlier. The only thing this trip might do was return the sense of control she'd once prided herself on.

"Well, I *could* put you on the standby list."

The barely veiled reluctance in the female ticket agent's voice broke into Jillian's thoughts. She glanced to her left as the woman continued, "But I must inform you, sir, that this flight is overbooked. There's little chance you'll get on."

"I'm willing to take my chances, miss," the man replied. "If you will be so kind as to make note of my name? Devlin Sinclair."

Devlin Sinclair's words had been spoken in the most polite of British accents, sending tingles up Jillian's spine. The hint of steel in his voice added a distinct chill to that sensation. Jillian glanced at him sharply. The smile curving his wide mouth appeared politely bland. His hands rested open palmed on the counter. Still, Jillian sensed a banked fury in the man.

She shifted her attention to the woman on the other side of the counter. The clerk seemed blissfully unaware of the effect her words were having on her customer.

"All right," the woman said as she tapped on her keyboard. "Devon Sinclair."

"No. Dev*lin*."

The woman shrugged, as if to say that this minor misspelling didn't matter, given his chances of getting on the flight.

Jillian waited for the man to explode. When he said nothing, she released her breath. She was being silly. Her attempts to control the hollow ache in her chest as her wedding day collapsed around her had apparently made her hypersensitive, inflaming an imagination accustomed to being held carefully in check.

The man standing next to her was no doubt annoyed by the treatment he was receiving, but it was ridiculous for her to think that he would assault the agent for her less-than-caring attitude, any more than she was likely to reach across and slap the clerk who was "helping" her.

"Mrs. Turner?" the man behind the counter demanded with little-disguised impatience. "What will it be? Will your husband be joining you, or can we sell his seat?"

As Jillian watched the Englishman step away from the counter, her mind raced madly down heretofore uncharted paths. She looked at the large rectangular watch, held on to her wrist with a worn brown leather strap. Eight-fifteen. The flight was due to depart in forty minutes. She still had time to decide.

The sound of the ticket agent clearing his throat impatiently pulled her attention back to the cold eyes above his oh-so-polite smile. The voice in her head that had been urging caution was silenced by her sudden desire to exact some kind of revenge on officious clerks who treated all and sundry with such uncaring civility.

"I'm not really sure," she replied at last. "There's a slight chance that Brett might be able to make it. Go ahead and check *me* in for the flight, though. I'll get out of line and wait a bit. If he doesn't show, I'll just go on to the gate, and have the agent there release his seat."

Moments later the strap of Jillian's oversize purse was digging into her shoulder, her tan all-weather coat was flapping from the crook of her elbow and her heart was racing as she hurried down the terminal after the man in the leather jacket.

What she was about to do was insane, she told herself. It wasn't like her to make snap decisions. She was a planner, a strategist. She thought things out, weighed her options carefully, played it safe.

And a little over two hours ago it had appeared that her plans were about to bear perfect fruit. She had been about to marry Brett Turner, a man who'd somehow managed to both sweep her off her very sensible feet and at the same time hold out the promise of the secure future she so craved.

All this became a cruel mockery when the person who was to be Brett's best man, the vice president of the company they both worked for, arrived at the old Victorian house in which she and her three sisters had grown up. The house where a small contingent of guests waited in her grandmother's carefully tended garden for Jillian to walk toward the white arch entwined with pink roses.

Between her boss, Roger Williams, and Agent Carter of the FBI, she'd learned that all the romance and all the plans Brett had offered for the future had been elaborate lies, lies that robbed her of everything she'd worked for, every dream she'd ever had.

Except for this trip.

Jillian's fingers tightened on the shoulder strap of her purse as she neared the swiftly walking man in the leather jacket. Taking a breath to fill her laboring lungs, she called out the name she'd overheard at the ticket counter.

"Mr. Sinclair!"

The man stopped and turned. Under the scrutiny of his narrowed eyes, she closed the five-foot distance between them.

"I need to speak with you," she said.

His eyes, a deep shade of blue, sharpened with suspicion. His dark eyebrows met in a frown.

"Do I know you?" he asked.

His tone lacked the courteous lilt that had colored his words while dealing with the ticket agent. The anger Jillian had sensed in him at the counter had surfaced, sculpting such harsh lines in his face that a startled breath caught in her throat as she gazed up at the barely controlled fury in his dark eyes.

She uttered, "I'm sorry," and turned to walk away.

"No, *I'm* sorry," he said in a deep voice, and with a firm grip on her elbow pulled her back around.

The man's grim expression had softened slightly, and though his sharp features still held a wary expression, his lips had eased out of their tautly drawn line to offer a ghost of a smile as he spoke again.

"Please, excuse my rudeness. You caught me by surprise, I'm afraid, while I was imagining various ways of exacting revenge on a certain airline employee."

Despite the nervous flutter in her stomach, Jillian found her own lips curving slightly as she replied, "Well, as a matter of fact, I might have the perfect answer to that."

"Oh? You have a vat of boiling oil handy, have you?"

Midnight blue eyes glinted down at her with an expression that straddled the line between fierceness and jest, sending a wave of needlelike prickles up the back of Jillian's neck.

"Uh, no," she replied slowly. "But I may have a way to get you a seat on that flight to London."

Her words were greeted with several moments of silence as the man continued to stare into her eyes. When his gaze began to travel slowly downward, her cheeks grew warm. They grew even warmer when she realized that she was blatantly returning his examination.

He wore a gray turtleneck under the brown jacket, and dark jeans. Up close he was even broader of shoulder than he had appeared in line. Taller, too. Jillian had to tilt her head back to study his face.

Upon closer scrutiny, she could see that any resemblance he might bear to the classically handsome Brett Turner was only superficial. Brett had possessed the kind of smoothly fashioned features that drew second glances from women who always seemed surprised to learn that Brett was an ordinary investment banker, not the male model suggested by his turquoise eyes and his thick black hair, which somehow managed to maintain styled perfection even on the windiest San Francisco day.

This man's hair was black, but there was one streak of white that blended with the darker strands over his left eye. The thick black mass fell in loose waves over his forehead in a rumpled manner that almost begged to be caressed into place. He looked a bit older than Brett's thirty-one, but that might have been due to the lines etched into the corners of his eyes, which were a much darker shade than her former fiancé's.

There was a hint of arrogance in his glance, which Jillian might have found intimidating if it weren't so familiar looking. Her grandmother, British to her core, often employed a similar air. Jillian and her sisters had learned long ago this was a demonstration of bark being worse than bite, the old woman's way of "toughening them up."

Jillian found her back straightening, her own eyes narrowing as the man continued to size her up. She felt stronger than she had all day. Stronger, she realized with a rush, than she had in a very long time. She couldn't recall when she'd last had to assert herself. Brett had made everything so easy. Too easy. All part of his plan, no doubt, to lull her into placing her complete trust in him.

This man asked no such thing of her, however. When his eyes met hers once more, they reflected every bit of the wary caution that she was feeling.

"All right then, love. Would you mind telling me how you would manage that?"

His deep voice filled Jillian's ears. The smooth inflection vibrated through her, accomplishing in one sentence what his quelling look could not—make her knees turn to soft rubber.

Jillian clenched her fingers into a fist, mentally cursing her almost pathological susceptibility to British accents. Some women went weak in the knees for men with rugged features, others for broad chests or nice tushes. Jillian admired all these things, too, and as far as her examination had gone, Devlin Sinclair possessed two out of three. But it was his deep-throated accent that had her gazing mindlessly into his midnight eyes and wondering, *How would I manage* what?

Her silent question was answered by a voice that sounded exactly like her granny's.

This is ridiculous, my girl. Your life has been destroyed by a man you thought you knew perfectly. You've absolutely no business reacting like this to a total stranger. Sell him the ticket if you must, but don't be thinking of him as anything other than a convenient bit of luck.

Hearing the crisp British tones that her grandmother had never lost in the twenty years she'd lived in the States made Jillian blink, pull her thoughts together, then answer the man's question.

"I have an extra ticket for that flight. I'd be willing to sell it to you, if you're interested."

His eyes narrowed again, held hers for a long moment before he spoke. "That's *quite* interesting, actually," he said. "You know that such activity is illegal, I suppose?"

"No. . . I didn't know that."

Jillian shifted her trench coat from one arm to the other to counteract the sudden nervous quiver his words had awakened in her stomach. Or perhaps it was the amused regard in his eyes that had done that? It didn't matter. What mattered was that she had to get to London, that she had to reach the privacy of her hotel room while the horror of everything that had happened to her still seemed like something out of a bad dream, before the wall holding her emotions back crumbled in the face of reality.

"Well, that sounds like a stupid law to me," she said. "*And* unfair. This is a refundable ticket that *I* paid for. I should be allowed to use it as I wish."

Jillian paused. If she didn't know her own voice so well, she might have thought someone else had been speaking, someone who hadn't spent a lifetime living by the rules. But then, for the past couple of hours she'd felt as if some alternate version of herself had taken possession of her body, forcing her off the path of reason.

"I agree," the man said. "Besides, the airline would only take your ticket, without giving you any cash, then sell the seat to some desperate soul like myself at a ridiculously inflated price. I should much rather see my money go to you."

Devlin Sinclair punctuated the end of his sentence with what could only be called a wicked wink. Jillian stared at him blankly before she nodded.

"Good," she said. "Are you saying we can make a deal?"

Devlin permitted himself a small smile. Not five minutes earlier he'd been thinking that his Irish luck had finally run out. Of course, as he was only one-quarter Irish, he'd occasionally feared that the good fortune he'd counted on for the past twelve years was bound to come up short eventually.

But, apparently, that was not going to happen today.

Today luck had appeared in the guise of the slim woman with light brown hair who stood gazing up at him with expectant golden brown eyes. Somehow he had imagined Mistress Fortune to look more flamboyant, a gypsy sprite in a flowing diaphanous gown, perhaps. He certainly hadn't expected her to show up attired in a businesslike tan jacket over a crisp white blouse and tan pants, wearing brown leather loafers.

One eyebrow lowered in a frown. Now that he thought of it, this woman was something of a study in contrasts. His first impression, when she'd approached him, was that she was not a woman to be trifled with, that like him, she was someone perfectly capable of taking charge of her life.

However, he now noticed that her sensible attire was completely at odds with the tiny flowers that appeared to grow out of the loose curls tumbling from her upswept hair to frame her wide, squarish face. The faint blush that colored her pale complexion as they'd sized each other up seemed to contradict her direct gaze.

And, neither her businesslike clothes nor the lavishly romantic hairstyle seemed to go with the slightly nefarious deal the woman was proposing.

This disparity appealed deeply to Devlin's love of the absurd. As did the suggestion that he travel on a ticket with someone else's name printed on it. After all, this last was actually most fitting, given the fact that "Devlin Sinclair" was already an alias.

Devlin's musings took a sobering turn. Ever since reading that coded message in the *Chronicle,* he'd been battling time. And it appeared that the clock was winning. He needed to get to England, but he was well aware that just simply purchasing this ticket wasn't the answer. As tempting as this woman's offer was, it presented many more problems than it solved.

Slowly he shook his head in response to her questioning eyes. "I'd love to buy the ticket from you," he said. "But with the constant threat of terrorism these days, airline and customs officials are more careful than ever about checking documents. If the name on the ticket I present and the one on my passport don't match, I'd be arrested on the spot. You, too, if I should get caught."

He was completely surprised when she responded to his words with a smile. She had a wide mouth with full lips. Their gentle curve and the tiny dimple appearing at the left corner altered her sober features, granting her a soft loveliness more in line with the tendrils twisting past her cheeks.

He was further surprised by her words.

"What if I were to tell you that I happen to have a passport bearing the same name as the one on the ticket, complete with a picture of a man possessing your coloring and similar features?" she asked. "Not an exact match, of course, but passport pictures are a lot like the ones on driver's licenses, you know. No one expects them to be a good likeness."

Devlin did know. It had been, after all, the way he'd gotten into this country. Controlling his rising hopes, he lifted his left eyebrow skeptically as he extended his hand.

"Well, if that's the case, give us a look then. Perhaps we can make a deal, as you put it, after all."

The woman reached into the deep tote slung over her shoulder, efficiently retrieved one of those agenda notebooks that all the dressed-for-success businesswomen seemed to carry. Unzipping the tapestry cover, she drew out a thin blue booklet and handed it over for his inspection.

One side of Devlin's mouth twitched as he noted the name Jillian Gibson, then studied her photo. It was a good picture, as passport images go. But the honey brown hair curving down to just above her shoulders from a side part didn't match the no-nonsense clothes she was wearing today any better than her current romantic upsweep.

Something else was at odds with the photo and the woman who'd accosted him with her half-baked plan. First off, the picture didn't do justice to her pale, almost luminous, complexion. But it was something more than that. Devlin's attention was drawn to the eyes in the picture. They gazed back with a wide, almost dreamy expression, as if, when sitting for the photo, she'd been imagining all the places the passport might take her to.

He transferred his attention to the woman in front of him. Yes, that was it. There was a tightness about her eyes now, a tinge of sorrow shadowing the honey brown irises, along with the barest hint of some slightly wild emotion that responded to his own throw-caution-to-the-wind outlook.

"I think you gave me the wrong passport, Miss Gibson," he said quietly as he handed it back to her.

"Oh." Her eyebrows moved together in an impatient frown. "One second."

She flipped a page in her agenda, then drew out a matching booklet. She handed this to him, along with a plane ticket. Devlin studied the documents. The name on the passport, Brett Turner, did indeed match the one on the ticket, just as she'd said. And the picture of Mr. Turner could certainly pass as one of himself, once he made a few adjustments to his own appearance.

"I think the fact that this fellow in the photo has a mustache will be an advantage," Devlin said as he met the woman's waiting gaze. "It should compensate, at least at a glance, for the other differences in our features."

He saw a hint of hesitation cross Miss Gibson's features before she nodded.

"But to be on the safe side," he said, "I think I should straighten my hair out and style it like Mr. Turner's as much as possible, and perhaps cover this gray steak. Do you have some hair spray and mascara I might use?"

A slight frown puckered the woman's brow. A tingling at the back of Devlin's neck warned him that he'd aroused her suspicions, had made her wonder if perhaps this wasn't the first time he'd done something like this.

"This all sounds rather cloak-and-daggerish, doesn't it?" he asked, then eased his lips into his best imitation of a sheepish grin.

It worked. He saw some of the tightness ease from her features.

"I do have some styling gel and, of course, mascara," she replied as she reached into the bag slung over her shoulder.

Again the looked-for items came quickly out of the tote. As Devlin took them from her hand, he said, "Well, then, I have just have one more question. A rather vital one, however. Won't Mr. Turner be missing his passport?"

He watched her face carefully. Other than a brief glance to one side, her features remained immobile as she replied, "I rather doubt it. The man is in jail at the moment."

Devlin's jaw tightened as he studied Jillian Gibson's matter-of-fact expression. What was wrong with this woman? She appeared to be intelligent. However, any logical, thinking person would have to realize that using the ticket and passport of a felon *might* pose a problem or two.

"Excuse me," he said. "I think we need to discuss this situation a *little* more."

His gruff tone had the desired effect. The young woman blinked, and her eyes opened wide. He saw no fear in her gaze, only dawning awareness.

"I'm sorry," she said softly. "I'm afraid I hadn't thought much past getting some cash for Brett's ticket."

"Well, before we go any further down *that* particular road, I think perhaps you'd better tell me what's going on."

He watched Jillian's slow nod, noticed that her face had gone several shades paler. Curving his fingers around her arm, he led her to an empty row of chairs. After taking a seat next to her, he studied her face again. Seeing that she was staring blankly ahead, he tapped her on the shoulder.

"Why don't you start by telling me just who this Brett Turner fellow is," he said.

She turned to him and began speaking slowly. "According to the police, the real Brett Turner is an investment banker who quit his job in New York about a year ago, and is now a fishing guide up in Washington State. The name of the man whose picture is on the passport is actually Brett Waters."

Jillian paused. Devlin saw her gaze shift slightly, so that she was staring sightlessly down the length of the terminal. When she didn't go on, he spoke.

"All right, then. Who is Brett Waters and what has he done?"

"I think the question might be what *hasn't* he done," Jillian replied. Her eyes met his again. "Apparently he's quite an accomplished con man and thief. He joined the investment firm where I work about six months ago. Today I learned that he has managed to divert over four hundred thousand dollars of other people's money into a foreign account."

Devlin lifted his eyebrows appreciatively. "I see. So how do *you* happen to be carrying his passport and plane ticket? Don't tell me you were part of his getaway scheme?"

Jillian shook her head, opened her mouth to answer, then blinked. She stared at him for several seconds before breathing, "Oh . . . my . . . God."

Devlin controlled the urge to roll his eyes heavenward. With each thing she said, his chances of getting on that plane grew even more faint. He was just about to stand up and wish this odd young lady bon voyage, when she spoke.

"That was it, of course," she said. "He needed an excuse to plan a trip out of the country."

Devlin got the feeling that her words were some form of thinking out loud. Curious, he kept still as she went on.

"What an idiot I am. I was part of his plan all along. Steal a fortune, find someone foolish enough to go along with a whirlwind romance, plan a honeymoon in England, and you're out of the country, free as a bird."

She stopped speaking, then continued to stare past him. Devlin broke the silence.

"This trip was to be your *honeymoon?*"

Jillian looked at him. "Yes. I didn't learn that Brett was in jail until my boss and the FBI arrived at the house, where all the guests were listening to prewedding music in the garden. So—" she lifted one shoulder "—instead of walking down the aisle, I had the pleasure of being questioned for an hour in my wedding gown."

Devlin was surprised by her dry-eyed assessment of what must have been a devastating turn of events. Her reaction suited his purposes well, however. He was beginning to believe this situation might be salvaged, after all.

"Are you suspected of being an accomplice?" he asked.

"Hardly." Her eyes narrowed. "Twenty thousand dollars of that money was mine, from an account I'd set up toward buying a home of my own. Within three months of meeting Brett, of course, it became a home of *our* own. I guess he took this a bit too literally."

She paused again. A frown brought her slender eyebrows together. "Anyway, apparently this isn't the first time he's pulled something like this. From what Agent Carter said, Brett's committed similar crimes under various aliases around the country, and in Europe, as well."

"So, I take it they caught him before the money actually disappeared?"

Jillian shook her head. "No. He made some computer transfer that they've so far not been able to trace. He's not speaking about this, of course."

Only half of Devlin's mind was listening to her words. The other part was running ahead, searching for any possible obstacles.

"Did the agent say anything about you not leaving town?" he asked.

"No. Just the opposite. I told him I wanted to take this trip, to salvage what I could of the disaster Brett had made of my life. All he asked was that I leave a copy of my itinerary, so he could contact me if he had any further questions. As to having Brett's ticket and passport, I packed them in my tote yesterday, so that we wouldn't forget anything in our rush to get from our reception to the airport."

Jillian Gibson was obviously a very organized young woman, Devlin thought. Very controlled. Good. Having been brought up in a thoroughly stiff-upper-lipped British home, he was ill equipped to deal with emotional women. And with Brett Turner, or Waters, or whoever this fellow was, safely in jail there wouldn't be any APBs out on the man to interfere with the use of his passport and ticket.

So he might as well take the gift fate was offering.

"All right," he said to Jillian. "I have thirteen hundred dollars in cash. I'll need a bit to get me from London to my home. Will one thousand buy that ticket from you?"

Chapter 2

A half hour later, Jillian breathed a sigh of relief as she stepped onto the jetway that sloped down to the waiting aircraft. Before she'd gone more than five steps, she felt a restraining hand close over her elbow.

"Slow down. We have to discuss what just happened."

The words were spoken loudly enough to be heard above the muffled whir of the plane's idling jets. Jillian glanced at the frowning man next to her, then drew her own eyebrows together.

"Discuss what?" she asked.

"Well," he started, "it seems that the first ticket agent you spoke with was apparently so anxious to coerce you into giving up Mr. Turner's ticket that he failed to study the reservation completely. Judging from the way the gate agent smiled and offered her congratulations on our recent nuptials, I would guess there must be some reference to marriage or honeymoon in the record."

Jillian didn't want to talk about that. Her lips were still

numb from the smile she'd forced them to maintain as the woman gushed over their romantic honeymoon plans.

"It's no big deal." She shrugged. "My sister, Holly, is a travel agent. Her gift to us—to me, was to make all the reservations for the trip, using her contacts to get special upgrades and provide the best accommodations available with the money I'd allotted. Holly must have put a note in the reservation to let the flight people know that this was a special occasion, with hopes that Brett and I would get extra consideration."

Glancing toward Devlin as she finished her explanation, she saw him lift one eyebrow.

"We're traveling in first class," he said. "I believe that good service comes with the price of the ticket. Of course, if this means we're treated better than we were back at the ticket counter, that's fine. It does, however, mean that we shall have to take care to act the part of newly wedded bliss."

These words stopped Jillian in her tracks. Devlin took two more steps then halted and turned toward her, eyebrows raised quizzically as the people entering behind them began to stream past.

"Why should we have to act like newlyweds?" she demanded in a hoarse whisper. "You're safely checked in for this flight. What anyone thinks of us from now on isn't important in the least."

"Not true, I'm afraid. If we don't seem to be the honeymooning pair mentioned in the reservation, an observant flight attendant might become suspicious. Not a good situation, love, especially if this person decides to pass his or her questions about us along to a customs agent in Heathrow."

This was too much. Jillian felt the last ounce of the wild determination and reckless abandon that had brought her to this point seep out of her weary body and even wearier soul.

She shouldn't be here. She should be home, accepting the condolences of her sisters and her grandmother. All she'd wanted to do was escape the rubble that remained of her once-stable life, to get some distance from what happened so she could regain a sense of control. Now, not only had she broken some ridiculous law by selling a ticket to this person, but a total stranger was suggesting that they act the part of a starry-eyed couple, anxious for their wedding night.

The kind of intimacy this suggested both embarrassed and unnerved Jillian. Breaking eye contact with the man, she stared at a picture of Big Ben on the travel poster hanging on the metal wall. A sudden chill slid down her spine as it occurred to her that she had absolutely no idea who Devlin Sinclair was or what kind of man he might be. When she'd overheard him mention a family emergency to the ticket agency in that devastating British accent of his, she'd just accepted that he was telling the truth about why he had to board this particular flight.

Well, what if that stuff about family was a lie? Recent events had demonstrated rather dramatically that any ability she'd possessed to judge people had deserted her when she met Brett Turner. What if there was some sinister reason behind Devlin Sinclair's desperate need to get on this plane? For all she knew *he* was running from the police. The man could be anything. A scoundrel. A thief.

A murderer.

"Miss Gibson."

The softly uttered words brought Jillian's eyes back to Devlin's face. He was smiling broadly. This smile was unlike the brief twitches that had previously lifted the corners of his mouth from time to time. This was a dazzlingly white, heart-stoppingly attractive grin that deepened the creases fanning out from the corners of his eyes.

"I wasn't suggesting that we attempt to join the mile-high club during the flight," he said. "Just that we appear less like strangers. For starters, I will call you Jillian. I suppose you'll have to call me Brett. And, like a properly besotted new husband, I suppose I should be holding your hand."

His hand closed around hers as he spoke. Jillian was stunned, both by the action and her skin's tingling response to the warmth of his fingers. His smile appeared to fade a degree or two, but the corners of his eyes continued to crinkle as he held her gaze.

"Well, Jillian, my little bride, what do you say? Do we get on the plane and continue with our charade?"

The dark blue eyes neither coerced nor demanded. The decision was completely up to her, they seemed to say.

Once Jillian could have trusted herself implicitly to make the right choice. But that was before she had given her heart, her money and almost her life to a man who had effortlessly convinced her that he was the kind of person who could be trusted with all this, even as he lied and deceived her.

And now she was supposed to trust a complete stranger.

Jillian drew a deep breath. Devlin Sinclair was not asking her for anything she hadn't already offered. The man hadn't suggested anything remotely threatening, now that she thought about it. Besides, they would be surrounded by people on the plane. If he attempted to take advantage of the situation in any way, she had only to call for an attendant.

"Sure," she said at last. "Let's go for it."

Devlin rewarded her with a one-sided grin. "Come along then," he said.

Minutes later they took their seats in the forward section of the aircraft, the last two places on the right side of the first-class compartment, across from an elderly couple and directly behind a gentleman accompanied by a huge cello.

"I do hope that thing is properly strapped in," Devlin said softly, cocking his head toward the neck of the instrument that extended above the aisle seat directly in front of him.

"Well, if the man thought enough of it to buy it a first-class ticket," Jillian whispered back over the click of Devlin's seat belt, "I'm sure he's taking good care of his traveling companion."

Devlin smiled a reply, then drew a magazine from the seat pocket. Jillian started to do the same, then remembered a small detail that would give further credence to the roles they were to be playing. Reaching under the seat in front of her, she retrieved two small, white velvet boxes from her purse.

"Here," she said to Devlin. "See if this fits."

She saw him glance over, then stare at the gold band resting on her open palm for several moments.

"It won't bite," she said softly.

"And it *will* wash off, I suppose," he said with a smile as he picked it up and slid it onto the third finger of his left hand.

As Jillian did the same with her band, her fingers suddenly began to tremble. When they wouldn't stop on her mental command, she grasped her left hand with her right, shoved them into her lap and took several deep breaths.

"No diamond?"

Devlin's question made her turn to him sharply and shake her head. "Silly me, I told Brett, No, honey, not if it means the choice between an engagement ring and the down payment on a house. Of course, that was when I was under the delusion that there was going to *be* a house."

The slight lifting motion of Devlin's eyebrows quelled Jillian's rising fury. This was *not* the time to get into this. She'd have time to vent later, in private, where she could rage and stamp her feet or beat the mattress, until her anger at Brett Turner and at her own colossal stupidity faded.

"Welcome to Flight 234, nonstop from San Francisco to London."

With the announcement echoing through the cabin, Jillian clicked her buckle into place. The plane began to move backward and the safety announcements started as she stared at the back of the seat in front of her. She took several slow, deep breaths, willing her angry thoughts away and the ache that had risen to her chest back down to the pit of her stomach, where she could control it.

Slowly the attendant's words seeped into Jillian's consciousness. Words about nearest exits, lights that would guide passengers in that direction and seats that could be used as flotation devices in the unlikely event of a descent into water.

Then she heard her granny's voice. *Your mum and dad won't be coming home, Jilly. Something happened to their plane. But I'll be here, just like always. Be brave, my dear, and help me explain this to your sisters.*

Suddenly Jillian was ten years old again, her throat so tight with fear and grief that she could hardly breathe. She glanced at the tiny window to her right, saw buildings and tarmac moving by. She felt an occasional bump as the noise of the jet engines grew louder and louder.

Her fingers tightened convulsively over the end of the armrest as her heart began to race. She forced herself to take a deep breath, then slowly blow the air back out. Her heart only pounded harder. Again she tried to breathe away the tightness in her chest.

"Miss Tur—Jillian. Are you all right?"

Devlin's deep voice made her blink. Slowly she turned to him. A frown darkened his blue eyes, making them look nearly black.

"You're not looking particularly besotted...or even happy," he said softly. "Don't tell me you're afraid of flying?"

Jillian supposed she was hardly presenting the picture of newlywed bliss they'd agreed upon. But, at the moment, she was having enough trouble just breathing. Playing the role of blushing bride was completely beyond her abilities.

"No," she replied. "I'm afraid of crashing."

"I see." One corner of Devlin's wide mouth lifted. "Well, that is, at least, a logical fear. But you do know that statistics have proven—"

Jillian interrupted his words with an emphatic shake of her head. "My parents died in an airplane crash when I was a kid. I haven't flown since."

The vertical line between Devlin's eyebrows grew more pronounced. Again he said, "I see."

In the silence that followed, Jillian sensed a wariness on his part, an unwillingness to become entangled in her emotional battle. She could hardly blame him. *She* didn't want to deal with it. But it was, after all, *her* battle.

Just as she was about to pull her gaze from his, she felt warm fingers touch her left hand hesitantly, then close slowly over hers.

"Come on, then," Devlin said. "After all you've been through today, I would think the possibility of a crash would seem rather minor."

Jillian stared at him for several moments. That was just the sort of thing her granny would say. And normally, this would make her smile, make her straighten her shoulders and face life with the determination she so prided herself on. But there was *nothing* normal about this situation. All her fight was gone, along with all the money she'd worked so hard for, along with the security she so craved.

She wanted desperately to enjoy the feel of the plane gathering speed, to anticipate with excitement the moment of takeoff, of *flying,* soaring above the clouds, weightless and free, that had so thrilled her as a child the few times she'd traveled with her parents. But even as memories of those long-ago trips awoke a flicker of excitement in her breast, a male voice echoed through the cabin, ordering the flight attendants to their seats.

Her fingers gripped the armrests. Devlin's fingers tightened gently over hers.

"Talk to me," he urged.

Jillian turned to him. "Talk?"

"Yes. It'll take your mind off things. Tell me what made you decide to head off to London on your own. Somehow you don't strike me as the spur-of-the-moment type."

Jillian started to shake her head, to tell him that talking just wasn't possible at the moment. Some tiny shred of what had once been inner fortitude rose to halt the gesture. She *had* to deal with this. If she started to break down now, she might not stop until she'd crumbled into thousands of tiny pieces.

"You're right." She managed a tight smile. "I am someone who likes to plan things out. I had everything set up for the wedding weeks in advance, for example. No last-minute rushes for me. Fat lot of good it did me, of course. Everything fell apart, the wedding, the beautiful reception my gran and sisters had worked so hard on, and the future I had all planned out. The only thing salvageable was this trip."

"And how does England fit into the grand scheme of things?"

This time Jillian's lips curved naturally. "I've been wanting to return to England from the time I was eight. Holly and I spent the summer there with our Granny Weston, the year our sister Sarah was born. Gran took us to London. I fell in love with the lush green of the country, running down hedge-lined paths and searching for the fairies that my granny insisted lived in the gardens. I thought Holly and I had found never-never land, and I didn't want to leave."

Jillian paused, sighed and continued. "We had to, of course. My mother needed us home—Gran, especially. My parents made nature films and Gran had agreed to be their live-in *child-care provider,* a term she absolutely loathes. Anyway, I just always dreamed of returning someday."

"Well, I hope you won't be disappointed."

The harsh, almost angry tone of Devlin's voice made Jillian blink away the vision of cottage gardens that had been dancing before her eyes. She found Devlin frowning at the seat in front of him. His hand still rested on hers, though, and when a sharp thump announced the raising of the landing gear, his fingers tightened slightly around hers.

When he turned to look at her again, the frown was gone. "So," he said, "I take it that the trip to England was your idea, not Brett's?"

Jillian started to nod, then stopped as an old conversation teased her memory.

"Well, no, Brett suggested it, actually."

Jillian found herself staring at the back of the seat in front of her. She was aware that the plane was climbing sharply, but she was too occupied with the swift pattern forming from remembered snippets of dialogue with Brett and others to react to any of the slight bumps or sways that accompanied the motion.

"Very clever," she said softly.

"Who?"

Jillian, blinked. She hadn't realized she'd spoken out loud. Just great. She wasn't sure she wanted to share the conclusions she'd reached with this stranger, but she didn't want him to think she was a complete nut, either.

Slowly she turned to him again. "Brett," she replied. "I just realized how he did it."

When Devlin gave her a puzzled frown, she sighed and tried to clarify herself. "How he fooled me so completely. I just remembered that one of the other secretaries was telling me last week that all the women in the office had been jealous when Brett first joined the firm and showed such an instant interest in me. She mentioned that he'd driven them crazy, asking all about my likes and dislikes. When I heard this, I felt flattered and at the same time vaguely uncomfortable. However I was too immersed in my wedding plans and attempts to get the office organized before I left to give it much thought. Now I realize that Brett must have taken all the information he'd gathered and fashioned a personality for himself that would match *my* likes and dislikes, to make me believe we were the soul mates he insisted we were."

When Jillian had started speaking, she wasn't sure how Devlin might respond to all this personal information. Embarrassed, perhaps. Bored, maybe.

The last thing she'd expected was for him to shake his head and say, *"Soul mates?"* The disdain in his voice only deepened as he continued. "Well, I must say I wonder if this granny of yours was a truly good influence on you. First she has you looking for fairies, and the next thing you know you're looking for a soul mate. Personally, I think you'd have a better chance locating the former."

His words stung. Jillian slipped her hand from beneath his as she replied, "You're right, of course. Not that I need to be reminded of what a fool I've been."

As she turned her head away, his hand captured hers again. "I'm sorry," she heard him say. She shrugged in reply as she clenched her jaw and resolutely stared out at the cloud bank they were rising through.

"Jillian, look at me. Please."

His softly spoken plea made her feel silly. Slowly she turned back to him.

"Look," he said. "I know how you feel. I've been there, too. When I was too young to know better I fell in love with a lovely young thing who managed to convince me that we were the proverbial match made in heaven. That match lasted only until she saw I was turning my back on all the things she'd wanted to marry into—the nice house, the money, the—"

He stopped speaking abruptly. A muscle at the corner of his jaw bunched. His eyes narrowed as he began speaking again.

"Hell, it's the same with most people, I suppose. We all buy into this fantasy that we aren't complete unless we find the one perfect person, made just for us. Walking around with this in mind, it's hardly surprising that we're completely open to being fooled by people who are less sentimental and far more cunning. Tell me, did this gran of yours ever tell you of the piskies?"

The change of topic brought a lift to Jillian's eyebrows, but she nodded. "The little folk who like to play tricks on people? Of course."

"Well, then—" his eyes narrowed "—she should have warned you that if you go looking for fairy-tale endings, you're just as likely to end up the butt of a piskie's cruel joke."

With these words, Devlin let go of her hand, drew a magazine from the seat pocket in front of him and began flipping pages.

Jillian turned her head and stared out the window. Anger churned in her stomach. Though her granny had never actually said that she didn't like Brett, the woman *had* warned Jillian about the vagaries of love, in almost exactly the words Devlin had used. This didn't change the fact that this man, this classic, handsome *stranger,* had no right to comment on her dreams, foolish as they might have been.

Jillian crossed her arms, pressing them against her waist, holding her sudden fury down. Any emotion was dangerous right now. She recognized the signs, knew just how to keep pain and fear at bay until she could find a private spot where she could let the tears flow until the pressure eased and she could regain her composure.

The rest room in the airplane would do, but the display panel overhead still ordered that seat belts be in place. So she had no other option but to force her tight chest to draw in calming air.

"Ladies and gentlemen."

The flight attendant's low, well-modulated tone drew Jillian's attention to the woman at the top of the aisle, wearing an apron embroidered with the name Sue.

"We're about to begin our beverage and snack service," Sue said. "And tonight we have a special offering, since four of our passengers are celebrating a very special day. Mr. and Mrs. Fitzwater, seated in the rear left corner, are commemorating their fiftieth wedding anniversary, and—"

A burst of applause interrupted the attendant's speech. Jillian felt all the warmth drain from her body as the sound echoed through the cabin. Her chest began to ache as she watched the elderly couple across from her blush and exchange a tender kiss.

"And," Sue said over the resulting aahs, "directly across the aisle from the Fitzwaters are Mr. and Mrs. Turner, who were married just this afternoon."

Married? Jillian's throat grew tight as she recalled the sympathetic glances of her wedding guests as they slipped past her. She blinked away the vision, then swallowed and tried to draw a calming breath.

"So, you're all welcome to share the complimentary champagne we'll be offering, along with our warmest congratulations."

More applause rang in her ears. Jillian noticed that Devlin had turned to her. The conspiratorial smile curving his lips invited her to join him in their private joke. She tried to make her lips form a smile, but found that they were suddenly trembling and realized that her eyes were filling with tears. Devlin's face registered concern, followed by an expression that bordered on sheer terror, before his features melted into a watery blur.

Jillian wanted to speak, to assure him that she was going to be all right, but her throat had closed. She tried to swallow the anger and the hurt, but the ache just increased. The only thing she could think of doing was to close her eyes and try to trap as many tears as she could.

"Is something wrong?"

At the attendant's soft inquiry, Jillian squeezed her eyes more tightly shut.

Devlin replied in a deep voice, "No. It's just been a rather long day for her. I think she may have a delayed case of bridal jitters."

If Jillian's chest weren't so painfully tight, if her throat didn't feel completely blocked, she might have burst into laughter at this combination of lie and understatement. She couldn't truthfully be called a bride. But the day *had* been the longest one in her life.

And it wasn't over yet.

Jillian shook her head ever so slightly, barely able to believe that she'd lost control like this in front of people. In front of a whole *planeload* of people.

It had been years, eighteen to be exact, since the last time she'd lost a battle with emotion like this. The powerful grief that had washed over her on the day that she'd learned of her parents' deaths had terrified her. The emotional undertow had dragged her down again and again. Hidden in the attic of the old Victorian house, she had alternated crying and sleeping until Gran had found her. It had taken all of her grandmother's considerable strength of will to pull Jillian out of that private hell. To convince the girl that her younger sisters were just as bereaved and frightened as she, that they needed their older sister free from tears.

"Not quite up to celebrating just now, are we, love?"

Devlin's wry tone offered comfort without a hint of pity, reminding Jillian of Gran's no-nonsense approach and soothing her emotions far better than words of sympathy would. Jillian felt some of the tightness ease from her throat. After a few seconds, she was able to open her eyes. As she blinked back the little remaining moisture, she saw that Devlin had turned toward her, was using his body to shield her from any curious stares.

His dark blue eyes held hers with an expression that bordered on panic. "You've got to help me here," he whispered. "Tell me what to do. Is there something I can get for you? A blanket? A pillow? Some fresh air?"

The image of Devlin trying to open a window at thirty-five thousand feet did the trick. The pain in Jillian's chest didn't disappear completely, but the tension eased enough for her to draw in a deep, quivering breath, and the remains of the sob huddling in her throat become a laugh.

Well, not exactly a laugh. More like a croak as Jillian shook her head and forced out the words "I'm okay now."

His eyes continued to hold hers a moment. "You're sure?"

"I'm sure," she replied as she raised a hand, intending to brush away her tears.

"No," Devlin said.

His fingers closed around hers. Jillian blinked at him. He smiled and spoke again.

"I have something here that will do a much better job."

As soft fabric dabbed at the moisture on her cheek, Jillian's attention drifted to the large, strong hand holding her icy fingers. She often suffered from cold hands, especially when she was under stress, but she hadn't realized how truly frigid her fingers had grown over the day until she felt them tingle and begin to thaw within Devlin's grasp.

The slow warming made her aware of how cold the rest of her body was. This had her wondering what might happen if Devlin were to take her into his arms and hold her to his broad chest. Perhaps the chill might leave her body as it had her fingers, perhaps she would stop feeling as if her insides were shivering.

On the heels of this thought came a mental image in which she saw herself standing within the circle of Devlin Sinclair's arms, safe and secure and oh so warm. The image moved, took on movielike life. She watched herself look up, saw Devlin's dark head come closer. As a heated current flowed down her body, she closed her eyes, willing the image to sharpen.

She opened them when something soft and warm touched her cheek, then traced the curve down to the corner of her mouth.

Jillian blinked. Instead of the pair of lips she'd imagined waiting inches above hers was a white handkerchief.

Drawing in a deep, ragged breath, trying to calm the embarrassed racing of her heart, she lifted her eyes to Devlin's. "Thank you," she said. "I . . . I'll be fine now."

"Are you sure? You look a little flushed."

She felt a *lot* flushed. That little daydream had raised her body temperature way past normal, to near fever pitch. A silly, impossible image, and yet it had left her more breathless and hot than actually kissing Brett Turner had ever done.

Not that she hadn't enjoyed kissing Brett. But she had been so taken with the way their personalities seemed to fit so perfectly that she'd happily overlooked the fact that her physical reaction to any romantic situation with him was warmly pleasant rather than wildly hot.

Not, of course, that *this* was a romantic situation. It was an odd situation, one that both she and Devlin Sinclair had entered into out of necessity. It would be a short-lived one, too, Jillian told herself, one that wouldn't be made any easier by engaging in silly daydreams. Especially when she was still reeling from the morning's emotional shock.

"I probably do look a bit pink," she said as she forced a smile and withdrew her fingers from Devlin's grasp. "Crying does that, you know. I'm sure my eyes are red, too. I must look horrible."

"Just dreadful."

The brief twitch of his lips, and the deepening creases at the corners of Devlin's eyes softened his dry tone. As she stared at him, Jillian found that she was once again having difficulty breathing.

"Is everything all right here?"

The flight attendant's voice broke the silence. Jillian turned to find the woman leaning over the cello's seat, peering anxiously at them.

"Yes," Jillian replied.

"Are you sure? Can I get you something? A beverage? A pillow? A blanket?"

Jillian and Devlin replied at precisely the same second. "Some fresh air might be nice."

Devlin glanced at Jillian with an ironic amusement that mirrored her own, then back to the attendant.

"I think we could both use something to drink. Jilly, what would you like?"

Devlin turned to her as he spoke. For a moment, Jillian couldn't do anything more than stare at him. Only her family called her by that particular pet name. No one else, not even Brett. Yet it sounded so very right coming from Devlin Sinclair. Hearing it brought a smile to her lips and a final release of the knot beneath her breastbone.

"I think I'd like some of that champagne," she said at last.

Sunlight filled the cabin after the all too brief night. Devlin had managed to get *some* sleep before the bright-eyed attendants came around with lunch. His body said it was early morning, but the watch he'd set on London time said it was close to two o'clock in the afternoon, making the meal brunch, he supposed.

"Not bad food, for airline fare."

As Devlin spoke, he glanced at Jillian, who gave him a smile and nodded before taking a sip of coffee. Devlin downed some of his, as well, grateful for the surge of energy imparted by the caffeine. He was considerably revived and ready to face whatever the day brought.

Careful, lad. You know better than to let yourself get overconfident.

The unbidden thought brought a frown to Devlin's brow. He glanced at the scar on the back of his right hand. Yes, he did know better. But the situation was different this time.

When he'd left England all those years ago, secrecy had been of the utmost importance. Two years later, when he finally made his way into the States, he'd felt reasonably sure that no shadows had followed his gypsy wanderings. So surely it would be impossible for anyone to know that he was coming back to England now, anyone except for the person who had placed that ad in the personals column. And *he* wasn't likely to tell anyone.

With a decent bit of sleep under Devlin's belt, along with a fair meal, the world did look good. The edginess he'd felt the day before had slipped away, leaving his whatever-will-be-will-be attitude back in place, and restoring his faith in his instincts, the instincts that had zigzagged him through the past twelve years, kept him alive, prosperous and unencumbered.

Well, almost unencumbered. There was the matter of the woman sitting next to him to deal with. Devlin had no idea how she'd done it, whether it was the tears she'd fought so hard against, the way she had of turning pink at the oddest moments, or those rare, dimple-punctuated grins, but Jillian Gibson had managed to slip beneath his well-constructed barriers and make him care what happened to her.

He didn't like that. He liked it even less that he'd loosened up enough to share a bit of his past with her. He still couldn't figure what had prompted him to tell her about Prudence. *Dear* Prudence.

Worst of all, though, was the way Jillian obviously idealized England. He was used to that, of course. Anglophilia, that strange love of England that seemed to afflict a good number of Americans, drew a nice crowd to his pubs. He used that interest to his advantage, but never once, as he'd gone about making his places look as English as possible and telling stories of his homeland, had he actually felt the least bit of nostalgia for the place in any portion of his cynical heart. Not until this damned woman had started going on about hedgerows and gardens and fairies.

Just like his mum.

For the first time in twelve years, he'd found himself recalling with fondness the places and the people that he'd forcefully thrust to the back of his mind so very long ago. It was the price of banishment, he'd told himself. True, his exile punishment had been self-imposed, but there'd been no choice, and no looking back. Until now. Until some apparently serious problem had arisen to prompt Colin to place that ad.

He wished he had more to go on, wished that the call he'd put through to the house before he'd left for the airport had produced more than a cool male voice stating that Colin was "not at home at the moment."

"May I take your things?"

The attendant's question made Devlin look up to find Sue giving him a practiced smile as she said, "We'll be getting ready to land soon."

Once the tray had been whisked away, Devlin pulled a magazine from the pocket in front of him and opened it. Out of the corner of his eye, he noticed Jillian writing in her date book.

"Mapping out a new future?" he asked quietly.

Her sharp glance confirmed that his words had sounded more sarcastic than he'd meant for them to.

"No," she said as she closed the agenda and zipped it shut. "Just the next day or so."

During one of her trips to the rest room, she'd removed the last traces of her aborted wedding, by literally letting her hair down. With it waving to her shoulders, she now looked very much like the picture on her passport, except that her eyes held none of the dreamy excitement that the camera had managed to catch. There was no hint of the throw-caution-to-the-wind glimmer of the day before, either. Just the same calm, determined look that she regarded him with now.

"How about you?" she asked. "Are your plans set?"

Before Devlin could reply, a flight attendant's voice echoed through the cabin.

"We're beginning our final descent into London's Heathrow airport. It's two-thirty in the afternoon, local time, and a light mist is falling. Please check that your seat backs are in an upright and locked position and that your seat belts are securely fastened."

Chapter 3

Devlin stowed the magazine and snapped the buckle of his seat belt. An echoing click from the seat next to him reminded him of Jillian's shaky response to takeoff. He glanced her way. Her head was turned toward the gray sky outside the window, so he had no way of gauging her expression.

She's probably fine, he told himself.

But what if she wasn't? he thought a second later. She would need to appear the bright and excited bride when they went through customs, not red eyed and looking emotionally drained.

"Jillian?" he said softly.

She turned to him, her eyebrows lifting in inquiry above her amber eyes.

"Yes?"

"Are you going to be all right?"

Her slender eyebrows moved together in a frown before she replied. "Sure. I'm going to be fine. Holly set up my entire itinerary, so all I have to do is take a cab to my hotel and I'll be—" She came to an abrupt stop. "Oh. You mean about the landing?"

Devlin nodded.

"It should be all right. I think I was just a bit overemotional when we left San Francisco." She gave him a tiny smile. The dimple appeared as the smile widened, and her eyes began to shine as she went on. "I'll be fine, especially once I get out of this plane and on the road to London. What about you? Is a family member going to meet you at the airport?"

"No. I never got a chance to call them and confirm my arrival time before we got on the plane," he lied. "Besides, I don't look down the road as far as you do. My family learned long ago not to look for me before I got there."

"Oh." Her dimple disappeared as her smile was once again reduced to an expression of mere politeness. "I see."

He hoped she did. He recalled with painful clarity the smile Jillian had given him after he'd brushed her tears away, and the soft expression in her eyes. She needed to know that he was no white knight on the lookout for a damsel in distress.

Devlin frowned at his thoughts. They were hardly fair. Since this thing had begun, Jillian Gibson had hardly been acting like a victim. True, she'd had a few rough emotional patches, but she'd been more than prepared to deal with them on her own.

A slight jolt and the screech of tires on tarmac pulled Devlin from his thoughts. They'd landed. His stomach tightened.

He hadn't been exactly truthful when he'd said he never made any plans. His standard procedure was to take things in steps, keeping an eye on his options so that when the time to move came, he could do so quickly and effectively. He needed to go over those options now.

It was two-thirty. Getting through customs and into London via the underground would eat up anywhere from an hour and a half to two hours. Unless things had changed greatly, there was a midnight train leaving Paddington for the West Country. It would get him to Exeter quite a while before dawn, but he'd be able to catch the first bus east, and be home around noon.

Devlin was so busy with his thoughts that by the time he was up the jetway and striding across the terminal's polished granite floor, his mind was moving faster than his feet.

It felt good to be on the move, ready to respond to the moment. He liked living by his wits. Which was just as well, since his brother had inherited Devlin's title, estate and money, leaving him with little other than a need for constant change.

Not fair, nor entirely true.

The thought slipped to the front of Devlin's mind before he could prevent it. He shoved it back ruthlessly. No regretting the past. He had to keep his eye on the future, and his attention in the present. That was how he'd survived this far.

"Brett!"

He heard a woman's voice rise above the rumble of hurrying feet moving toward the door marked Immigration. Devlin continued to walk. He heard the voice again, this time from directly behind him, accompanied by a tug on his right sleeve.

He turned to see Jillian, her cheeks pink, her chest rising and falling with rapid breaths, staring up at him with wide frightened eyes.

"You haven't forgotten about customs, have you, *Brett?*"

Of course he had. He'd forgotten all about the act that had yet to play itself out, the ruse that was to get him anonymously into the country. But Jillian's concern puzzled him. He was the one who should be worried about this, not her.

"We have a problem," she whispered as she leaned toward him. "The passport department wouldn't issue a passport to me under my married name until I could present an official marriage certificate. I was to bring *that* document along with me to justify the fact that my passport says Jillian Gibson, and my ticket shows Jillian Turner. Since there was no wedding, I, of course, don't have a marriage certificate."

Devlin stared into Jillian's worried eyes, then slowly began to smile. This, he could handle.

"Well, first off, I'm sure the officials here have run into this sort of situation in the past. Well, maybe not young women left at the altar by con men, but certainly brides who have only their new husband to vouch for them. And since you do have one of *those,* you can wipe that terrified look off your face."

When Jillian took a deep breath, he gave her an approving nod. "Next, I shall need to borrow your styling gel again, to make sure that I look as much like *my* passport picture as possible. And then, you must promise not to laugh at my attempt at an American accent. I've been told it's an abominable mix of Boston, South Bronx and East Texas."

Devlin paused. He watched Jillian and saw her lips twitch ever so slightly. They slowly widened into a smile, awakening that corner-of-her-mouth dimple. He stared at that a moment, realizing that this was one of those moments that wanted responding to.

"Most importantly," he said with a slow grin, "you must remember the role of love-mad newlyweds we are playing, and must not, under *any* circumstances, pull back when I do this."

On that last word, before Jillian had a chance to anticipate what was coming, Devlin slipped his arms around Jillian, bent his head and lowered his mouth to hers. Covering her parted lips, he caressed them lightly with his as he gently tightened his arms around her and increased the pressure of his mouth on hers.

He had been prepared for her to resist. He had not expected her to lean into the kiss, to melt against him, to slowly begin to move her soft lips beneath his in a way that sent his blood coursing wildly through his veins, pounding in his ears, making it so damnably difficult to pull away.

"Thanks for your help with this."

Jillian glanced at Devlin as they stepped away from the bank and back into the bustling terminal. The act of changing some of her dollars for pounds had really not been that difficult, but she felt she had to say something more or less mundane in an attempt to return the situation between them to a more neutral footing, after spending the past half hour with his arm around her as they made their way through immigration and customs.

Despite all efforts to appear calm and collected, her lips still tingled with remembered heat, a banked fire still smoldered on her cheeks. She couldn't remember how she'd come to give herself so completely to that kiss. One moment she'd been thinking, *I've only known this man twelve hours,* and the next minute she'd been unable to think at all as the warmth of his lips on hers seeped into all the empty crevices of her soul.

The heat had flowed swiftly through her, building to a fever pitch that finally woke her to the scandal of what she was doing. Now, over an hour later, she still didn't know why she'd surrendered so completely to the moment. True, she was past being simply tired. Between the time difference and what little sleep she'd had this preparation-filled week, she was dangerously near exhaustion. And, of course, there was the emotional trauma of her ruined wedding, finances and future that she still hadn't truly dealt with.

But when it came down to it, she knew that her reaction had been primarily due to the fact that Devlin Sinclair was simply the best kisser she'd ever had the good fortune to be kissed by.

"No problem," Devlin replied. "Actually, I need to thank you. Did you happen to notice the fellow in line behind us going through customs? Your height, slim, light blond hair and glasses?"

Jillian nodded. "Vaguely."

"Well, I went to school with him, and because of our little Mr. and Mrs. Brett Turner charade, Sedgewicke apparently failed to recognize me."

"Would that have been a problem?"

Devlin shrugged. "He was always quite a talker. I didn't want to get stuck chatting up old times."

He glanced up and down the terminal, then spoke again. "The ramp down to the tube station is that way. I need to get to London and check on train connections." He looked down at her. "The underground is the quickest and least expensive way into the city. Do you want to join me, or did you have other plans?"

Jillian had originally envisioned sharing a quiet, romantic ride in the rear seat of a large black taxi—with Brett. The idea now sounded less than appealing.

"The tube will be fine," she said. "Lead the way."

Jillian stepped up her pace as Devlin moved toward the arch marked Underground, where they joined the luggage-laden crowd marching down the serpentine ramp. She let him forge a path ahead and she followed, tugging her wheeled suitcase behind as they made their way toward the ticket booth.

His recent words made her recall another aspect of the Mr. and Mrs. Turner charade. Now that she thought about it, the performance had been almost comical, like something out of the "Benny Hill Show," with the two of them constantly interrupting each other, so as to thoroughly confuse the agent, and make him happy to send them on their way.

It was even funnier when she recalled Devlin's accent.

She was still smiling twenty minutes later as they stood at the front of the crowd waiting for the subway train to arrive. She was aware that she was bone tired, in spite of the snatches of sleep she'd caught, and hungry, even though she'd eaten less than an hour earlier. She hadn't expected jet lag to set in quite so soon, but that was the only explanation she could come up with for the giddy, schoolgirl silliness behind the grin that curved her lips.

Over the combined noise of their fellow travelers and the hum of the approaching train, she heard Devlin's deep voice. "Want to share the joke?"

Jillian glanced up. His hair had once again rebelled against the styling gel that had held it combed so neatly to the side. The humidity in the subway, along with Devlin's habit of raking his fingers through it impatiently had worn away most of the mascara from the gray streak and freed the thick waves, which now tumbled onto his forehead.

"Your accent," she said softly.

Devlin frowned and shook his head to indicate he hadn't heard. When he leaned toward her, she raised her voice a little.

"Your *accent,*" she repeated. "When we were going through customs, I noticed that you were telling the truth. Your reproduction of American speech patterns is every bit the hodgepodge you claimed."

Devlin smiled, then shrugged. "Well, I'm nothing if not honest about my shortcomings."

"Well, how refreshing."

Jillian was surprised at the arch, joking tone in which she said those words. She'd been told that she was too serious for so long that she'd just accepted that role. But not today. Today she was in England, land of fairy tales and castles. Today she had pulled off a coup, broken some silly, victimless law and found she felt no remorse, only a wild, crazy sense of freedom.

"However," she conceded, "honesty is not quite in character, Mr. *Turner.*"

The half smile Devlin gave her said that he understood her joking reference to her former fiancé's larcenous ways, while his half frown suggested that he might be a little concerned about her mental state. Thinking to reassure him, she placed a hand on his arm and opened her mouth to tell him she was fine, just a little overtired.

The words never got past her lips.

Before she could say one thing, she saw Devlin's eyes grow suddenly wide. At the same moment, she felt his arm slip from beneath her hand. Some instinct made her fingers convulse over the leather as he tilted sideways. She felt his arm slide away under the sleeve. Time seemed to stop. For one very long second, Jillian had a clear picture of Devlin leaning diagonally over the lowered tracks. Not one hundred feet away, the front of the engine moved into view.

Her heart was racing, her mind tumbling as the fabric beneath her grasp slid down to his fingers. She wasn't going to be able to stop him from falling further. He was too heavy. Already she was being pulled with him.

"Here, mate."

A male voice broke the spell. A pair of strong hands trapped Jillian's fingers as a man grabbed her hand and Devlin's arm, then pulled them both back, away from the track.

The next few moments were lost in a blur of activity as Devlin, Jillian and the stranger backed away from the train, while the crowd of travelers pressed forward.

"You all right, mate?"

The question was slow to register in Devlin's mind. He turned as the tight hands were easing from around his arm, and found himself staring into the pale green eyes and round face of a rather portly gentleman with gray hair.

"Yes, I am," he replied slowly. "Thanks to you."

"Well, you gave me a fair turn, you did, almost fallin' onto that track," the man said as he took a step back. "Got dizzy, did you? Gettin' off a plane and all that waitin' in line can do that to a body."

Devlin forced his lips to curve. Getting a sharp, sudden push from behind could do that, too.

"I guess I didn't realize just how tired I was," he said. "Thanks for thinking and moving so fast."

"Well, if the little lady hadn't a screamed like that, I doubt I'd have noticed your predicament. You need to thank her. And I need to make that train."

With those words, the man turned and stepped away. In a matter of moments, Devlin's rescuer had joined the crush of people at the side of the nearest car. A loud whoosh accompanied the opening of the door. Barely waiting for disembarking passengers, the crowd surged forward like a human river moving through a narrow culvert.

"I don't recall screaming."

Devlin looked down at Jillian. There was no trace of the wild, reckless expression he'd been about to question when he felt himself begin to fall. Her light brown eyes were wide, her face pale, her expression even more serious than he'd seen it before.

"Well, I'm glad *one* of us managed to make a sound," he said.

She smiled at that. It was a rather weak smile, though, and the frown above her eyes deepened as she said, "Hey, why don't we forget the subway, and get a cab. I'll treat. All of a sudden, I really don't feel like spending thirty to forty minutes doing an impression of a sardine in a can."

From his seat on the right side of the taxi, behind the driver, Devlin stared across the multilane highway at a misty landscape done in shades of green and gray. With his back pressing against the comfortable cushions of the large, black vehicle, his arms crossed over his chest, he cursed the pace at which they traveled.

The road from the airport to London was clogged with traffic. The cab's leisurely pace made it impossible for him to ignore the view outside the window. The panorama of silvery skies embracing green meadows and ancient trees awoke long-forgotten memories, recalled days when he was very young, before large tracts of land came to represent a heavy burden of responsibility to him.

Devlin glanced to his right, where Jillian sat forward, her nose practically touching the window. He was glad that *one* of them was enjoying the trip. He was even more pleased that gazing at the passing countryside had distracted her so thoroughly.

He frowned. He should never have told her that he'd been pushed. But she'd been so concerned about his "dizzy spell," that he'd blurted it out. Then he'd had to assure her that it must have been a simple accident, a result of too many anxious people crowded onto the platform. No doubt someone had turned to someone else, he'd told her, and inadvertently bumped him with some bit of shoulder-laden luggage.

And in the process, he'd managed to convince himself of this, as well. After all, it would have been impossible for someone to have been lying in wait for him. Only Colin had any idea that he might be coming into the country, and even his brother would have no way of knowing *when* he would be arriving, or at which airport.

As to running into Sedgewicke, well, if the man was still working for the trading firm his father owned, he most likely spent a lot of time in airports.

However, for one moment Devlin had found himself recalling other *accidents*, cars that had careened toward him down a dark, narrow Oxford street. The fishing boat that had sprung a leak, miles off the Devon coast. The brakes that suddenly quit working on a steep road. Enough clichéd perils to make for a month of "Movies of the Week."

The mark of the Suttons.

Pushing a man into the path of an approaching train would fit right in with their flair for the melodramatic, as well as the lack of imagination that marked the crime family that seemed to glory in copying tactics depicted in B versions of *The Godfather* saga.

But even if Colin *had* called him back to England in response to some revival of their old threats, the Suttons wouldn't have any way of anticipating his return. As far as the rest of the world was concerned, Marcus Devlin St. Clair had disappeared twelve years ago, and no one in the world knew where he was, or even if he was alive.

"Oh, how adorable."

Jillian's words drew Devlin's attention to her window. Just past the tall grass growing by the roadside, a small, ivy-draped stone house peaked out from the surrounding pocket of trees. A picture postcard of England. Rare now on this highway these days, but an example of many places, some smaller, some far more grand, that sprouted out of the English countryside like mushrooms.

"I've always dreamed of having a place just like that."

Jillian turned to Devlin as she spoke. He frowned.

"Well, if it's cottages that you're in the market for," he said, "you've come to the right place. Be warned, though. They might look snug and cozy, but most of them fail to live up to the promise without extensive, and expensive, repairs."

Jillian blinked. "Tell me, Mr. Sinclair, are you always such a cynic?"

"Tell me, Miss Gibson," he returned with a frown. "Are you always such a wide-eyed romantic?"

The frown puzzled Jillian, but the term he'd used stunned her. *"Me? A romantic?"*

"You're denying it?"

Jillian stared at the man for several seconds. "Not denying it," she replied at last. "More like questioning your perception of me. My friends and family would all tell you that I'm the most practical, down-to-earth person they know."

"Well, I'll concede that you are alarmingly organized. But practical? What makes that word describe you? A truly practical person would have scrapped this trip and gotten whatever refund they could manage."

Jillian thought about this a moment before she replied. "Well, given the circumstances under which we met, I guess your opinion of me is understandably skewed. But believe me, I have never done anything like this in my life. I've been far too busy supporting myself and my three sisters."

Devlin's eyes narrowed. "Why?"

"Why?" Jillian shrugged. "I was the oldest. When our parents died, they left us with one of those century-old Victorian homes you see on postcards of San Francisco, but very little cash. The constant repairs it needed and rising property taxes ate through that money by the time I was sixteen. Gran took in dressmaking, but that wasn't enough, so I went to work after school as a part-time file clerk in a bank. I gave up any idea of higher education and built a career in the financial world. You don't call that *practical?*"

"No. A practical person would have sold the old place, and moved to something less demanding."

Jillian stared at Devlin. Her muscles tightened as she shook her head. "We were all born there. That was our home, not just a house."

"There you go again." Devlin's lips eased into a wide smile and the weary look disappeared from around his eyes. "Only a romantic falls in love with a house. It may be true that you realized the need to get a job at a young age. I've no doubt that you are efficient and responsible in your work. But, I contend that, deep in your heart of hearts, *you* are a romantic."

Jillian couldn't believe this. She was the one with the agenda, with the plans, while he continually talked about not looking down the road too far.

"Oh," she said. "And I suppose you are an expert on being a romantic, Mr. Live-for-the-Moment?"

Devlin gave her one of his half smiles. "Ah, there you go again, confusing things. I am not a romantic. I'm the most practical person I know. When I left home, knowing it to be best for all concerned, I never looked back." The smile disappeared as he paused. "What's more, I learned that a house, big or small, is nothing but a building and not something to get attached to. That is how a practical person views things."

With these words Devlin turned to stare out his window. Jillian did the same, but the view had changed, grown more suburban than rural. No longer magic.

Magic?

Good grief, he's right about me.

Jillian was stunned by this new take on her personality. Ever since she could remember, people had commented on her maturity, on her business sense. She had taken great pride in doing what had to be done, had even found a practical way to console herself when she'd passed up on the scholarship she'd been offered to design school—by using some of her earnings to restore and redecorate the big old house off Filmore Street.

Closing her eyes, Jillian pictured each room, painted and papered in true Victorian splendor. Oh, dear. What could be more romantic? And less practical? Her lips curved. A cottage, she thought. A cottage with flowering vines climbing the stone walls to a thatched roof. A cottage with a riot of flowers crowding the front yard, and a stream running past a tall oak in the back.

Her eyelids had grown too tired to open. She let them stay shut, rested her head back against the seat and told herself that truly practical people did view houses as empty shells. She, on the other hand, saw a house as a still-life entity, something with a soul, a personality.

It was so lovely the way that people in England named their houses, from the largest mansion to the humblest cottage, she thought. Perhaps Devlin had been in the U.S. too long, she thought sleepily, and had forgotten his roots. Pity.

The next thing she knew, Devlin's voice was saying, "Jillian, wake up. We're at your hotel. Let's get you checked in."

Feeling half-drugged by her nap, yet craving even more sleep, she forced her eyes open and dragged herself out of the cab. She followed Devlin, who carried her suitcase along with his duffel, up a wide set of steps. She was too groggy to do more than glance at the magnificent granite building before entering through wide glass doors, or to pay proper homage to the red Aubusson carpet she walked across as she approached an elaborately carved mahogany front desk.

But with each step, she became aware that a sense of dread was leaking into her half-awake state. She was going to have to check in now, and somehow explain why she was doing so alone. When she reached the front desk, she met the bespectacled eyes of the older gentleman on the other side, managed a smile and opened her mouth to speak.

Before a sound passed her lips, Devlin's voice echoed in the high-ceilinged vestibule, "Mr. and Mrs. Brett Turner."

Jillian turned to Devlin in surprise. He didn't so much as glance at her, just continued to stare at the desk clerk until the man said, "Yes, that would be the honeymoon suite. We've been expecting you."

The sharp ring of a bell made Jillian start. A moment later, a young man in a gray uniform marched up to Devlin and held his hands out to accept their luggage as the desk clerk announced, "Room Seven-O-Eight."

As she followed the bellboy to the elevator, Jillian told herself that it was very thoughtful of Devlin to help her over this little hurdle. Of course, eventually she would have to explain her situation to the management at the hotel. But right now, she could get herself up to her room and out of her travel-rumpled clothes without saying another word to anyone.

Which was just as well, because when she passed through the door that the bellboy held open for them, she was rendered completely speechless as she gazed at the old-world splendor of the sitting room.

A molded ceiling soared a full twelve feet above her head. The walls were paneled in dark wood to the tops of the mahogany doors, and above that painted a pale blue. A sapphire sofa, oversize and overstuffed, lined the wall to her left, bracketed by two wing chairs. An ornately manteled fireplace filled the opposite wall. Jillian's gaze slid past that to the dining table and chairs in the left corner of the room, set within the angle of two wide windows draped in more dark blue velvet.

And this was only one room of the suite.

In something of a daze, Jillian turned toward the door to her right just as Devlin and the bellboy reentered the sitting room. Walking past them, she stepped into the bedroom to stare at the huge bed with thick wooden pillars that held a burgundy canopy above a matching velvet coverlet.

The deep voices echoing indistinctly from the living area caught her attention. At the sound of a door being opened, Jillian roused herself and stepped back into the other room just as Devlin was saying, "Please tell the manager that we find the suite satisfactory in every way."

Before Jillian could say or do anything, the bellboy nodded briskly and placed his hand in his pocket as he backed into the hall, drawing the door shut behind him. She frowned as she turned to Devlin.

"What?" he said before she could speak. "The suite isn't up to your standards?"

"Not up to my standards?" Jillian glanced around again. "I'm overwhelmed by it. Holly wouldn't tell me anything about the places she booked me into, other than that they were all nice. She told me she cashed in some favors to get special discounts, but this goes far beyond nice."

"Then why the frown?"

"Oh, because I realized that my stunned response to this place put you in the position of having to tip the bellboy. You'll have to let me reimburse you for that—and for the cab fare that I'd promised to pay."

Devlin shook his head as she reached into her purse for her wallet. "Forget it. That's what husbands are for."

"I *won't* forget it." Jillian pulled out some of her newly changed money. "I've been paying my own way since I was sixteen. Besides, I think we can drop the Mr. and Mrs. Turner business."

"Well, actually." Devlin gave her a sleepy grin as she walked toward him. "I've been thinking about that, and wondering if we couldn't keep it going, at least for tonight."

Chapter 4

Jillian felt a sudden chill as Devlin's words echoed through the room. She stared at him, noticed that his heavy-lidded eyes and the dark stubble on his jaw gave him a sinister, threatening appearance.

Her heart began to flutter like the wings of a trapped moth. What had she done? What kind of stupid mess had she gotten herself into? *Don't ever go anywhere with a stranger.* Three-year-old kids knew better than to do what she'd done.

"Jillian. I'm not the big bad wolf."

Devlin's deep voice made her blink. His amused tone turned her panic button down a notch or two.

"I didn't think you were," she replied.

She knew her words sounded defensive and less than convincing. Devlin apparently found this funny, because he smiled quite widely. His teeth gleamed as he shook his head.

"You did, too. This must be that practical thing you were mentioning." His smile faded. "And you're right. That was a very improper suggestion I just made. It's just that I suddenly realized how tired I am. I thought it would be nice to stretch out on your couch for the night, and get an early start in the morning. But perhaps it's better I go ahead and catch the late train. Here."

Devlin extended his hand toward her as he spoke. The card key lay on his open palm. Jillian frowned as she took it from him, then lifted her eyes to his.

"That's not necessary," she said. "I'm so tired, I can hardly think. You must be, too. If you go now, you'll probably fall asleep the moment you sit down on the train, then sleep right through your stop. Besides, I noticed a lock, complete with key, in the door to the bedroom."

Devlin's eyebrows gave a quick lift. "Rather odd for a honeymoon suite, wouldn't you say?"

"I'm not so sure." Jillian managed a weary smile. "I doubt that I'm the first *bride* to arrive after a transatlantic flight too exhausted to do anything in the bed but sleep."

"Or I the first *groom,*" he replied. He gave her a smile that looked only slightly like a leer, followed by a quick wink. "My other appetites are less affected, however. I'm not sure, but somewhere along the line, I think we've missed at least one meal. Are you hungry?"

Jillian glanced at her watch. Nearly five-thirty. The last time they'd eaten had been on the plane, a good hour before they landed. Suddenly she was starving.

"Yes," she replied. "But I don't have the energy to go out looking for a restaurant. I guess we could order something up."

"Well, as a matter of fact, the bellboy mentioned something about a dinner that was already on order for us. He said it was to be delivered at our convenience. Your sister's handiwork, I imagine. He said to ring room service, and it would be up in a half hour."

Jillian felt a little of her weariness lift at this bit of news. "That sounds great. Would you mind calling down? I'd like to unpack a few things, then take a shower. It might wake me up long enough to eat."

Devlin nodded, then watched her turn and enter the bedroom, shutting the door behind her. He smiled at the soft *click* of the lock, then glanced around till he located the telephone. It sat on a small table next to the sofa, where he was more than happy to take a seat while he rang room service.

After hanging up, he lifted the receiver again and dialed an outside number. Three long rings later, a female voice answered. Even though all she said was a short hello, Devlin recognized the voice.

He found himself fighting the urge to say, "Hello, Mum, it's me, Devlin. Read any good books lately?"

It was an old joke, their standard greeting when she would return from a trip to London, or he came home from school. Now the words clogged his throat. They would hardly be appropriate, given the harsh ones that had been exchanged when he'd announced his decision to leave.

His eyes narrowed as he heard her repeat, "Hello?"

"Hello, is Colin in?"

"No, I'm sorry. He's out of town at the moment. Is there a message?"

Devlin frowned. "No. Thank you."

Slowly he replaced the receiver. Out of town? That made no sense at all. Twelve years ago, he and Colin had made a solemn pact. Whenever he changed cities, he was to send his younger brother a package, containing some insignificant item. There would be no return address to identify that it was from him, but the item would be wrapped in the local daily newspaper from his new temporary location.

If something of a dire nature were to arise that required his presence in England, Colin was to place a personal ad in that particular paper, and Devlin would leave for home immediately. They'd never stipulated what the nature of such an emergency might be. At the time, several possible events had sprung to mind. Over the years, those fears had faded.

Other than a major illness in the family, the only other circumstance he could imagine prompting Colin's message would have something to do with Nigel Sutton or his family.

Devlin ran an impatient hand through his hair. All that had been over, years ago. It was more than a bit paranoid of him to imagine that the incident at the underground station had been anything other than a simple accident. It was patently absurd to imagine that the Suttons could have been lying in wait for him, that one of them had tried to push him in front of that train.

He probably shouldn't have called the house, but he needed answers. Now he only had more questions. His brother shouldn't be "out of town." Colin had to know that he'd leave for England as soon as he read that ad.

Devlin closed his eyes, relaxed against the couch cushions, and told himself to quit fretting over it. He was too tired to think properly, for one thing, which was why he'd decided against leaving for Exeter this evening. His mind wasn't functioning at top form. He needed one full night's sleep before he tackled the rest of his journey and faced whatever it was that needed facing.

The next thing Devlin knew, a series of loud knocks was waking him from a deep doze. Forcing his weary body to rise from the sofa, he opened the door to admit the room service attendant. Pushing a cart laden with silver-domed plates, the white-coated fellow crossed the room and began to set the table. He'd just finished arranging the plates and lighting several tall candles in the center, when Jillian entered.

She looked refreshed. Some of the color had returned to her cheeks, and her hair seemed to shimmer in the candlelight, making Devlin suddenly aware of the stubble that darkened his jaw. She'd changed clothes, too, into a black long-sleeved tunic over matching wide-legged pants. The knit fabric skimmed her slender curves as she approached the table. As the attendant began backing his cart away, she handed the man a tip, accompanied him to the door, then opened it to let him exit.

"I found some extra blankets in the wardrobe closet," she said as she crossed back toward the table. "And you can have one of the pillows from the bed."

Devlin nodded as he held a chair out for her, but she walked right past him to stand in the center of the angle formed by the two corner windows.

"Look at this magnificent view," she said softly. "I can't believe it. I'm finally here."

Devlin moved around the table to join her. She was right, it was a fantastic view. The afternoon mist had lifted, leaving a few thin clouds shimmering in shades of mauve and lavender beneath the jagged skyline. From the right-hand window they could see Waterloo Bridge crossing the Thames. Out the left one the river wound up to pass beneath the Tower Bridge on its way toward the dome of St. Paul's Cathedral.

"Postcard perfect," he conceded. "Your sister did well."

"Yes, she did."

Jillian swayed slightly as she peered from one window to the other. Though London was no stranger to Devlin, it had been a long time since he'd seen it. As he stared out over the huge city, where ancient stone towers rose alongside those made of metal and glass, something twisted in his gut, a deep ache that rose to tighten his chest.

His mind reacted immediately. *Good God, not some delayed sense of homesickness. Not at this late date.*

No. You're hungry, he told himself. Nothing more.

"Jillian," he said. "You can see the view from the table. Come on, have a seat before the the food gets cold."

Jillian nodded and turned to take her seat at the table. As the meal progressed, she had to admit that Holly had ordered well. Cream-of-broccoli soup was followed by a small Caesar salad, then Beef Wellington, succulent within its golden crust, and rosé wine served with the meal hit just the right note.

"Your sister made some great choices."

Jillian nodded and swallowed a sip of wine. As she lowered her empty glass to the table she shifted her gaze to Devlin. "Yes, she chose all my favorites. And Brett's, supposedly."

"Supposedly?"

"Well, who knows which things he said were true and which were lies? I was thinking about this in the shower, and it occurred to me that almost anything the man said is suspect now."

He lifted one eyebrow. "Oh, singing a chorus of 'I'm Gonna Wash That Man Right Out-a My Hair,' were we?"

Jillian found her lips trembling slightly as she thought about the tears that had mingled with the shower spray falling on her face. They had released a great deal of pain from her chest, and once much of the hurting was gone, her mind had cleared, too. Now she was able to smile more widely and nod.

"Sort of. It occurred to me that Brett went to a great deal of trouble to ensure that I'd be attracted to him. I'm fairly certain that the women in my office not only filled him in on my tastes in food and entertainment, but also mentioned that I had an aversion to men who were too charming."

Reaching for the bottle of wine, she poured another half glass. "So, even though I feel like a fool for having fallen for his act, I take some comfort in knowing that I was tricked by a well-armed expert. And once I realized this, everything else made sense, too."

"Such as?"

Jillian stared at the candles glittering between them as she considered her reply. She was feeling very serene and relaxed after all that good food. She realized the wine had loosened her tongue, but being able to talk about what had happened to her without tensing with anger or fighting off tears gave her a sense of strength, as if she were in charge of herself once again.

"Well," she said. "It occurred to me that my instincts may not be as defective as I thought. My alarms didn't go off in his presence, because he had the ammunition to disable them."

Jillian paused as she placed her empty plate to one side. She reached for the dish of chocolate mousse that had been tempting her all through the meal, and poured herself a cup of what Devlin had assured her was decaffeinated coffee.

"And now," she said, "I even understand why he never pressed me into having sex."

"You've got to be kidding."

Devlin's words brought a quick blush to Jillian's cheeks. She hadn't planned on saying *that*. "I'm sorry," she said. "I guess wine on top of jet lag is more than I can handle."

"I'm not offended by what you said if that's what you're thinking," Devlin replied. He shook his head as he poured coffee from the silver pot into his cup. "Just rather surprised. From what you'd told me earlier, I'd decided that Brett Turner was a clever, rather heartless fellow. But this last bit tells me he either had some scruples, or he was a complete idiot."

Jillian's face grew even warmer beneath his gaze. She shook her head.

"I don't believe it was a case of either of those things. I think it's very likely he didn't want to rock the boat, that he needed to get to the wedding and the honeymoon so he could make arrangements to leave the country without raising suspicions. The agent from the FBI said they believe he has an accomplice over here. I wouldn't be at all surprised if this was where he was going to pick up the money he'd transferred on the computer."

Devlin raised his eyebrows. "You might have something there."

Jillian took a sip of coffee and stifled a relieved sigh. Thank God, her brain was working well enough to move the conversation to less personal matters. Now, if she could, she'd like to escape the spotlight all together and learn a little about the man on the other side of the table.

"You know," she said. "I just realized that I've never asked what it is that you do for a living."

Devlin lifted his eyebrows as he placed his coffee cup back in the saucer. "Me? I own a couple of English-style pubs."

"How apropos. In San Francisco?"

"Well, the newest one is there. I have half interest in a couple of others in different cities."

He wasn't giving much, but he was at least responding. And increasing her curiosity.

"Well, how did you get into that?"

Devlin shrugged. "I started out as a bar back, a stocking clerk of sorts, in New York about ten years ago. I worked my way up to bartender, and decided I liked the work so much that I wanted my own place. So, I saved an old building from the wrecking ball near the financial district, restored it and fixed it up so that anyone walking in would swear they'd stepped into a British local. It went over rather well."

Jillian found herself smiling. "Oh, so you like fixing up old buildings in the same way that I like restoring houses."

"One difference, my girl." Devlin leaned toward her, his eyes creasing in the corners. "I don't get attached to my places. I get 'em running and move on to start again."

Jillian couldn't help returning his smile. Or liking this man. He made no pretense of being anything other than a pleasant, self-serving rogue. An honest rogue, she thought as she turned to gaze out the window. Not like Brett, purposely fooling others into believing that he was something he wasn't.

It was dark now outside now. The only light in the room came from the three flames atop the tapered candles in the center of the table. Devlin turned to share the view with Jillian, and saw that London had been transformed into a world of glittering lights beneath a dark sky powdered with stars.

He looked at Jillian again. Her face wore none of the weariness he'd noticed earlier. There was no trace of determination, or sadness there, either. None of the expressions he'd become familiar with in the past...was it merely twenty-four hours?

The only word he could come up with for the look he saw shining out of her amber eyes was *wonder.*

He couldn't remember the last time he'd experienced that particular emotion. Seeing the Grand Canyon, he supposed. The Statue of Liberty rising above New York Harbor. Lake Tahoe, looking like an enormous aqua stone set within the granite peaks of the Sierras.

But never when he'd looked upon a city.

"What are you thinking?" he said softly.

Jillian turned to him. Her lips twitched into a hesitant smile, then she shook her head.

"What?" he persisted.

"You'll laugh at me."

"No, I won't. Look, I've seen London lots of times. I think it's a great looking place. But you seem to see something beyond that. Tell me what it is."

Jillian shifted her gaze to the window again. Her eyes glittered as she shrugged. "A story come to life. Wendy staring out over London from the nursery window. Peter saying 'Second star to the right, and straight on until morning.'"

Devlin sat silent for a moment as Jillian shifted her gaze back to the window. She'd mentioned her sisters before, and her grandmother, all with a tone that spoke of affection.

"Your gran read *Peter Pan* to you often, I take it," he commented softly.

Jillian nodded as she lifted a hand to her cheek with a quick, brushing motion. "Yes. My sisters and I used to put on little plays based on the story."

Her words unearthed long-forgotten visions of Devlin's own childhood.

"Really? My brother and I did the same thing. The sword parts, of course. So, tell me, which of you played Peter Pan?"

Jillian continued to stare out the window as she replied, "Holly, usually. She also played Hook."

"Rather schizophrenic, isn't that?"

She responded with a tiny shrug. "We all alternated roles, depending on the needs of the story we were playing out. Emily and Sarah took the roles of the lost boys, including John and Michael."

"And you?"

Jillian turned to him and brushed her hand at the corner of her eye again as she gave him another small smile.

"I think you know the answer to that."

"Wendy," he said.

"Right. Always the little mother."

Devlin frowned at the suspicious-looking glimmer in her eyes. "Are you all right?" he asked.

Jillian blinked, then her smile twisted into a wry grin. "Sure. I just got to thinking how great my sisters all were yesterday, after they learned there was to be no wedding, and why. They handled everything for me."

"And what did they have to say about your plan to go on your honeymoon alone?"

A frown tightened Jillian's brow as she considered his question. "They were all rather surprised, at first," she said at last. "Then they were all for it. They gave me what cash they had, and wished me all the best."

"Hmm. Quite a bit different from *my* family's reaction when I announced my decision to leave," Devlin said.

He waited for the anger to tighten his jaw, as it always did whenever he slipped and allowed himself to recall the arguments, the recriminations, the harsh words that had followed him out the door. But anger was silent tonight. Instead, he became aware of a deep sadness, welling up within his chest, straining at the walls he'd so carefully built to hold it back.

There had been a great deal of concern beneath those angry exchanges with his family. He had chosen to ignore that, to forget the days when his mother had read to him and his brother as Jillian's gran had for her and her sisters. His father had read to him, as well, and played with his sons, before his grandfather had died.

"You parted in anger?"

Devlin nodded in response to Jillian's soft question, recalling how he'd held on to that anger, used it to keep him strong, so he would not weaken and stay, and continue to put them in danger.

The pain in Devlin's chest deepened, making him frown. He must be far more tired than he thought. He'd never spoken of any of this before. Pushing his chair back, Devlin stood. He needed to get some sleep under his belt. That would take care of these aberrant emotions, along with the foggy thinking that seemed to have crept into his brain.

"I'm going to get those blankets and that pillow, if you don't mind," he said.

"Not at all," Jillian replied. She got to her feet and began stacking plates. "I'll see to putting all this into the hall. Now that I've eaten, I've revived a little. Why don't you take your turn in the bathroom first?"

She watched him nod, walk across the room to retrieve his duffel from the chair nearest the bathroom.

After he was gone, her shoulders sagged. She'd lied. She was exhausted. But at this particular moment, even more than sleep, she needed some time to get herself in hand.

It had been obvious that Devlin hadn't been truly comfortable once the subject of his family came up. The expression of pain in his eyes had kept her from asking anything about the family emergency he'd mentioned at the ticket counter. She knew all too well how it felt to open one's mouth and reveal more than one was ready to handle.

That thought brought a burning sensation to her cheeks as she recalled what she'd said about never having slept with Brett.

She finished stacking plates on the silver tray, carried it to the door that led to the hall and placed it just outside. As the door clicked shut again, Jillian crossed her arms and leaned against the wall.

That statement had most likely made her sound like some sort of prude or ice princess. But maybe that was just as well. Maybe this would keep Devlin from realizing just how strongly she'd reacted to that kiss in the airport, or from guessing that just thinking of those moments could make her knees weak and her heart race.

Like they were doing now.

"Jillian."

Devlin's deep voice made her start, then turn to find him standing in the doorway. A pillow was under one arm, and a blanket under the other. The strap of his duffel bag dangled from his fingers.

Jillian noted these things in some recessed corner of her mind. Most of her attention was drawn to the dark blue T-shirt he'd changed into. It hung loosely past the waist of his jeans, but fitted snugly across his shoulders and chest. Apparently he hadn't packed any pajamas. Perhaps he never wore pajamas to bed.

Or anything else.

Blinking away the image created by this thought, Jillian concentrated on staring at Devlin's face. She noticed that the five-o'clock shadow was gone, and that the dark waves falling on his forehead glittered wetly in the glow from the candles. But it seemed that not even his face was safe territory. His eyes regarded her with a heavy-lidded, questioning look that made her stomach tighten and twist.

"Yes," she responded.

"The bathroom's all yours," he said as he stepped into the room and deposited his duffel and pillow on the chair and the bedding on the couch.

Jillian crossed the room silently. She had just reached the door to the bedroom, when a deep voice made her turn around.

"Wait a minute."

Devlin stepped past the furniture to stand in front of her. "Jillian."

His voice was slightly hoarse, his eyes shadowed with weariness as he gazed down at her. Jillian swallowed as she felt the warmth of his hand along her cheek, held her breath as he leaned toward her.

"You're a good lass," he said, then paused again.

Chapter 5

"I want to thank you for the use of the couch."

Jillian held her breath as Devlin finished speaking and stepped back. The tips of this fingers grazed her jaw slightly as he moved away. In response to his lopsided grin, she managed to sketch a smile before closing the door between them.

The moment it clicked shut she turned and leaned against it, grasping the knob to prevent her body from sliding down the smooth mahogany surface.

For a second there, she'd been afraid that he was going to kiss her. Afraid? Or hoping? Her lips were tingling with anticipation and her heart was making feeble, fluttering beats. She felt warm all over. Her face, especially.

And she *should* be blushing. She was reacting like an idiot. She barely knew the man. Yes, he had very nice lips—nice and talented lips, judging by her body's reaction to the kiss they'd shared earlier in the day.

But he was a stranger. A not very communicative stranger, at that. She knew his name, that he'd come to

England because of a family emergency and that he owned some pubs. Nothing more.

A frown pulled Jillian's eyebrows together. As she straightened from the door, she wondered how Devlin Sinclair had managed to reveal so very little about himself. Crossing the impossibly thick mauve carpet to the rack holding her suitcase, she couldn't help but wonder if his reticence had simply been some natural quirk of the British need for privacy, or if he'd skillfully kept her talking about *her* life and plans, so that he wouldn't have to talk about his.

These questions gave rise to others. For instance, had it been simple gentlemanly consideration that had urged him to escort her to her hotel? Or had he counted on her allowing him to stay with her all along? And what about that business in the subway?

The sudden image of seeing Devlin fall toward the tracks and the oncoming engine made Jillian shudder. She blinked away the vivid picture and told herself that it was too late at night to be thinking about all this, especially if she wanted to get some sleep.

And she desperately wanted to do that.

Not, however, in the silvery nightgown she found herself staring at as she looked down to her open suitcase. Her sisters had all pitched in on this shower gift, an expensive gown and matching robe made of heavy satin and edged in silver gray lace. Elegance, romance and seduction in one sensuous package.

What a waste.

With one sweep of her hand Jillian pushed the fabric to the side, then lifted the corner of one folded item after the other until she found a pair of dark green leggings and an oversize pink T-shirt. In a matter of moments, she had her knit tunic and pants on hangers in the closet across the room and had changed into her sleeping attire.

A few more moments later, she returned from the bathroom, ready for bed. She flicked off the light, then guided by the small glowing lamp atop the table next to the bed, she crossed the room. The covers had been turned back to reveal pristine white sheets. Not satin, thankfully, she noticed as she slid between them.

She turned off the light and pulled the covers up to her chin. Now, in the dark, she could pretend that she wasn't in a room that screamed, in the most understated manner, *honeymoon suite.*

As the bed warmed beneath her, she realized that some of her anger at Brett Turner had faded. Oh, the situation still made her furious, but the bulk of her anger was now directed inward. It was clear that she'd done a very good job of conning herself during the past six months, of falling in love with love. It was amazing that she could see so clearly now, what she'd refused to face during their courtship.

She had hardly known the man she'd planned to marry. She had fallen in love with an image, not a person, all because of her growing desire for a home, and a family to fill it.

She could have bought a house on her own a couple of years ago. Why hadn't she? And why had she waited all these years to make this trip? Not because of her parents' accident, she knew, though losing them so suddenly had definitely had a strong effect on her, making her even more cautious, placing her in a highly responsible role at a very young age.

But it had been a long time since any of her sisters really needed her. Holly and Emily both had their own incomes, and Sarah had a part-time job to supplement her college scholarship. A year ago, Gran had received an inheritance from a cousin that made her quite comfortable. Yet, Jillian thought, she'd persisted in waiting until Prince Charming came along before giving in to her long-held desire to revisit England.

Well, she was not wasting any more time. Neither was she going to be bound to doing sensible things anymore. Tomorrow she would start a whole new life in which she would leave herself open to the moment and see where the moment would lead her.

The only sensible thing she was going to do was forget what it had felt like to kiss Devlin Sinclair.

Jillian shifted her attention from her London guidebook to the neatly printed lines in her agenda.

So much to do, so little time.

With a sigh, she reached for the pot of tea in the center of the table and poured herself another cup, then leaned back in her chair and gazed out once again over London, where the dome of St. Paul's Cathedral glittered beneath the sun streaming through some light clouds.

Her first reaction, upon discovering that Devlin had already ordered up breakfast, was to eat as quickly as possible, then run down and catch the first bus going anywhere and just gobble up London as she found it.

But breakfast had settled her down somewhat. As she sipped a second cup of tea, she'd come to the conclusion that she was likely to see far more if she made some plans.

Running true to form already, a little voice chided her. *What happened to living moment to moment?*

Devlin Sinclair, that's what.

She'd entered the sitting room to find the man sitting at the table wearing a crisp white shirt that was opened at the neck to reveal the tiniest triangle of black chest hair. The quick rush of warmth to her face in response to his good-morning smile had made her decide that as long as Devlin was around, with his bedroom eyes and his knee-weakening, seemingly ever thickening accent, it might be a good idea to hold on to her sensible, practical habits a bit longer.

With a sigh, Jillian placed her cup in the saucer and returned her attention to the itinerary she'd been struggling with for a half hour.

"May I ask what it is you are doing?"

Devlin was surprised to see an almost embarrassed expression cross Jillian's face as she glanced up at him from across the table.

She was dressed more casually today, in a long-sleeved white T-shirt and khaki slacks. The waves in her honey brown hair were more pronounced, softening her square features. When she'd entered the room a half hour earlier he'd seen a flicker of the spontaneous, defiant glint he'd noticed in her eyes more than once the day before. But as they ate, she'd retreated into a quiet, polite, but definitely reserved, shell.

Which, he supposed, was just as well. He'd half expected Jillian to bombard him with questions when she came in this morning. Now that she'd had some sleep, he'd been afraid she would decide to ask some of the questions he'd dodged yesterday, like where his family lived, perhaps, or what was so important that he had to get there so quickly?

Since he had only suspicions regarding this last subject, he'd joined her in silence to enjoy the huge English breakfast of eggs, ham, kippers, toast and jam, served on delicate cream-colored china.

Now that he had all that food and half of his third cup of tea in him, he knew he should make some move toward putting his loosely formed plan into action. But the sight of Jillian gazing into a tour book of London and scribbling in her zippered notebook had raised his curiosity. And before he'd had the chance to remind himself that what Miss Jillian Gibson did now was none of his business, he'd found himself questioning her actions.

"Making a list of the things I'd like to do today," she replied as she returned her attention to the page she'd been writing on.

"I see."

Devlin took another sip of tea, to keep from offering his assistance. He knew London well, after all, and could easily suggest a day's outing that wouldn't be too taxing for a newcomer. But she hadn't asked his advice. Besides, it was high time he got on with his own plans, such as they were.

Just as he started to get to his feet, Jillian glanced up and gave him a rather sheepish smile.

"Last night I promised myself I was going to take things moment by moment, sort of follow my nose," she said, "but I only have the one day in London before I take the train to Bath tomorrow. My accommodations are all paid in advance, which means that no matter how much I might want to go where the wind blows me, I really can't afford to deviate much. I'm going to have several days in London at the end of the trip, to do some shopping and see the plays Holly got tickets to, but when Brett and I—"

She stopped. Her features hardened slightly, she took a deep breath, then went on. "When *I* planned the itinerary with Holly, I told her it would be more relaxing to see the countryside first, then take London a day at a time at the end of the trip."

Devlin gave her a brief nod. "Sounds like a right good plan, if plans are the thing for you."

Her eyes narrowed. "Well, what would *you* do, if you only had three weeks to see a country you've been dreaming of all your life?"

"Me?" Devlin shrugged. "Well, first off, I'd give myself a lot more time than just three weeks. You could run yourself ragged just trying to see all there is to see in London in that time, and still miss half of it. Oh, unless you're one of those people who consider staring at a building and snapping a photo *seeing* something. To really experience a place, you need to spend some time. Stop for a cup of tea, or bend an elbow at one of the local pubs, that sort of thing."

For one moment, as he watched her eyebrows move together, he thought Jillian was going to tell him where to get off. Then she sighed and shook her head.

"You're right. And I plan on doing exactly that. In fact, I've already crossed out half of the places I was trying to cram into my schedule for today."

"Good girl. So, what are you left with?"

"Covent Garden. I figured I'd take the bus, and just stroll through the shops. I'll probably have lunch there, and I noticed that a couple great-sounding bookstores are located nearby." She glanced at her notebook. "My itinerary shows that I've got reservations this afternoon to take a tour of the city that leaves from the hotel. I'll do that, but I think I'll cancel dinner at R. S. Hispaniola."

Devlin was familiar with the restaurant, created from a ship docked near the Waterloo bridge.

"Why?" he asked. "It's on a nice spot, right on the Thames. You couldn't ask for a nicer view."

Jillian glanced up, then lifted her shoulders in a brief shrug. "I think I'd feel more comfortable eating here."

Here, in the hotel room, where she wouldn't be surrounded by other couples dining in the romantic atmosphere provided by the water view. Here, where she'd have some chance, no matter how slight, of forgetting that this was supposed to be a honeymoon.

Devlin found himself wanting to congratulate Jillian on her attempt at a thoroughly British stiff-upper-lipped approach to her situation. He also found himself wanting to pull her to her feet and into his arms and kiss her until she was dizzy.

An utterly insane idea, if he'd ever had one.

Getting to his feet, Devlin crossed the room to rearrange the clothes in his now-bulging duffel. He'd seen her fight with her emotions and noted a strong sense of self-directed anger and doubt the day before. She deserved to know just how attractive and desirable she was, and if circumstances were different, he would love to be the one to demonstrate this to her.

In truth, he'd almost done something of that sort the night before. When they stood at the doorway to the bedroom, the memory of holding her in his arms and kissing her in the airport had sorely tempted him to repeat that moment.

But circumstances weren't different. He didn't have the luxury of time to help Jillian explore London, to introduce this pathologically organized woman to the joys of lolly-gagging, or to see if the spark ignited by that kiss would blaze into something more powerful.

Devlin frowned. That was a dangerous thought, not to mention a rather aberrant one for him. He'd had his share of relationships with women, but they were always based on mutual mental and physical attraction. Emotions, like a desire to offer a healing hand to a wounded soul, had never played a part in any of these situations. He'd lost all faith in matches made in heaven, and preferred to be with women who were too involved in their careers to look for anything permanent.

Yet now he found himself strongly attracted to a woman who had definitely expected permanence in her last relationship, a woman with an absurd fondness for a country that was barely holding on to the last shreds of former glory, a woman who needed time to recover from the disaster of her near-marriage. Now, when his time wasn't his, when, for the first time in twelve years, he faced some real obligations.

Obligations and doubts.

Devlin pulled the zipper shut. He'd pretty much convinced himself that his little brush with death the previous afternoon had just been an odd accident. However, caution would still be wise.

Caution and speed.

"Are you leaving now?"

Jillian's soft question drew Devlin out of his thoughts as he slipped on his jacket.

"Yes," he replied.

"Well, I'm going down, too." She stood, notebook in hand. "If you'll wait while I get my purse and coat, I'll be right with you. We can take the lift down together."

Jillian saw him smile. Figuring that it was in response to her use of the British word for elevator, she gave him a saucy grin.

"Oh, I can speak the lingo, old chap. That's what comes of being raised by a native Brit, don't you know?"

His chuckle followed her into the bedroom, where she continued to smile as she slipped her arms into her beige trench coat. Her skin tingled. Little shocks of electricity coursed through her as she placed her agenda, guidebook and her folding umbrella into her large purse.

She had no idea why she suddenly felt so light and carefree. She told herself that this could be due to the fact that Devlin was going on his way. With him gone, she'd be free to do whatever she wanted to do, without any obligations toward anyone else, for the first time in far too many years.

A small frown tightened her brow as she retrieved her hotel key from the table beside the bed. So why had she decided that it would be best to say goodbye to him in the hotel lobby? Was it because she knew that the presence of other people would keep her from asking if the two of them might meet up somewhere during her stay in England?

That would sound foolish, if not rather forward. It would also most likely cause him to wonder if being jilted hadn't made her so desperate that she'd leap into the arms of the first man she bumped into. Not that they weren't nice arms, she reminded herself as she stepped back into the sitting room to find him holding the door to the hallway for her.

"I suppose you also know that you get the best rate of exchange for your dollars at the banks, not at the hotel desks?" Devlin asked as she passed in front of him.

"Actually, I remember reading that, but I might have forgotten it if you hadn't mentioned it. Thank you."

The lift was slow to arrive. Jillian stared at the buttons flashing on and off as it approached their floor and concentrated on keeping her hands relaxed and at her sides. She found herself wanting to thank Devlin—and she didn't really know why. *She'd* been the one to save him, really, by providing a way to get to his homeland as quickly as possible. Not to mention the use of her couch.

Maybe she felt this sense of gratitude for the patient way he'd listened to her, cheered her on, encouraged her to plan less and enjoy more. Not once in her life, even before the death of her parents, had she been encouraged to be anything other than a "big girl"—responsible and levelheaded.

No one else had ever seen her as a romantic.

"I want to thank you, Jillian."

Devlin's words took her by surprise. No, not his words, she told herself as she turned to him, but the completely serious tone in which they were spoken.

"I know you had your own reasons for offering the plane ticket to me," he said, "but letting me stay in your hotel room went above and beyond. Now, I'm going to ask you one more favor."

Jillian stared into his eyes. "What's that?"

"Don't trust anyone else that way while you're here."

Devlin's dark blue eyes held hers as he spoke. For several seconds Jillian continued to stare up at him, trying to decide if she was angry at him for thinking her foolish enough to do such a thing, or pleased at his show of concern.

Before she could respond to either emotion, a soft *ding* announced the arrival of the lift. The doors opened to reveal a nearly full car. Once inside, Jillian was highly aware of Devlin standing next to her, even more so after three more people got in on the next floor, forcing her arm into contact with his.

The slight musky scent she would always think of as being Devlin's filled her every breath, reminding her of the security of his arm around her waist as they'd gone through customs, the warmth of his hand holding her frozen one, the heady sensation of his lips claiming hers.

By the time the car reached the ground floor and the door opened, these memories had sent such a dangerous rush of heat through her veins that Jillian couldn't decide if she was relieved or sorry to step out and away from him.

"I have to use one of the pay phones, but you should probably be about your sight-seeing," Devlin said.

He led her to the double glass doors that opened onto the circular driveway, where a pair of cabs were just pulling up to deposit more patrons.

Devlin stared through the glass, then looked down at Jillian.

"There's a Barclay Bank on nearly every corner, by the way," he said.

After Jillian's soft thanks, Devlin's lips twitched up briefly. "Don't mention it. One more favor?"

Jillian noticed the frown above his dark eyes. Before she could respond, he spoke again.

"Be careful . . . and have a good time."

His voice was deep, his eyes suddenly serious. Jillian felt her face grow warm, her insides melt. A dangerous and ridiculous combination that screamed to be controlled.

"That's *two* more favors." She managed to keep her voice light. "Besides, I got the impression you thought those things were mutually exclusive."

The amused glint she'd been more accustomed to seeing returned to Devlin's eyes as he responded.

"Ah, but I'm an expert. You are merely a novice. I think it best to employ caution when learning anything new."

"If you insist."

Jillian shrugged elaborately. She flashed him a smile then turned to step toward the door. A gentle but firm hand on her shoulder made her stop and look up at those dancing blue eyes one last time.

"Again," he said, "thank you."

Resisting the impulse to rise on tiptoe and kiss him goodbye, Jillian replied simply, "My pleasure."

When his fingers slid from her shoulder, she gave him another smile and then stepped forward and passed through the doorway.

Cool air greeted her, but once she was out from beneath the awning that covered the hotel entrance, the sun warmed Jillian's back. Walking briskly down the street, she followed the path she'd marked out during her session with the tour book at breakfast.

With each step, the vague feelings of sorrow and regret at leaving Devlin faded, replaced by a sense of excitement and adventure. The bustle of cars in the street filled her ears, the mixture of old and new architecture claimed her vision, the riotous color of the flower stalls, the newspaper stands filled with tabloids exclaiming impossible headlines, the red double-decker buses.

Bobbies on bicycles, two by two.

No, she told herself, she was not going to break into song, even if she did feel lighthearted. *And* a little lightheaded. So nearly giddy, she realized a few moments later, that she almost walked right past the line—no, she reminded herself, the *queue* at the bus stop.

The red double-decker vehicle that would take her to Covent Garden arrived in less than five minutes. As Jillian mounted the stairs, the conductor took Jillian's money, then shifted his attention to the person behind her.

"Excuse me, sir. The young lady is the last I'll be able to let on this bus. We're all full up."

"Oh, come on, then. There's room for one more, isn't there?"

Jillian turned. The man behind her was dressed in a dark suit and tie, a somber combination that made his red hair look all the brighter. His square, ruddy face bore an expression halfway between angry and pleading, a comic sight that made her want to laugh, but one that apparently had no such effect on the conductor.

"Not a body more," he replied evenly. "Another bus will be along soon."

With that, the conductor signaled the driver to move. As the bus lurched forward, Jillian watched the flushed face below tighten into a full scowl, pinning her with an accusatory glare, as if to indict her for having had the audacity to be in line before him.

Shrugging off a slight shiver, Jillian gazed up the winding stairway leading to the top deck, then turned to the conductor and said, "I don't suppose there would be any point trying to get a seat up top."

He shook his head. "Not unless some of the folks get off within a stop or two. It's not likely, however. Summer crowd, you know, making for the Garden."

Jillian nodded and turned her attention to the shops lining the streets as the bus rumbled along, consoling herself with the thought that when they arrived at her destination, she'd be one of the first passengers off the crowded vehicle.

Actually, she was the very first to disembark, and once on the street, she headed immediately for the arched entrance that she'd seen in countless pictorial tours of London. She gazed at the curve of glass and iron that covered much of the enclosed area. For a moment she could almost hear the echoes of long-gone food- and flowermongers calling out from their stalls, hawking their wares to bustling Victorian patrons this place served in the past.

The current-day proprietors had converted those stalls into bright, modern shops. Spying a kiosk that offered free maps of the two-level shopping area, Jillian crossed the cobblestone courtyard and pulled one out of the plastic pocket.

She'd decided she'd only window-shop today. She wanted to buy something special for Gran and each of her sisters while she was in England, but she didn't want to be lugging these things around the country for the next three weeks. She would check out the shops here, and if she didn't find the perfect items during her trip, she'd feel secure knowing that she could get something here before she flew home.

Jillian strolled down the row of shops, her eye on each window, looking for something to appeal to someone on her short souvenir list. Three stores down, she stopped to admire a grouping of miniature pewter knights that she knew would please her youngest sister, Sarah.

Jillian had just drawn her daybook from her purse to make a notation of the item and the name of the shop, when she realized that the large window was offering a perfect reflection of everything going on behind her. Most of what she saw was in motion, except for a figure standing near a display of topiary animals.

She recognized the bright red hair immediately as belonging to the man who'd been denied access to the bus. He'd removed his jacket. His white shirt was open at the collar, his tie loose and dangling in a manner that completely reversed his earlier natty appearance.

She watched him a moment, saw him glance in one direction, then the other, as if he were waiting for someone, before she opened her date book. She made her notes, then studied the guide to the Covent Garden shops once again.

Spying the name of a bookstore several stalls down the line, she placed the guide back in her purse and started walking. She found herself standing in front of a coffeehouse named Jeans and Beans. Figuring she must have read the guide wrong, she stopped and glanced around.

In the center of the courtyard, a troupe of mimes was surrounded by a small crowd. Jillian gazed past them and a second later, spied the store she'd been looking for, directly opposite the coffee shop. Turning, she worked her way to the right, circling the knot of people. She was halfway across the cobblestones, when a flash of orange-red caught her eye.

She glanced to the right and once more saw the man from the bus. He was about thirty feet away, walking parallel to her, staring straight ahead.

Jillian jerked her head forward and continued toward the bookstore. Her loudly pounding heart almost, but not quite, obliterated the echo of the man's shoes on the stones. She forced herself to breathe slowly as she drew open the door. Stepping into the maze of bookshelves, she took a jog to the left then slipped quickly down the row to the back of the store, where she gazed sightlessly at a row of books.

She was being followed.

No, that was impossible. That sort of thing only happened in movies, not to real people.

Just like real people didn't get pushed into the path of an oncoming subway?

Of course they did. Accidents happened all the time, especially where crowds were involved. Devlin's brush with danger had nothing to do with this man with the red hair.

"Can I help you find anything?"

Jillian turned to the small, dark-haired woman standing at her side. Large brown eyes peered up at her from behind thick wire-framed lenses.

"Well, not really," Jillian said. "I just came in to browse."

And to escape some horrid man who is following me.

The thought echoing in her mind sounded so ridiculous that Jillian found her face growing every bit as warm as it would have if she'd uttered it out loud.

The man had, after all, been trying to get on a bus headed this way. He probably had some very legitimate reason for wandering the shops. Maybe he had to purchase a gift for a birthday or wedding. That chore would easily account for his surly looks, if he was like most men she knew.

Jillian drew a deep breath, then smiled at the saleswoman.

"Actually, I'm interested in interior design. Could you direct me to books on decorating?"

As she glanced at the beautifully photographed rooms in the book the woman had directed Jillian to, an idea slowly took root. She wanted to make some changes in her life when she returned home. The bank offered tuition for continuing education. Perhaps she could take a course or two in interior decorating. Or, for that matter, maybe she'd just look for a new job altogether. It was possible that one of the many decorating firms in the San Francisco area would take on a willing apprentice.

Twenty minutes later, when Jillian stepped out of the shop, her thoughts were so full of possibilities that she had to remind herself to look for the man with red hair.

Not a sign of him anywhere. Releasing a half relieved, half embarrassed breath, Jillian turned and let the bright colors and the heady perfume of a flower stand draw her to her right.

Spires of blue delphiniums and yellow gladiolus rose above bouquets of white daisies and purple irises in the display out front. A wire stand crammed with seed packets, all brightly illustrated, caught her eye. Thinking of Gran's garden at home, she reached for an envelope of double hollyhock seeds, then stopped when she spied the shock of red hair through a space between the packets.

Jillian jerked her hand back. She pivoted around, and without a backward glance to determine if the bright red hair really did belong to the man in the rumpled shirt, she walked briskly over the cobblestones and mounted the first set of stairs she came to.

Did she hear footsteps on the stairs behind her? She thought so, but she might just be hearing the scrape of her own soft-soled loafers on the risers. She wanted to look back, but didn't want to give the impression that she was aware of the man, if indeed he, or any other person, was actually behind her. She just wanted to get somewhere safe, somewhere she could collect her thoughts, and observe without being observed.

She found that place in The Mad Hatter.

Stepping inside, she was greeted by row after row of hat racks, filled from the floor to several inches above her head with headgear. She couldn't see anyone in the place, but a high-pitched voice floated forward from the rear of the store.

"Ooo, yes, that one looks absolutely *smashing* on you. Would you like to see it in red, as well?"

Hoping that the clerk would stay busy while Jillian played her game of spy versus spy, she slipped down the second row. Next to a mirror that reflected the front of the store, she grabbed a black, broad-brimmed hat that looked like something Eliza Doolittle would have worn, and placed it on her head, all the time watching to see if anyone entered behind her.

She saw absolutely no movement.

When Jillian glanced again in the mirror, a reluctant smile curved her lips. Not only could she see no hint that anyone stood outside the shop, waiting for her, but the hat looked absolutely ridiculous on her.

Her imagination was definitely working overtime, she decided. But perhaps she shouldn't be so very surprised at this, considering how many of the books, movies and TV series that she enjoyed had originated in England. There was probably something in the air here that bred mystery and intrigue.

With a sigh and a shake of her head, Jillian removed the hat, placed it on the rack, turned and walked slowly toward the front door.

The glass inset gave her a wide view of the area in front of the store. If anyone was waiting for her, they would have to be lurking alongside the wall on either side to miss her sweeping glance. Telling herself for the third time that day that she was being silly, she pushed the door open, stepped out and turned to her right.

She hadn't taken more than two steps before strong fingers gripped her elbow.

Chapter 6

"Jillian, I thought we'd agreed to meet at The Crusting Pipe for an early lunch."

Devlin pulled Jillian around to face him as he spoke. The look on her face as she glanced up at him was an almost comic blend of panic, surprise and relief.

"What are you doing here, Dev—"

"I'm starving," he interrupted. He was aware that he was talking more loudly than necessary, and continued to do so as he went on in his best Americanese. "I don't know what's going on with my stomach—probably the time change, or the long flight. Let's get something to eat now, and shop later, okay?"

Following these words, he whispered, "Play along with me."

The expression on Jillian's face changed slowly. A hint of panic remained, but it was softened with a look of dawning comprehension.

"Sure," she replied finally.

Devlin loosened his grip on her elbow, then slipped his

arm around her waist to urge her toward the stairway she'd just recently ascended.

"You're doing fine." He spoke barely loud enough to be heard over the echoes of their feet on the steps.

"Thank you," she replied in the same tone. "Might I assume, then, that my imagination has not been working overtime, and someone *has* been following me?"

"Very observant, my dear Watson," he said. "Now give us a smile."

She turned to him as they reached the bottom step and did as he asked. Her lips were a bit tight, and her eyes were wide beneath a slight frown. Devlin leaned toward her right ear and spoke softly.

"Just go along with me on this, okay?"

"It depends," she replied. "Am I going to learn what all this is about?"

"I'll explain once we're in the restaurant." He let his lips graze her cheek as he pulled back and stared down at her. "All right?"

When a hesitant look crept into her eyes, Devlin took both of her hands in his and squeezed them lightly. She took a deep breath, then nodded.

"All right." Her voice was low, even. "But it better be good."

He knew she was talking about his explanation, but the restaurant was a good choice, as well. The entrance was located in the piazza section, and led them down to a cellar-like area. They were shown a booth that was lit by candlelight. An intimate situation, perfect for the honeymooning couple they seemed destined to play for a while longer.

Both of them ordered the salmon and salad. As soon as the waiter left, Jillian leaned across the table and spoke softly.

"Okay. I've been watching the door, and the fellow who's been following me hasn't come in. Will you please tell me what's going on?"

Devlin hesitated. He still only had suspicions, rather improbable sounding ones, at that. "Well," he said, "I'm not quite sure myself."

Jillian's narrowed eyes said she wasn't at all happy with his response. "All right then," she said, "why don't you start with telling me how you knew I was being followed?"

"Ah, that one I can answer. When I was walking toward the old phone booths near the hotel entrance, I happened to notice a fellow with bright red hair standing outside the door, watching you as you walked by."

Jillian nodded very solemnly. "I see. And this raised your suspicions."

Devlin smiled. "No, actually. I mentally congratulated him on his ability to recognize quality when he saw it."

When Jillian's cheeks immediately turned pink and she lowered her gaze to the cup of tea that had just been placed before her, Devlin sobered. This was hardly the time for him to become flirtatious.

"It was what happened next," he said quietly, "that raised my suspicions. Carrot-top turned to the fellow he was standing with, and they both glanced around in a rather suspicious-looking manner. Then the redheaded fellow broke away. From my spot in the booth, I was able to watch him follow you, carefully keeping his distance. That was when I remembered the second cab."

"What second cab?"

"Last night," Devlin replied. "After we arrived at the hotel, I noticed that another taxi had pulled in behind ours. As I was holding the front door for you, I happened to see that it followed the first one away, without letting anyone out.

Jillian glanced toward the door. When she looked back to him, her golden-brown eyes were dark beneath a frown.

"Then you think that someone followed us from the airport? Who would want to follow me? And why?"

"Those are questions that only raise more questions," he replied.

Lifting his glass of ale to his lips, Devlin took a brief sip. "You should know," he said quietly as he lowered his glass to the table, "that I doubt you are their target. I had a good job eluding the other fellow when I left the hotel. The first bloke most likely followed you figuring that we were together, and would hook up again sooner or—"

"Dev. He's here."

Panic sharpened Jillian's whisper. Devlin reached across the table and took her hand in his. "Look at me," he said.

When she obeyed, he held her gaze, conscious of her fingers, slim and cold within his. He spoke softly. "Don't look at anything but me. Remember, we are newlyweds. Madly, wildly in love with each other. The rest of the world does not exist for us. We shall act this way all day long, taking in the sights in London like any other two tourists, pretending we know nothing about this fellow and his friend. As I said, I suspect that they are trailing me, not you. I think if we convince them that we are just-married Brett and Jillian Turner, perhaps they'll leave off."

Jillian was silent for a moment. The frown over her eyes grew tighter.

"No, Devlin," she said. "Don't you see? That's it—Brett Turner. The FBI suspected that he had an accomplice or two over here. He probably informed his associates when he would be arriving. They were probably waiting at the airport, and assume that you are Brett."

Devlin stared at Jillian as he considered her words. Her conclusion made sense, in a nonsensical way. It was certainly more logical than assuming that the Suttons could have magically found out that Colin had sent for him.

After a full minute, he began to chuckle. Releasing her hands, he took another drink of ale, then shook his head and said, "I hadn't considered that. You see, I have a bit of a checkered background myself. But now that you've pointed this out, I think something of the sort you've suggested is probably exactly what is going on."

Jillian wasn't smiling. "Well, I can't tell you how comforting that is. I just barely escaped marrying a con man. Now you're hinting that you were once a small-time hoodlum, or something?"

Pain edged her voice, and something akin to fear huddled in the light brown eyes that glowed so softly in the candlelight.

"No," Devlin replied. He reached across the table to place his hand over hers. "The problems in my past are a result of a misspent youth, not a criminal one."

Their food arrived before Jillian could ask the questions he could see lurking in her eyes. As Devlin ate, he became aware of the unnatural silence that stretched between them. He could almost feel her curiosity growing. Hoping to forestall her questions about his past, he said the first thing that came to his mind.

"The owl and the pussycat went to sea, in a beautiful pea green boat."

These words elicited a puzzled stare from Jillian.

"It's considered traditional for happy couples to converse, but I'm short on small talk," Devlin murmured. "Beam me up, Scotty."

A hesitant smile curved Jillian's lips and awaking comprehension glimmered in her eyes. A few seconds later, she swallowed a sip of her tea, smiled widely and said, "The fat's in the fire."

"The cat's in the meadow, and the cow's in the corn," he replied.

Her laughter rang out softly over the sounds of silverware clinking against china. Devlin's smile of approval brought renewed warmth to her chilled body and almost made Jillian forget the red-haired man in the corner booth.

She continued to play the game Devlin had invented as they left the restaurant, then made their way up to the street. It helped her concentrate on the role she was supposed to be playing, but when Devlin hailed a cab, curiosity got the better of her. As the black vehicle neared them, Jillian began to glance behind them.

The next thing she knew, strong fingers were gripping her upper arms. She was being twirled back toward Devlin and pulled into a fierce embrace. She didn't even have a chance to draw a breath before Devlin's lips captured hers in a deep kiss. For five thudding beats of her heart, his mouth caressed hers. When her lips parted under his, she thought she heard a deep groan from Devlin's throat. Then the kiss ended as abruptly as it had begun.

Jillian gasped as his mouth lifted. She stared into the eyes so near hers. He'd done it again, made her feel weak and helpless, caught up in a response she seemed unable to control.

Her body, warm with the warring sensations of pleasure and anger, grew suddenly stiff.

"Let me go," she said.

"As soon as you promise not to do that again," he answered.

"Do what again?"

"Look around to see if we're being followed."

She was aware of the waiting cab. She could hear its engine above the more muted sounds of the traffic in the street, could feel cool air rush by with the wind that had brought in darker clouds to blot away the morning's sun. But all these sensations were mere whispers when compared to the feel of Devlin's arms around her, his chest tight against her breasts and the tingling remembrance of his lips on hers.

"I won't do that again," she promised. "Now, please, let go of me."

Devlin released her, then pulled open the door. Inside the cab, she allowed him to sit next to her, his arm over the back of the seat behind her stiff, straight form.

"Look," he said to her after giving the taxi driver the name of their hotel, "I'm sorry about that. But we have to keep up appearances."

She stared past the driver's head at the traffic in front of them.

"I understand," she replied.

"You didn't cancel those dinner reservations, did you?"

Jillian turned to Devlin with a frown. "Not yet. Why?"

"Well, it occurred to me that if these people are indeed after the man you were supposed to marry, and if all your reservations were made by computer, our shadows should have little trouble finding out where you are expected to show up. If we don't want them to know that we've spotted them, then we'd best follow along with your plan."

Jillian raised her eyebrows. "Follow a plan? You?"

She couldn't resist the gibe, despite the knot of fear in her stomach. Devlin's ghost of a smile in reply told her that he was finding the situation almost as unnerving.

Suddenly this was no game, no little one-act play. The fact that they were being followed was very real. And this frightened her.

"How's this for a plan," she said. "We go to the police and tell them someone is following us."

Devlin glanced at her sharply. "And do what, admit that I entered the country on someone else's passport? I think not."

"We could just tell them that someone is following us," she countered.

Devlin shook his head. "And what do you think they'll do with that information? Ask us for details, which would have to be vague if we want to avoid being arrested. Then they'll listen politely while we make utter fools of ourselves while describing phantom shadows and odd behavior. This is *England,* my dear. We pride ourselves on a certain level of eccentricity. Except, of course, when it eats up the time of a constable who has better things to be doing."

Jillian considered his words. As the cab pulled up in front of the hotel, she nodded. "All right. We take the bus tour of London, and play the part of tourists, then go out to dinner. And after that?"

Devlin had just gotten out of the cab. He turned and leaned toward her just as she scooted over to the door. Their eyes met. "That is all the planning we can do for now, love. We'll figure the rest out at dinner."

Soft music echoed across the small dance floor of R. S. Hispaniola. Jillian was vaguely aware of the gentle motion of the seagoing vessel turned restaurant riding its mooring on the Victoria Embankment. From their table near the window in the dining area, she gazed at the shadowy shapes of boats floating past, their running lights dancing over the Thames like water sprites.

Holly had outdone herself here. The restaurant provided the perfect romantic atmosphere for two just-married people.

Or for two strangers, for that matter.

Jillian stole a corner-of-her-eye glance at Devlin.

It was so odd, even looking almost intimidatingly formal and James Bond-debonair in his rented tuxedo, he no longer felt like a stranger. It was true, she thought as she stared at the water again, that she still didn't know a lot of facts about the man, but already she felt more in sync with him than she ever had with Brett.

But perhaps that wasn't so surprising after all. She'd already come to realize that she couldn't lay all the blame for the wreckage of her life on the calculated actions of a con man. She'd been more than ready to be fooled. She was nearing thirty, and according to the time schedule she'd worked out for herself, it had been time to find a serious relationship, to let her domestic side have its say after years of playing the little businessperson.

So when incredibly handsome Brett Turner had entered her life, as if on cue, seeming to possess the traits of honesty, caring and concern for security she'd been looking for, she'd granted him the role of "soul mate," ignoring the little voice that kept complaining that something didn't feel right. Not to mention that, for someone who was to be her leading man, his kisses certainly lacked the proper chemistry, unlike those of a certain Englishman.

"Penny for your thoughts?"

Devlin's deep-voiced question made Jillian blink and brought instant heat to her cheeks. *Penny* for her thoughts? She wouldn't tell him about those musings for a million dollars.

"Oh, just wondering if it was all that necessary for us to continue with this charade," she lied. "We didn't see the red-haired gentleman again, before or after that bus tour we took. Maybe he and his friend weren't following us, after all. Or maybe they gave up."

"And maybe they sent two different people to tail us. Any of the other couples in this restaurant, for instance."

Instantly Jillian lost the languid feeling that had been imparted by the wonderful meal they'd just shared. When she started to glance around, Devlin took her hand.

"No-no, love," he said. "Play it cool. If you want to check the people out, I suggest a dance."

He got to his feet as he spoke, still holding her hand. His smile widened as she hesitated.

"Hey," he said, "think of it as part of our little play."

Their little play was beginning to get out of hand, Jillian decided as they reached the dance floor and began swaying to the slow music. With her hand in his, and her waist warm beneath the arm holding her so near his lean form, her heart began to pound wildly, while a strange fever heated and weakened her muscles.

It was getting more and more difficult to dismiss her physical responses to this man as being the result of jet lag.

"Jillian," Devlin whispered in her ear, "you have to act happy if you want to convince our audience that we are the honeymooning pair we're trying to appear."

She glanced up. He wore a wide smile that almost glittered in the dance floor's dim light. She forced a matching curve to her lips and held it as she spoke.

"I think you are actually enjoying all this cloak-and-dagger stuff."

Devlin raised an eyebrow and the broad shoulder beneath her left hand lifted in a shrug as he replied, "I suppose I am, a little. Put it down to one of those quirks of the English personality."

"Oh, and which quirk would that be?"

Devlin twirled her around gently, then smiled. "Well, as a whole, we are a rather domesticated race. It takes a bit to get us worked up. But push us into a corner and we come to life. There's something about being the underdog, then rousing ourselves to save the day, that gets our blood moving. You know, the young Peter Pan, armed with only a short dagger, taking on Captain Hook and his sword."

"I see," she said. "And why do I get the feeling that you are something of an expert at this sort of thing?"

Devlin frowned at the question. He considered answering with a quick, noncommittal line. But this was Jillian, who, unless he missed his guess altogether, was beginning to grow a little frightened about all this stuff.

Oh, she'd managed to smile and converse easily enough most of the evening, and she'd certainly dressed the part of a woman ready for a night of romance. The black-shot-with-gold number with the cowl neckline that ran from shoulder to shoulder across the front, and dipped low in back, was made of a knit fabric that hugged her small breasts.

Sudden awareness of those soft breasts brushing against his chest made Devlin's mouth go dry, then say the first thing that came to his mind.

"I have, actually."

"You have had people following you?" Her eyes opened wide. "That misspent youth you were talking about?"

"Right. I..." He paused. "God, it's a long story."

"Well, you said we had to converse to keep up appearances."

Devlin had evaded questions about his past for so long that the thought of revealing even a little made him uncomfortable. Besides, he could think of much more pleasant ways to promote the appearance of newlywed bliss.

Unfortunately, the way his mind was working recently, he was afraid they would all look like newlywed lust. Each time he'd kissed this woman he had found he needed a deeper taste, needed to hold her in his arms more tightly, needed more control to break away. He wasn't sure how much willpower he had left. And even as he acknowledged the danger inherent in such a move, his body wanted to pull her into one of those kisses.

Telling Jillian a little of his story wouldn't be nearly as dangerous.

"I had to testify in a murder case quite a few years ago," he said slowly. "The family of the lad who'd committed the crime tried to discourage this—using some rather drastic measures. After he was sent away to prison, they apparently decided to exact their revenge on me and my family. I decided to leave before anyone got killed."

Jillian stared at him for a moment. She glanced at the jagged ribbon of a scar that marked his right hand, which was lightly holding hers, then back up to his face.

"Are these people responsible for your scar?"

Devlin shook his head. "No," he said ruefully. "The person responsible for that little item is a woman."

"The one you mentioned before? The one who fooled you into thinking she truly loved you?"

The music ended as Devlin nodded. He released Jillian from his arms but continued to hold her hand as he led her back to their table.

"The very same," he said. "It seems Prudence didn't appreciate the notoriety that came with my testimony. It threatened to affect her social standing. She was even less appreciative of what I considered to be a most romantic proposal, that she run off with me."

Jillian raised her eyebrows. "So, how does the scar fit in? Did she try to pin you to a wall with a knife to keep you there?"

Devlin found himself smiling, in spite of his remembered anger. "Well, actually, I shouldn't have said she was responsible for the scar. That would be me. I was so enraged when I realized that I'd failed to see her for the coldly calculating young woman she was, that I wanted to hit someone, or at least *something*. Worst luck, the item I chose in my moment of fury was a small glass window."

Jillian's features tightened ever so slightly as she gazed up at him, no doubt remembering the tears she'd shed over being similarly fooled. Hoping to distract her thoughts and lighten the mood, Devlin gave her a mock scowl as he spoke again.

"So let this be a lesson to you, young lady. When you get angry at Brett, punch a pillow."

They had reached their table as he spoke. He held her chair while she sat, then took his own seat. When he looked across the table at her, he saw the corners of her mouth twitch ever so slightly.

"I'll remember."

Devlin downed the last mouthful of wine. As he placed the glass back on the table, a waiter stepped up to inquire about dessert.

"No, thank you," he replied.

"No dessert?" Jillian's incredulous tone drew Devlin's attention to her as she gently reprimanded, "Darling, you know me better than that."

She turned to the waiter and requested that he bring her some *crème brûlée*. When he left, she leaned forward and spoke softly.

"You really don't know me very well, do you? I *never* skip dessert. It's one of my rules."

"You have rules?" Devlin asked, then before she could reply he said, "Of course, you have rules. I suppose you make them up into lists, as well?"

"No," she replied. "I memorized them."

"I see. Care to recite them for me while we wait, then? What comes after Always Eat Dessert?"

Jillian shook her head. "No, it's Never Pass Up Dessert. A subtle difference, perhaps, but it does keep my sweet tooth from ruling my life. And I have no intention of reciting my rules. You'll only laugh."

"You're right," Devlin said as the waiter presented Jillian with a small crystal bowl.

She scooped up a discreet spoonful as the waiter poured the decaffeinated coffee she'd requested.

"You have no rules at all, I assume," she said when the man left.

"Well, you're wrong. But I will admit, I do tend to make them up as I go along."

The look Jillian gave him as she glanced up from spooning another bite was an odd mixture of amusement and something akin to regret. Devlin fought the sudden urge to further explain the origins of what must certainly appear to be a less-than-responsible outlook on life. For some incomprehensible reason, he wanted Jillian to know that he was a trustworthy, stand-up guy.

But there was no point in such an endeavor. He'd learned to keep his distance from women like Jillian, the ones looking for happily-ever-after. And for good reason. He wanted nothing to do with any of that hearth-and-home stuff. He knew far too well the pain of losing those dreams, and refused to set himself up for such pain ever again.

Once Jillian was finished with her dessert, Devlin escorted her out to the street. As they strolled along the banks of the Thames toward the hotel, he realized that the atmosphere outside was just as charged with romance as the restaurant had been.

The air was cool, the sky a deep blue, lit by a full moon. Jillian's hand rested in his, small and fragile feeling. Her footsteps matched his, and the silence between them felt comfortable. She was very easy to be with, Devlin found himself thinking. Her mind clicked rather well with his, considering how organized she was and how spontaneous he preferred to be. Wendy to his Peter.

Right, he thought with a frown. As if there had been a happy ending for *that* couple. Wendy had grown up, stayed in her childhood home. Peter had continued to live in Neverland.

And like Peter, he preferred being on his own, free to wander where he wanted.

The following morning would see the two of them setting out on their own separate paths. Those paths would most likely never cross again, unless Jillian should happen to walk into Ale's Well That Ends Well on Hyde Street before he turned the property over to Al's management and moved on to another location.

"Devlin."

Jillian's fingers closing tightly around his hand drew Devlin's attention to her panic-widened eyes.

"Don't look," she said, "but I think I just saw the red-haired man at that newspaper stand across the street."

Devlin stared down at her pale face. Slowly he lifted his head, ignoring the increased pressure of her fingers around his, and looked directly at the two men standing in the streetlamp's beam. The redhead met Devlin's gaze, then elbowed his friend. When the blond one looked up from the paper he was reading, his companion lifted his chin, not breaking eye contact with Devlin for one second.

Now both men were staring across the street, the hard set to their features issuing a silent dare. In one quick second, twelve years of avoiding trouble rose to stick in Devlin's gorge.

He decided to take the dare. Slipping his hand from Jillian's, he said, "Wait here," then started across the street.

Neither man moved as he approached. Good. He was damned tired of running, of watching over his shoulder. Not just for the past day, but for the last twelve years. Somebody should have to pay for that, it might as well be these blokes.

The redhead smiled as Devlin drew near. "Nice night, gov'nor."

Devlin frowned. "Yes, it is," he replied. "Or it was, until I noticed the two of you. Mind telling me just why you have been following us all day?"

The blond shook his head, while the redhead opened his green eyes very wide.

"I have no idea whatcha mean, old man. Me and George 'ere are just takin' the night air."

Devlin was only half-aware of the light footsteps hurrying across the street behind him, only half heard Jillian's whispered, "Dev—*Brett.*"

The man was a blatant liar, and an arrogant one at that. His red hair and florid face reminded Devlin very much of another arrogant chap, one Robbie Sutton. Robbie owed him dearly, for twelve long years of exile. Since Robbie wasn't around, this man might just have to pay the tab.

Devlin stepped forward, and in one quick move crushed the front of the man's shirt in his fingers. "You're lying. We've seen you. Several times." He jerked the man forward. "I want to know what's going on."

The redhead opened his mouth, but before he could say a word, a thick fist crashed into Devlin's left cheek, just as the redhead pushed on his chest. The sudden pain broke Devlin's hold on the shirt. He reeled backward and was only saved from falling into the street by a pair of slender hands grabbing on to his arm.

He heard the sound of running feet, and by the time Devlin had regained his balance, the two men were halfway down the street.

"What were you thinking?"

Devlin turned to look down at Jillian. She still held on to his arm. The eyes that met his were narrowed beneath a deep frown as she went on.

"I thought the idea was to pretend we didn't see them."

Devlin took a deep breath. "You're right. I guess I just got tired of the game."

Jillian gazed up at him for a moment. Her frown eased slightly as she shook her head and said, "I think we are both just tired, period. Let's get back to the hotel."

Jillian's fingers relaxed slightly as he nodded, but she continued to hold on to his arm as they started walking. Her legs were shaking badly, and her heart raced as they closed the distance between the embankment and the hotel.

Reaching the safety of its front doors did little to soothe her. As she rode the lift with Devlin and another couple, watching the lights indicate the rising floors, her fear turned into sudden and irrational anger.

This was all so unfair. She'd been having such a nice time, dining with Devlin. She had actually forgotten for a while that she'd been moving across the dance floor in his arms for any other reason than that it felt so wonderful to be doing so.

Her fury grew. Was it too much to ask that she be allowed to have one little moment to enjoy a bit of the romance she'd expected when she planned this trip? One space of time without those men following her around, a sharp reminder of the destruction Brett had brought to her life?

By the time she and Devlin entered the room and the door clicked shut behind her, she was not only angry but feeling desperately sorry for herself. She tried to deflect this emotion by turning her attention to Devlin.

"Your cheek is red. Let me get a cold cloth for it."

When she returned from the bathroom, Devlin had removed his jacket and was staring out the window. He turned as she approached, and she lifted the cool moistened cloth to his face. Before she could place it on his already darkening cheekbone, he raised his hand to take it from her.

"Thanks," he said.

Jillian nodded. Her throat was too tight to speak. Ministering to Devlin's wound hadn't worked, hadn't distracted her from the emotion that had risen with her anger.

Blinking rapidly, she turned to the window, completely ignoring Devlin.

"Jillian, are you all right?"

His hand touched her shoulder. He turned her to him. Jillian blinked again and her vision cleared enough to see the concern in his dark eyes, to see him bend toward her. Before she closed her eyes and tried to trap the tears behind her lids, a sob, a silly weak sob, rose to her throat.

It never made it past her lips. Devlin's mouth was there, covering hers, blocking any sound from leaving, as well as any breath she might want to draw. Kissing her deeply, his arms enfolded her, drew her firmly to him. His heat filled her with warmth, soothing the tightness from her chest and throat.

Leaving in its place a deep, strong hunger. For more kisses. For deeper contact.

Jillian parted her lips. Devlin's tongue entered, touching hers, igniting fires deep in her stomach that spiraled lower and lower. She reached up to bury her fingers in the thick waves that had tempted her from the moment she'd met him. She held her hands there when she felt his head lift, tasted his moan against her lips.

Devlin followed this with another kiss, tightening the arms that held her to him. With his hips cradling hers, there was no doubt that he was every bit as aroused as she.

But, apparently, in better control.

His mouth slid from hers, grazed her jaw until his lips were just brushing her ear. "Jillian, it's okay." His voice was rough. "No one is going to hurt you."

No one was going to hurt her?

Jillian blinked, then leaned back into his arms to stare up at him in confusion. He gave her a slow smile, then asked, "Are you all right now?"

All right? No, she wasn't all right. Her body was surging with desire. It was certainly clear that his body was similarly affected. But the concern in his eyes told her he'd mistaken the reason for her tears, that he'd assumed they expressed fear of the men he'd just confronted.

And, perhaps that was just as well. Nothing good could come of letting him know that she was crying over a spoiled romantic atmosphere.

"Yes, I'm fine," she lied.

Jillian stepped back. Devlin's arms loosened as she did so. When she was free of them, she decided to embroider her little cover-up.

"I'm sorry for losing it like that." She forced a breezy tone to her voice. "In the movies when women go to pieces, someone usually slaps them to make them snap out of it. I like your way better. So, what do we do now?"

Devlin gave her another tight smile. "Get some sleep. We need to get up early tomorrow. We're going to the train station, where we're going to shake those tails of ours for good."

"What makes you think we can do that tomorrow?"

"Because I have a plan," he said.

When Jillian raised her eyebrows, his lips eased into a grin.

"Yes, me, with an honest-to-goodness, almost foolproof plan. Of course it may call for some changes in your itinerary, but we'll discuss all that in the morning."

Chapter 7

The morning was gray above the arched iron-and-glass roof of Paddington Station. Jillian shivered in spite of the lining in her trench coat as she stood near the ticket booth, pretending to peruse a brochure, "Things to Do in Bath."

As a train rumbled out of the station, she glanced at her watch. Ten o'clock.

She hadn't seen any sign of the red-haired man or his companion, but Devlin had told her that didn't mean they weren't being watched. His confrontation with the redhead the night before would dictate that new shadows be assigned, if someone was still determined to follow them.

Jillian had spent her time covertly studying the others in the station, trying to decide which of these people might have gotten the new assignment, while Devlin queued up for their tickets.

She'd picked out a tall, thin man with black hair who stood behind Devlin as he quite audibly requested tickets to Bath for two in that abominable fake American accent of his. The man's companion, a small woman with short brown hair, waited across the open space, beneath a sign directing passengers to Platform Two.

Placing the brochure in her large purse, Jillian checked again to make sure that the two BritRail passes she'd brought with her were where they belonged. They were an important part of Devlin's plan, which called for the two of them to board the train bound for Bath, where the next accommodations for Mr. and Mrs. Brett Turner had been made.

Once they were sure that their shadows were safely aboard the train, he and Jillian would disembark and slip onto the one headed toward Oxford, loading on the same platform. From there they would make some calls and see how they could reconfigure Jillian's reservations. Then she would set off on her trip and Devlin would make for home.

Wherever *that* was.

Jillian shivered again. She didn't even know where the man lived, yet the night before, she'd been more than willing to let the passion that had flamed between them blaze into something more. She was just damned lucky that Devlin had assumed that the reason behind her tears had been fear, and that he was apparently too much a gentleman to take advantage of such a situation.

She wondered, however, if he would have shown such restraint if he'd known that her tears weren't from a case of the nerves, that they fell because she and Devlin hadn't met under different circumstances. And because she had the sinking, impossible feeling that she was falling in love with a man that she'd just met and would probably never see again.

But he didn't know this, and would never get a chance to learn it if their plan worked out.

It did. Like clockwork. Soon after the train switch had been made, they were *click-clicking* over the tracks on their way to Oxford. They'd found a row of seats with one facing backward, so they could both sit next to a window.

Devlin had chosen to ride backward. He gazed out the window, watching the gray suburbs floating by beneath an equally gray sky, until Jillian spoke.

"You know, Devlin, you never explained why you chose Oxford for an alternate destination."

He turned from the view to meet her soft, questioning eyes. She was right. And she certainly deserved to know.

"My grandda—my mother's father—owns a pub there. Shaemus Devlin is the source of the touch of Irish in my otherwise impeccable English lineage."

Jillian lifted her eyebrows. "Your lineage, is it?" she said. "Your family traces itself back in an unbroken line to William the Conqueror, I suppose."

Devlin let his answering smile build slowly to a wide grin. "My father's branch of it does, actually. My mother's side is not so well pedigreed, however. Although my grandma did claim to be descended from a lady-in-waiting—to Anne Boleyn, worst luck. Her husband, Shaemus, on the other hand, is quite proud to trace his ancestry back through a line of farmers. Of course, as he says, they were all Irish, through and through, and what could be better than that?"

Jillian smiled, then turned to gaze out the window as the wheels clicked quicker over the iron tracks. Devlin shifted his attention to the houses that backed onto the track, as well, watching as the city slowly gave way to green countryside.

Little was said during the hour's ride into Oxford. Devlin glanced at Jillian from time to time, half expecting her to be looking over her agenda and comparing it with her guidebook of England. But each time he checked, he found that she was relaxing against the upholstered seats, gazing out over the green fields.

Pointed spires and tall towers rising above a band of trees in the center of a curve in the track announced their approach to Oxford. When the train stopped, Devlin helped Jillian retrieve her luggage, then led her out of the station and down a long street, between tall trees in full leaf and even taller gray buildings.

"Well, here it is."

Devlin came to a stop in front of a white building with black exposed timbers. As he stared at the familiar sign above the oak door that proclaimed the name of the pub, The Leaf and Fig, he tried to swallow something that seemed to have suddenly lodged in his throat.

A minute later, he opened the door and wordlessly ushered Jillian inside. Not a thing had changed. Sawdust still softened the sound of his shoes on the wooden floor. The dark wood that paneled the lower half of the whitewashed walls and formed the bar across the far end still gleamed of well-polished mahogany. A collection of dark-hued paintings and commemorative plates still decorated the walls.

It was only a little after eleven, so the place was empty, except for a tall man with iron gray hair who stood behind the bar, drying glass after glass, then placing them on a tray.

He looked up as Devlin took Jillian's hand and started walking toward him. A welcoming smile etched creases into the man's square face. Those features suddenly froze as Devlin drew closer.

"Hello, Grandda." Devlin came to a stop at the bar. "Have you finally managed to chase off all your customers?"

Shaemus Devlin shook his head slowly as a frown lowered over his dark blue eyes.

"Good God, Dev, what the hell are you doing here?"

"Happy to see you, too, Grandda," Devlin said quietly.

A sharp pain quietly burst inside his chest as he stared at the older man. His grandfather had changed remarkably little. A few more lines marked his features, perhaps, and his hair had more gray, but his dark blue eyes were just as bright, his voice every bit as hearty as Devlin remembered.

He also remembered the man's warmth, a warmth that seemed totally lacking now as Devlin met the man's deep scowl.

Shaemus Devlin was the one person he'd always been able to count on, the one person who never quibbled over feelings. He either liked someone or he didn't, and he made no bones about either. Devlin had always believed that his grandda loved him, would always welcome him into his life. Now he wondered if time and distance had destroyed all of that.

It had been the only way, Devlin had told himself a thousand times in the past twelve years. If his family didn't know where he was, if there were no communications to be traced, he would be safe. And more important, *they* would be safe. No one would die.

But, apparently, affection had. He'd always rather doubted that bit about absence making the heart grow fonder. Now he knew it was a lie.

With a sigh, Devlin took a step backward. Before he could take another one, Shaemus turned abruptly, strode toward the far wall, rounded the end of the bar, then walked back toward Devlin, his arms held wide. The old man's embrace was fierce and quick. Before Devlin could properly return it, Shaemus released him. His strong, weathered hands gripped his grandson's shoulders as he slowly shook his head.

"And I'm glad to be seein' *you,* lad. Many's the time I've wished to look up and find you walkin' through that door, wished we could share another game of darts. But the last couple of weeks, as it happens, I've been thankin' heaven that you were safely away from here."

Devlin's body grew suddenly very still as he asked, "And why these past weeks, especially?"

His grandfather started to reply, then stopped as the front door swung open. Shaemus looked past his grandson, lifted a hand in greeting to whoever had just entered, then spoke softly.

"I don't want to talk about it down here. Hold on a moment, and I'll get you upstairs," he said quietly.

Turning, the old man shouted for someone named Addie. A few seconds later a woman in her late forties entered. Her salt-and-pepper chin-length hair framed a wide, pleasant face that possessed the same short nose and wide smile as Shaemus.

"What is it, Da? You know that I've tarts in the oven and—"

The woman had flicked a glance at Devlin as she marched down the bar toward her father, said two more words, then stopped as she turned wide eyes to Devlin again to stare in silence.

"Aunt Addie. Good to see you." Devlin grinned. "I've sorely missed your tarts."

Addie's eyes began to shimmer. "I've missed *you*, my lad. What is it you've been up to? Nothing good, if that nasty-looking bruise means anything."

Devlin lifted his hand to his cheekbone and gave her a wry smile.

"Oh, you know, just a little scrape. Nothing to worry about."

"Oh, I'm sure," his aunt replied as she blinked. "As if I haven't been worrying about you every day for the last twelve years."

Devlin's throat tightened. He'd spent so much time trying to forget the people at home, blocking the memories that hurt far too much to examine, that it hadn't occurred to him that they might have done just the opposite, might have continued to think about him, to worry.

Before his thought could go further down that path, Addie stepped toward him. A second later, the two were trapped in a tight embrace, while Shaemus stood quietly by.

Finally he coughed, then said, "I don't want to hurry you through this reunion, Addie my girl, but I need you to watch the front for me while I get this boy out of sight."

Addie glanced at her father, her features suddenly somber. "Oh, of course."

She turned to go around the bar, then swiveled back to Devlin.

"Does your mother know you're here?"

Devlin shook his head. "And you're not to say anything to her. I need to sort some things out before I can get home."

Addie nodded as Shaemus led Jillian and Devlin through the huge old kitchen, where the well-remembered scent of shepherd's pie teased Devlin's senses, and up the stairs to a small room under the eaves that served as his grandfather's office.

"Have a seat, my dear."

Shaemus closed the door and directed Jillian to a worn, oversize brown chair. When Jillian didn't move, Devlin realized introductions had yet to be made.

"Jillian, I'm sorry. As you might have guessed, this old curmudgeon is my grandfather, the one and only Shaemus Devlin. Grandda, this is Jillian Gibson, of San Francisco."

His grandfather sketched a bow. "I'm most pleased to meet ye, Jillian Gibson. I must say, you must be far tougher than you appear, if ye've been bearing up with the likes of him for any time at all."

Jillian gave Shaemus that impish grin, the one that revealed the small dimple in the corner of her mouth, the grin that always caught Devlin by surprise and made him want to grab her and kiss her.

Not the time, he told himself, nor the place.

"Nice to meet you, too, Mr. Devlin," Jillian was saying. "And as to your grandson, he's been a perfect gentleman. If he hadn't been with me the last couple of days, I'm not sure what would have happened to me."

"Oh, makes a decent tour guide, does he? Well, that's a surprise, given he hasn't been around the last decade or so."

Shaemus's grin tightened as he glanced at Devlin.

"I wish it had been a simple case of showing me the sights," she said quietly. "It seems that somehow I attracted the attention of some less-than-savory men. They've been following me. Devlin brought me here to throw them off our track."

The man's smile disappeared at this and his wrinkled brow knitted into a frown as he turned to Devlin.

"Well, my lad, it looks like a case of out of the frying pan and into the fire, then."

Devlin grew very still. "Why do you say that?"

"Remember I mentioned bein' glad the last couple weeks that you weren't here? Well, three weeks ago Nigel Sutton was let out of prison. A fortnight ago, the man himself walked into my bar, askin' about you and about Colin."

"Did he say why he was looking for me?"

"Of course not, but we can guess, can't we? I'm thinkin' the man is plenty angry. He was up for parole several times, you know. On a manslaughter conviction, he should have gotten let out quite a while ago. Apparently, though, justice isn't always blind. I think perhaps she decided to hold on to this particular Sutton, bein' that they're as hard to catch as an eel in muddy water."

"You're right," Devlin said. "And if I hadn't been so damned busy the last month I'd have read about Nigel's release in the Sunday *London Times.*"

Shaemus narrowed his eyes. "Busy? You? Doin' what?"

Devlin found himself smiling in spite of the dark thoughts forming in his mind. "Starting up a new pub, I'll have you know."

"A pubman? You?"

"Why not? If for no other reason than to prove my father wrong. You remember how he loved to say that I'd never be able to make a living playing darts and sipping ale."

Devlin gave his grandfather a wide grin, then sobered as he went on. "I normally pick up a Sunday *Times* at the bookstore down the way, but the last several weeks I've barely had the time to glance at the *San Francisco Chronicle*'s personal ads. That's where I got Colin's message that I needed to come home."

Shaemus leaned forward, his gray eyebrows meeting in a frown. "You mean to tell me that you've been corresponding with your brother this whole time?"

"No."

Devlin shook his head quickly, then explained about the system they'd set up all those years ago. "But it's really odd," he said as he finished. "I tried calling the house when I got here, and I was told that Colin was out of town."

Shaemus nodded slowly. "Same here. I rang the place after Nigel left here, and that wife of Colin's informed me that the lad was in Italy on one of those digs of his. She also mentioned she'd seen Nigel in the village, said he asked for Colin."

So. Colin had a wife, and one that his grandfather didn't care about, from the tone of his voice.

Interesting, but not important enough to ask about while there were more pressing matters to discuss.

"Curiouser and curiouser," he said.

"And curiouser," Jillian added.

Devlin turned to her. He smiled at her puzzled frown and the arms crossed over her chest.

"I'm sorry," he said. "I imagine that you're wondering what we're talking about."

Her brown eyes met his from beneath slightly raised eyebrows. "Yes. Although I have figured out that this Nigel person must be the one you testified against."

"That's right."

"And now you think that he's somehow connected with the people who have been following us?"

Devlin frowned. "That's beginning to look like the case. Nigel is the oldest son in an underworld family—kind of a cockney version of the Corleones of *Godfather* fame. Only not quite so vicious, usually."

He dropped his gaze, staring at the floor as he remembered the Nigel he'd met at eighteen, conjuring up an image of rusty hair above a freckled face that seemed to be lit with a perpetual impish grin.

"You did say he'd murdered a man."

Devlin brought his head up to meet her eyes. "Not *murdered,* exactly," he replied. "It was...basically an accident. However, he did cause the death of another man."

"Devlin, my boy." Shaemus touched his arm. "I've heard this story before. Why don't I pop down and get you two something to eat, while you bring Miss Jillian up to speed on this."

Devlin nodded. When his grandfather opened the door, Devlin said, "Oh, do you suppose Aunt Addie could spare us one of her strawberry tarts? It's vital that I keep Jillian here in desserts."

"I see." Shaemus gave Jillian a wink. "I'm sure we can manage something, then."

Jillian smiled at the man. When he closed the door behind him, she turned to Devlin to find his smile gone, replaced by a frown that sent an unaccountably strong chill racing down her back.

"Sit down," he said. "I'll try to make this as simple as I can."

He took a seat in the ladder-back chair in front of the desk. Jillian lowered herself to the worn leather one to the right of it as he began to speak.

"I was assigned to room with Nigel Sutton my first year at Oxford University. He was a brilliant fellow, and knew more about having fun than anyone I'd ever met. I'd been a fairly steady fellow up to that point, believe it or not. Serious and responsible."

Jillian couldn't help filling in his pause incredulously. "You? *Steady?*"

Devlin lifted one corner of his mouth in a tiny smile. "Yes, me. Let me be an example of what can happen to youth gone bad, young lady."

He stopped speaking for a moment and his smile disappeared as he went on. "You see, I met Nigel just when I decided I was due to cut loose a little. Unfortunately, I had no idea who the Suttons were, or that the family was deeply involved in things like extortion and gambling. I only knew I'd never met anyone like Nigel, with such a talent for fun. I'm afraid that my main education for the next four years was in how to get the most enjoyment out of life."

Devlin paused. His eyes seemed to take on a faraway look. It didn't take psychic abilities to figure that he was recalling the great times he'd shared with this friend, here in this old city.

Jillian had already deduced that the story didn't have a happy ending. However, it was obvious that Devlin wasn't quite ready to get to this part. She didn't want to rush him and risk stemming this uncharacteristic flow of information, so she waited and watched.

Devlin continued to stare past her for several moments longer, his eyes dark beneath his frown. Then he drew in a quick breath, straightened in his chair and shifted his gaze back toward her.

"Sorry," he said. "Got lost for a moment on memory lane. Where was—oh, it doesn't matter. The long version isn't important. I'm sure you get the picture. I grew to trust the guy, and was soon spending far more time in this pub, and others, than cracking the old books. I managed to get by, though. We were three weeks away from graduation, when things got sticky."

Devlin leaned back in his chair, his eyes on the calendar on the wall. His voice seemed to grow harsher as he spoke again.

"Nigel had a younger brother, Robbie, who'd just started at Oxford that year. Robbie enjoyed playing every bit as much as his brother, but he lacked Nigel's quick intellect. Anyhow, I was just leaving for the library one night near the end of term, when Robbie came to ask Nigel to help him out of a spot of trouble. He'd taken an exam that day and failed."

Jillian saw the crease between Devlin's eyebrows deepen as he paused to sigh.

"When I came back to the room around midnight, Robbie was still in the room. Nigel came in a few moments later. His face was very pale as he handed Robbie his exam booklet and a blank one, along with the promise to help his brother with the correct answers. He was acting very un-Nigel-like, barely responding to his brother's effusive thanks. I assumed this was due to the urgency of returning this new response to the office before dawn."

Devlin's eyes were narrowed. Jillian could see that whatever memories were dancing in his head were painful. Out of the corner of her eye she noticed Shaemus enter the room, but Devlin didn't seem to be aware of this.

"The next day," he said slowly, "the don that taught that course was found dead on the stairway just outside his office."

"And to put a quick end to a long story," Shaemus said as he set a tray of food on the desk, "the lad here was placed in the sticky position of choosing to keep silent about Nigel Sutton's activities that night, or to give the story to the authorities. Dev spoke up and Nigel went to prison."

The expression on Devlin's face made it clear that he'd not come easily to this decision. Jillian reached across the space between them and placed her hand on his arm.

"I'm sure they must have had other evidence to get a conviction. Besides, a man lost his life because some spoiled kid was too lazy to do his own work," she said. "You did the right thing."

"I know." The corner of Devlin's mouth jerked upward ever so slightly. "And I've been paying for it ever since."

The long silence that followed Devlin's words was broken by Shaemus. "Eat, the both of you. I'll finish the tale for the lass."

He handed Jillian, then Devlin, a plate filled with shepherd's pie. She placed a forkful of the mashed potato crust into her mouth as Shaemus began speaking.

"Nigel's people did their best to discourage Dev here from giving evidence against their boy. At one point, they even tried to make it look like Devlin was involved. When that didn't work, someone tried to run over him in the dark. Then, right before the trial, a suspicious package was delivered to his parents' home. When the bomb squad was called in, a right bit of excitement in that little village, indeed, all they found were some pieces of metal and a note that said, 'Silence is golden.'"

Shaemus paused and said, "I brought your favorite ale up for you Dev, and some for you, my dear."

Jillian took the glass of dark liquid and tasted it. She'd tried ale in San Francisco and found the brew to be richer and stronger tasting than beer, but far from unpalatable. Shaemus's offering was much smoother, though. After taking another sip, she placed the glass on the edge of the desk as Devlin took up the story.

"I thought things would be over once Nigel received his prison sentence. I was wrong. Robbie and his gang of assorted relatives and associates made harassing the St. Clair family into their national sport. At first I thought they were just trying to make my life miserable, leaving dead birds on the hood of my car, sending me what seemed to be empty threats with notes cut out of magazines. I actually found it funny for a while. It all seemed so ridiculously melodramatic, and predictable, like something out of a bad movie."

"Robbie has no imagination," Shaemus interjected. "The lad was brought up on the worst that the telly has to offer. I doubt he's ever read anything more intellectual than a comic book. Unfortunately, even the unimaginative can be dangerous, with help."

"Right."

The way that Devlin bit the word out made Jillian glance sharply his way. He frowned at a forkful of the tender meat pie suspended above his dish, then continued to speak. "Someone managed to get to my car and cut the brake line. It's been done a thousand times in books and on-screen, but somehow you don't expect that sort of thing to actually happen in real life."

Jillian was aware of a deep chill spreading through her body as she nodded.

"Just like you don't expect strange men to follow you," she said. "Or for that matter, to have your traveling companion pushed into the path of an oncoming train."

Chapter 8

"Someone tried to *kill* you?" Shaemus asked. "Did you see who?"

"No." Devlin shook his head. "And I'm not even sure I was pushed on purpose. We were surrounded by a crowd of people."

"Well, it does sound just the sort of trick a Sutton might pull. Didn't see any familiar faces?"

When Devlin started to shake his head again, Jillian spoke up.

"What about that fellow in line behind us going through customs—the one you said you went to school with?"

Devlin nodded slowly, then lifted one side of his mouth in a doubtful smile as he turned to his grandfather.

"She's referring to Jerome Sedgewicke. You remember the lad. He did know Nigel, but they were never particular friends. In fact, they didn't get on at all well. Besides, I find it hard to believe that the next Earl of Cuppingham would been working with the likes of the Suttons."

"Oh," Shaemus replied with lifted eyebrows. "And why would you be surprised at that?"

Devlin shot a warning glance at his grandfather before turning to Jillian again.

"What Sedgewicke was, or wasn't doing at the airport is really beside the point. The point seems to be that the Suttons were also waiting for me there, although I can't imagine how they could have known that I was coming to London, let alone what time and which airport."

Jillian was wearing a puzzled frown. "Excuse me, but you just skipped right past a couple things, like why you left England in the first place and what brought you back here."

"You're right." Devlin drew his thoughts back to where he'd broken off his explanation. "Remember the sliced brake lines I mentioned?"

Jillian nodded.

"Well, I wasn't the next one to drive. My father was the one who almost died when it went careening out of control down the road toward the river. After that happened, it became clear to me that I had to leave England before someone got killed. So I simply disappeared."

"Simply?"

"No, it wasn't all that easy. First off, I had to do battle with my father and grandmother, who seemed more concerned over matters of honor and tradition than the fact that someone might die before I managed to arrange for a new passport. My full name is Marcus Devlin St. Clair, so I used a variation of my last name and made my middle name my first."

"We all called him Devlin, anyway," Shaemus explained to Jillian. "His father's first name is Marcus, too, but he goes by his middle name, Andrew. It's a family tradition that goes way back. So, Devlin—you got this passport. Then what?"

"I knocked about Europe for a couple of years, then I left for America, and started working in a bar in New York."

"Well, lad." Devlin straightened. "Although I'm dying to find out how you fared there, I think we need to be figuring out how to get you safely home. You know that we get a lot of tourists in here with the regulars. If it is the Suttons looking for you, you can bet they'll have sent someone to watch the place."

Devlin nodded. "I've been thinking about that. I figure—"

"Now, before you go pushing that brain of yours," Shaemus interrupted, "I've got a couple of ideas." He reached over to take Devlin's bowl and place it on the tray. "Let me go down and make some phone calls, and see what I can come up with."

"Don't ring the house," Devlin said. "I don't want anyone else to know I'm here until I've had a chance to get the lay of the land."

"Well, I think I can come up with some way for you to do that. Just sit a bit, and let me see if I can work it all out."

After he left the room, Devlin turned to Jillian. "Well, while he's gone, you and I need to decide what to do with you."

The concern in his dark eyes filled her with sudden warmth. "With me?" she asked quietly.

Devlin nodded. "I'm pretty sure that the two men we caught following us have been doing so from the moment we arrived at Heathrow. That would explain the taxi that left after the one we arrived in, and the fact that the men were waiting outside the hotel the following morning. But I'm still not convinced they are connected to the Suttons."

Jillian nodded. "I understand. If Colin is the one that placed that ad, then the Suttons would have no way of knowing you'd be coming. Unless... no, that would be silly."

"What?"

"Oh, I think that perhaps I have seen too many B movies. I was just going to say, unless Colin had been kidnapped, and these men had forced him to place that message."

Devlin gave her a slow smile. "Actually, I wouldn't put that past Robbie. But I think there's a simpler explanation."

"Which is?"

"The fact that we both brought some old baggage over here with us—your relationship with the less-than-honest Brett, and my past with the Suttons. We've been trying to make all the pieces fit one scenario or the other, but I think we're actually dealing with two separate problems. It's very possible that the reason Colin has asked me back has something to do with the Suttons. But I think that the men who've been following us are after you and Brett."

Jillian nodded slowly. That made sense. It didn't make her comfortable, but it made sense.

"Which brings us," Devlin said, "to the fact that just because we sent them on a wild-goose chase to Bath, doesn't mean they won't be dodging your every footstep if you try to resume your itinerary."

"Well, that's assuming that they have traced my plans on some computer, isn't it?"

"Yes." Devlin's frown made his eyes look darker as he gazed down at her. "And when one is trying to avoid trouble, I've learned that it's best to assume the worst. That gives you a better chance to hope for the best."

Jillian shivered slightly. She forced a smile to her suddenly stiff lips. "How cheery. And the best is?"

"Well, right now, it looks like the best would be for you to set up an entirely different itinerary, booking yourself under Jillian Gibson. And I don't want to hear about your lack of funds. You just get that guidebook of yours out and plan the rest of your trip. I'll borrow the money from my grandfather. He knows I'm good for it."

These words tightened the shaky sensation in Jillian's stomach. "No," she said. "You're not going to pay for my trip."

Devlin's features hardened, reminding Jillian of the suppressed anger she'd seen on his face at the airport. "I certainly will," he said. "I owe it to you. Remember, *I'm* the reason your honeymoon has been ruined."

"I beg your pardon." Jillian raised her eyebrows. "My honeymoon was ruined before I even met you. And I am quite accustomed to taking care of myself."

"Oh, really?"

Jillian found the slightly raised eyebrows and blatant doubt in Devlin's voice infuriating. She got to her feet.

"Look, I've made some mistakes. But I'm not about to let those things turn me into a frightened, needy child. It's been very nice of you to help me the way you have, but that has to end. Now."

Jillian could feel her throat tightening as she spoke. She turned and walked over to the dormer window that looked over the steep slate roof. The morning's gray clouds had finally produced a fine mist that fell with only the faintest patter.

She took several slow breaths as she asked herself why she was so angry. She'd always known that she and this man would part at some point.

"It's raining," she said at last.

The scraping of Devlin's chair against the floor told her that he had stood. Footsteps echoed on the wooden floor, then his voice, coming from her right.

"So I see."

She turned. He was leaning against the wall not two feet away, gazing out the window thoughtfully.

"I'm not going to take your grandfather's money," she said quietly.

Devlin glanced at her. "It wouldn't be *his* money. I'll pay him back."

"Well, I'm not going to take your money, then. I have always paid my own way in life. I'm not going to stop now. I can afford an inexpensive bed-and-breakfast on the outskirts of London." Jillian turned to stare out the window as she finished, "Someone once told me it would be impossible to see all of that city in such a short time, so I'm sure I'll see enough to make me happy."

"Jillian."

She turned her head at the nearness of his deep voice. He'd moved to stand next to her. As she gazed up into his eyes, he placed his hands on her shoulders and turned her to him.

"Is that what you *want* to do?"

Beneath his light touch, Jillian could feel her skin growing warm. The heat quickly began to spread, moving across her shoulders and down both arms. Her chest felt hot and tight, and warmth spiraled through her stomach.

Forcing herself to draw a deep breath, she said, "It'll do. And it will get me out of your hair."

His eyes held hers for several moments while his eyebrows lowered into a frown.

"Is that what you think I'm trying to do?"

Jillian tried to pull her attention from the fact that Devlin's body was disturbingly near hers, but her senses seemed determined to recall other times when he'd been so close. Her blood pulsed quickly at the memory of being pulled into one of those mind-searing kisses.

Forcing her thoughts from that path, she managed to ask, "Isn't it?"

"No. I'm trying to make sure you have the nice, safe trip you planned."

"I can never have the trip I planned. It was based on a lie. Besides, if it's safety you're concerned about..." She hesitated, then went on quickly. "I feel very safe with you."

Devlin stared into her eyes before slowly shaking his head. "Oh, Jilly-girl. You couldn't be more wrong," he said, then lowered his lips to hers.

Jillian was quite aware that she could have avoided the kiss, if she'd wanted to. She didn't want to, though. Even before his mouth touched hers, her lips felt its heat. As his fingers slid along her jaw until his hand was cupping the back of her head, her skin tingled, sharp pinpricks raced down the ridge of her spine. When he increased the pressure of his mouth on hers, she felt her lips part.

The touch of his tongue against hers awoke the most exquisite sensations in Jillian's body. Her arms seemed to act of their own accord, slipping around Devlin's waist. Her hands splayed out against his back. Beneath them, she could feel the play of muscles as his arms eased around her, pulling her to him.

And all this time, his mouth never left hers. His lips continued to caress hers, to tease her mouth into replying as her body eased even closer to his.

A soft *click*, however, was all it took to break the intense connection.

Jillian was aware that Devlin released her at the same moment she drew her arms away from him, that he lifted his head at the same second she turned hers to one side, that they took identical steps back, leaving them staring at each other from opposite edges of the small window.

"Well, I can get you as far as Lyme Regis, Devlin my boy."

Devlin turned at the sound of his grandda's voice. He gave Shaemus a questioning look, counting on the man's love of speech to do the rest. *He* certainly wasn't going to say anything yet. Even if he was capable of forming a coherent sentence, he was sure the timbre of his voice would give him away.

Damn it. Never, in his entire life, had kissing any woman affected him the way that kissing Jillian Gibson did. And each time he'd done so, the urge to go further, to increase the intimacy they shared, had grown stronger. And each time he pulled away, he was even more certain that this would have to be their last kiss.

For one thing, his life was a mess. For another, with the addition of the Suttons to the equation, the danger to him and to Jillian had become all too real. He would have to keep his wits about him if he wanted to keep Jillian safe, as well as his family. He'd given up a lot to protect other lives all those years ago. He didn't want his return to put them in danger again.

"I've a man comin' up from Exeter tomorrow," Shaemus said. "He's to remove a load of furniture from that cottage I rent out to married students. My last set of tenants have already left for their new place near Southampton. You can stay in the cottage tonight, and if you'll help the driver load the furniture tomorrow, he'll take a quick detour and drop you off on the coast. He offered to drive you right on in to Smeaton-on-Axe, but changed his mind when I told him how steep and narrow the road was."

"No problem. The hike from Lyme Regis will do me good. *Us* good."

Devlin released a quick breath, pleased that his voice sounded perfectly natural, no hint of passion. He turned to Jillian, smiled at the astonishment on her face.

"Now that I think about it, until we know who those men following us are, I think it's best we stay together. I hope you have some good walking shoes."

Her lips twitched into a smile as she nodded. "I have hiking boots in my suitcase."

"Good. But speaking of suitcases, it won't be possible to lug that thing with us." He turned to Shaemus. "Grandda, I'm thinking we can stuff a few days' worth of clothes each into a backpack. Do you know where we could get a couple?"

"No problem. I think perhaps Tim has left one or two around here somewhere."

"Tim? My cousin Tim?"

"The very one." Shaemus gave Devlin a wide smile as he turned to the door. "He's a ranger, down in Dartmoor. Comes up to visit his mother and stays here with us from time to time. I'll scare them up. I can also arrange for whatever you leave here to be sent on to Devon."

He gave them a wink, then exited. Once the door shut, Devlin turned to Jillian. Her questioning honey brown eyes met his. "Well, what do we do now?"

Devlin could think of several things, starting with resuming the kiss that had been so rudely interrupted by his grandfather's most recent entrance. Once again he found himself thinking, *not the time nor the place.*

Of course, he reminded himself, there was never going to be a time when it would be right to follow that particular path with this particular woman. She was too vulnerable right now. She might truly be grateful that fate had prevented her marriage to Brett Turner, but she wasn't the kind of woman who could go from that kind of hurt to a casual affair.

Which was all he could offer her. There was no question that she shared his physical hunger, but the soft expression in her eyes suggested that her feelings went far deeper than casual. To take advantage of this would make him a worse cad than Brett Turner ever thought of being.

"Why don't you go through your suitcase and pull out something appropriate for tramping through the woods." Devlin lifted her suitcase onto the desk as he spoke. "You'll need a warm sweater. It's usually fairly chilly near the coast any time of year."

While Jillian went through her things, Devlin pulled his jeans and a tan sweater from his duffel, along with a couple pairs of fresh socks and shorts. His grandfather entered a few minutes later, dropped off two brown backpacks, told them that one of his employees would be taking them down to the cottage in a half hour, then left.

Other than saying thank you in unison to Shaemus, neither Devlin nor Jillian said another word. The rain had begun to fall harder at some point. Besides the rhythmic patter of water on the window, the only other sound was the soft hush of fabric brushing against canvas as they both packed.

"All done."

Devlin turned. Jillian was sitting in the chair, the bulging backpack on the floor next to her. She had changed into a pair of leather hiking boots and was just finishing tying the leather laces when the door opened and Shaemus walked in.

"I can spare Roger just long enough for him to drive the two of you to the cottage and get himself back here before the late afternoon rush," he said. Turning to Devlin, he went on. "I'm sending some bedding with you. I'm sure the Bannisters' sheets and such are all boxed up. Your aunt packed a supper for tonight and things for breakfast in the morning. You can leave the cooler and the blankets in the cottage."

Devlin nodded in response to these orders, then stepped toward the door. Shaemus placed a large firm hand on his shoulder to stop him before he entered the hall. "Now, you watch yourself, my boy. And take it easy on the folks at home. Quite a bit has changed since you were last there. Some good and some bad. Too much for me to go into now."

With that, Shaemus walked them down the stairs and out the back to a courtyard where a rusted blue Mini-Cooper rattled at idle. The driver was a slight fellow with medium brown hair who looked to be about twenty. Devlin threw their bags on top of the cooler, which occupied the right rear seat behind the driver, then slid into the passenger seat on Roger's left.

Jillian smiled at Devlin's attempt to get his long legs into the small car, before she turned to Shaemus.

"I transferred my passport and anything else essential into the backpack," she told him. "My purse is in my suitcase, and there's room for Devlin's empty duffel in there, too, if it will make it easier for you to package it up for posting."

Shaemus gave her a warm smile. "You are a very efficient young lady, aren't you? How did you ever get hooked up with the likes of my grandson?"

Jillian gave him a wry grin as she shook her head. "You would never believe it."

"A good story, is it? Well, then, once all this is settled at Blodwell Hall, you'll have to give me the full of it. I'm particularly interested in those matching gold bands that you and the lad are sporting."

Jillian glanced at her left hand. She'd almost forgotten putting the ring on her finger. It seemed like those moments on the plane had happened months ago, instead of a matter of days.

So much had happened. So much running. Jillian thought she would like nothing better than to sit on a stool in Shaemus Devlin's pub and shock him with the story of how she'd met the man's grandson.

But there was no time to do that now, and she didn't have any illusions about seeing this man again. Once the mystery of who was following who was solved, she'd have no reason to hang about, either with Devlin or with any members of his family.

"I'll do that," she lied, then gave in to impulse and rose on tiptoe to brush the man's rough cheek with her lips.

As she dropped back down, Shaemus caught her eye and said softly, "Have patience with the lad. It may be rough going for a patch, but things should work out."

With that, he took her arm and escorted her over to the car. As she slid into the seat behind Devlin, Shaemus leaned toward his grandson's window.

"Mind you, be careful now. I've just been telling the lass I expect you back here within the week. You and I have some time to be makin' up." He paused, then raised his voice. "All right, Roger. Off with you now. Get back as soon as you can."

Shaemus might have said something else after Roger shifted into first gear, but the accompanying racket would have drowned out the howl of the hound of the Baskervilles. The ride was none too smooth, either, but Jillian was soon too lost in gazing at the passing view to pay the car's antics much attention.

The streets were packed with automobiles and bicycles that formed what looked to Jillian to be a potentially lethal combination. After seeing several heart-stopping near-collisions, Jillian craned her neck to stare at the intricate stonework topping the upper stories of the old, stained buildings until they passed out of the most congested part of the city.

Then she relaxed against the seat and watched shops and offices slowly give way to small square houses bordered with grass and trees, until eventually the suburbs were left behind, and the road entered a pleasant wooded area.

Jillian gazed at the trees until she began to grow sleepy. She had just closed her eyes, and rested her head against the window, when Roger swung the car into a hard right turn, sending the cooler sliding into her. After pushing it back in place, Jillian turned to see that they were driving down a narrow, winding road that passed beneath the arching branches of birch and oak trees.

As she gazed at the blue and pink flowers blooming among the tall grass at the side of the road, she drew a deep breath then released it, along with some of the tension that had collected in her shoulders.

For the first time since learning the truth about Brett Turner, she felt truly at ease. No one was following her, for one thing. And, since the coming night's lodging and the following day's schedule was set, there was nothing that she had to plan for.

Of course, now that she thought about it, she did find herself wondering about Dev's home. Blodwell Hall, Shaemus had called it. That sounded rather grand. Probably one of those great old country houses made of brick, or perhaps stone. She hoped it wasn't one of those places where people dressed for dinner, because none of the things she'd stuffed into her backpack was likely to pass muster.

Maybe she should have—

Jillian's thoughts came to a crashing halt as the car finished rounding another curve and she caught sight of a small cottage at the end of the lane.

Her dream house come true.

Chapter 9

The cottage was tiny, not much wider than twenty-five feet. Two small, curved-topped windows huddled beneath a thatched roof. A stone chimney peeked over the ridge above. Two rosebushes, bearing huge red blooms, climbed soft golden stone walls to meet in an arch above the thick oak door. Two more diamond-patterned windows bracketed the doorway above flower-laden window boxes.

Jillian didn't even look at Devlin as he opened the car door for her. She kept her eyes on the house as she slid from her seat and stepped onto the stone path winding through a yard dressed in riotous bloom, afraid if she looked away for even a moment the place might disappear.

At first glance, the inside of the cottage matched the fairy-tale exterior. Feeling a little like Snow White stepping into the dwarfs' home for the first time, Jillian stood on the threshold and gazed around.

Directly opposite the door, a huge iron stove sat upon a stone hearth. To her right, a flower-print couch and two dark green chairs bracketed an oval braided rug in front of an oak bookcase.

However, the small television sitting atop the shelves lent a jarring, modern look, as did the green Formica topping the table on her left and the matching counter that connected the small white refrigerator and stove in the corner beyond.

Those were things that could easily be changed, though, she found herself thinking. Refinishing would bring out the grain of the wooden cabinets and a new butcher-block counter would be make for a more authentic cottage look. The fifties-style dining set would have to go, of course, and—

"Pretty cramped with all these boxes in here, isn't it?"

Devlin's voice made Jillian blink, then glance around the room again. Oh, she had it bad. Not only was she mentally redecorating a place that was not hers, and never would be, she'd completely blotted out the sight of the assorted boxes and crates arranged along the wall behind the couch and in the corner near the dining room set.

"You all right?"

The concern in Devlin's voice brought a wry smile to her lips as she turned to face him.

"Yes," she replied. "I was just looking around and thinking how..."

"How *adorable* the place is?" Devlin filled in, mimicking the word she'd used to describe the cottage she'd seen from the highway leaving the airport.

There was a difference in his tone, however. He'd said that word in a scornful, even angry tone then. Now his voice, and the glint in his dark eyes, were gently teasing.

"Well, yes," she replied.

"Well, it might be picturesque, but you've got to admit I was right about the drafts."

Jillian felt the skin on her arms pucker against the chill air even before he finished speaking.

"Okay," she said. "You were right. It *is* cold in here."

"And," he said, "Roger just informed me, the power is off. However, Grandda did send along a lantern for us and there should be plenty of ice in the cooler to keep the food from spoiling."

Jillian glanced down at the ice chest at his feet. He and Roger must have brought it in while she was mentally giving the cottage a face-lift. It looked like it held more than enough food for the two of them.

"But what do we do for heat?" she asked.

Devlin smiled as she looked up at him. "We build a fire in that old stove. If I were a truly mean fellow, I'd make you chop the wood, just to demonstrate the price one pays for living in such unpractical digs. But far be it from me to dash a dream to pieces. I'll see to the fuel, and give you a chance to check out our accommodations."

The rest of the cottage consisted of a hallway that lay beyond an arch set into the dining area wall to her left, leading to the back of the house. There she found two generous-size bedrooms, bisected by a bathroom that was dominated by a large, claw-footed tub.

"Colin and I had our first swimming lessons in that."

Jillian jumped at the sound of Devlin's voice and turned to see him standing three feet behind her, gazing into the room beyond.

"We used to stay here with my grandma and grandda when we were little. She had a deep fear that we'd fall into the creek behind the house some spring and drown if we didn't know how to swim. She was a great one for worrying."

Devlin's bittersweet smile almost made Jillian's soft question unnecessary. "She died?"

"Yes." He continued to stare into the bathroom as he replied. "The year I started at Oxford. It was partly concern for Shaemus that made me spend so much time at his pub."

His half smile disappeared and was replaced by a frown. "Grandda was glad to see me, but he found a way to let me know that Grandma would be far from happy to see me hanging out with the likes of Nigel Sutton."

Jillian found herself frowning, too. "I thought you said you didn't know about Nigel's connections to the underworld."

Devlin's gaze shifted to her. "I didn't. Neither did Grandda. He said he just got a bad feeling from Nigel. Shaemus likes to believe he has fey powers, you know."

The left side of his mouth twitched up again. "Second sight and all that. Claims he knew that my grandmother was the woman for him the moment they met. And, although they got married after only knowing each other two weeks, their marriage lasted over thirty years." He paused. "Her death was very hard on him. It left him feeling...lost. I guess you know a bit about such feelings yourself."

Jillian acknowledged his reference to her parents' deaths with a nod. "Yes. And so do you."

At his questioning look, she continued. "You lost *all* your family twelve years ago," she said. "That must have been hard, too."

Devlin stared at Jillian for several minutes. It was on the tip of his tongue to tell her it hadn't been all that hard on him, to assure her that he'd been too busy, first traveling and then establishing his businesses, to think about the people back here, living their lives without him. After all, that was why he'd left, so that they would be able, safely, to do just that.

But it had been difficult, sometimes. Especially late at night, when he was alone and tired. Shadowy recollections of his past would slip into his mind, and grow into the most vivid memories in an instant, filling him with a mixture of joy and pain, pleasure and loneliness, forcing him out of bed to work on financial statements or purchase orders until the visions faded.

He had the oddest feeling that Jillian knew all this, too, though he couldn't imagine how.

You be careful with the lass, Dev my boy. Shaemus's deep voice whispered in his mind, echoing the advice the man had given him back at the pub. *She's a special one.*

Yes, she was, Devlin thought. Too special for the likes of him.

"I need to chop more wood," he said abruptly. "I used what kindling I could find to get a fire started in the stove, but we'll need more to make it through the night. I don't know about you, but I'm getting hungry, too. See what Addie sent for dinner, will you?"

Without waiting for Jillian to reply, Devlin turned and marched down the hallway, through the main room and out the front door. He traced the stone path leading to the back of the house.

Already the sun had dipped low enough for the light to be growing dim beneath the trees. Devlin crossed to the cavelike stone attachment to the house. Reaching in, he grabbed the ax that had always been kept here, and a log, which he stood on end atop the thick oak block scored with aged cuts. Taking aim, he raised the ax and swung, taking great pleasure in the resounding *crack* and the vibration of the handle.

He'd forgotten how soothing the act of splitting wood could be. During the twelve years he'd spent moving from city to city, he'd usually stayed in a room above his pub. None of them had fireplaces. Some of them had only been warmed by an electric heater. He'd forgotten what it was like to be in the country, where he could hear the burble of a brook, the whisper of the wind in the trees or breathe air like this, clean and moist.

The air in San Francisco, early in the morning, before motor emissions had a chance to sour the scent, was the closest he'd come to the air here. But even that didn't compare with the sweet scent that filled his lungs as he forced the ax blade through the heart of the log, dividing it into two pieces.

He bent to position one of his newly created half logs on the chopping block then started to raise his ax again. He stilled the motion as the distinctive sound of a wood warbler's song trilled through the woods on his left. He turned, just in time to see the yellow-and-green bird leap from the overhanging branch of a silver birch and take to the dusky sky.

Devlin lowered the ax head to the ground, then leaned against the handle.

He didn't need this. Didn't need the cottage or the memories of the pleasant days his family had spent here.

He didn't need to remember seeing his father swinging this very ax toward this very chopping block as he instructed his young boys in the fine art of log splitting. What Devlin needed to do was remember the stern parent, the man his father had become after inheriting Blodwell Hall, the one who'd continually told his oldest son how disappointed he was in him.

That was the man Devlin had left, the one he would have to deal with tomorrow. Remembered anger would help him do whatever it was that needed doing, so he could turn around and once again leave this country, with its memories of what could never be. Devlin hoisted the ax again, hoping the hard physical labor could make up for the fact that he was having a difficult time dredging up the anger that had once been so strong.

A half hour later, his body weary, but many of his demons exorcized, he made his way down the dusky path. With a practiced kick, he opened the front door. The rich fragrance of gravy wafted out as he stepped in. Jillian turned from the pot she was stirring on the iron stove.

"Perfect timing," she said. "The fire's almost out. If you want this stew that Addie sent to get any warmer than room temperature, we're going to need some of that wood. Now."

Devlin deposited his armful of split logs into the wood box, placed three lengths on the low flames and closed the iron door. When he stood, his thighs protested lightly, reminding him that chopping wood was the most physical exercise he'd had for a while. However, a few stiff muscles were a fair exchange for having relieved some of the tension that had sent him from the cottage. His more relaxed attitude enabled him to smile at the domestic picture that Jillian presented, standing before the stove.

"That really smells good," he said. "Will it be ready soon?"

Jillian glanced up. "I think so, now that the fire is blazing away. Addie sent along some carrot sticks, if you need to munch. They're over on the table."

Devlin turned toward the dining area. The raw vegetables sat in a dish on the blue-checkered tablecloth that matched the ones used at The Leaf and Fig. Two glasses and two bottles of his grandda's best ale were arranged to the right of each of two place settings. His grandda's old lantern commanded the center of the table, sending out a soft glow.

A most cozy scene.

The smile he'd given to Jillian faded as tension once more tightened his shoulders. Reaching up to rub the right one, he stifled a sigh.

He didn't need this any more than he needed English mists or bird songs he hadn't heard in over a decade. Jillian was yet another entanglement he couldn't afford. He was as drawn to her as he was to all these trappings of the home he'd left behind. But he couldn't have her, any more than he could stay in England for more than a couple days.

His life would never mesh with hers. Good Lord, look at this place. Even with the packing boxes crowded around, she'd managed to make it look more homelike than some of the places he'd lived in for a year.

"We're two different types of birds, you know?" he said as he turned to Jillian.

A frown tightened her brow as she looked up from the beginning-to-bubble stew. "What are you talking about?"

"Well, look around. You're here barely an hour, and it's all... homey. It's obvious that you're a nest builder. Me, I need to fly. I can hardly wait till tomorrow, when I can set out on the road again."

He thought his words might make her soft smile fade. If he was truly lucky, they might even make her argue with him. Anger might help break the cozy spell this place had cast over him.

Instead, Jillian gave him a wry smile.

"You know, you're right—about the nest-building thing. I can't believe I've ignored it all these years, when it was staring me in the face. I think I mentioned to you that I restored the old Victorian that I've been sharing with my sisters. Well, the other day in Covent Garden I decided that when I go back to San Francisco, I'm going to study interior decorating. However—" her smile took on a slightly wicked twist "—I really am looking forward to seeing some more of the country, too. Believe it or not, I really didn't plan on doing a lot of homemaking on this trip."

Devlin stared at her a moment. "I'm sorry. I forgot. I suppose that being a bride normally means that one is wined and dined on a honeymoon, not turned into chief cook and bottle washer."

Jillian took a deep breath and issued an exaggerated sigh. "Well, yes. But I did have that dinner on the Thames last night. I guess that little bit of romantic atmosphere will just have to do."

She grinned up at Devlin. He stared at the tiny dimple at the corner of her mouth, and remembered how he'd been tempted by it as they danced the night before, and later as they walked beside the river beneath the full moon. He recalled how good it had felt to give in to that temptation at the hotel, pulling her into that long, tear-spiced kiss. A kiss that had stirred his blood, that had built in intensity so quickly, and made it so very difficult to release her, to send her to her room.

"I understand what you mean about being a bird of flight, though."

Jillian's words brought Devlin back to the present. She glanced up from ladling thick stew into one of the plastic bowls his aunt had sent along.

"My parents were like that," she said. "They both preferred traveling to being at home."

She handed him a bowl, then began filling another.

"You mentioned that when we first met," he said. "Didn't you say something about them making nature documentaries?"

Jillian nodded. He followed her to the table, where they sat across from each other.

"Did they ever take you with them?"

Jillian glanced up from pouring her ale into the clear plastic glass. "Oh, yes. I don't remember the earliest trips, of course. They took me with them to Kenya when I was only three months old."

Jillian paused as she placed the bottle on the table, and a quick memory of her mother's reminiscing of those days flashed through her mind. Her lips curved softly as she reflected.

"My parents met in San Francisco, during the Summer of Love, you see, and I guess they never really outgrew their flower children sensibilities. Mom used to tell me that she just strapped me on her back and carried me into the bush to get the shots she wanted. She did the same with Holly, then Emily. By the time I was eight, I'd been to Africa, India, China, France and England."

Devlin lifted one eyebrow. "That's interesting. My parents had their hippie period, as well. My mother was a rather well-known fashion model in her day, and my father played keyboard in a rock band." His eyes narrowed as he paused. "However, I wouldn't ask him about that. Once Grandfather died, making my father head of the family, he sort of disavowed his youthful days."

"Disavowed his past?" Jillian asked. "You can do that?"

At Devlin's puzzled look, she explained, "Well, just think about it. If I could convince myself that I never had anything to do with Brett Turner, I would not only have peace of mind, I'd still have that twenty thousand dollars I'd saved up."

Devlin nodded slowly. "And you wouldn't be stuck with the likes of me."

Jillian had just finished scooping out the last of her stew. She held the spoon over the bowl as she considered his words.

"That's true. But then, I wouldn't be having an adventure, either. You know, for someone who had such an interesting upbringing, my life has become quite boring. I guess the ability to disavow one's past could be as much a curse as a blessing."

"You'll have to tell my father that."

Jillian shook her head as she chewed. After swallowing her food, she said, "No, thank you. My gran taught me to avoid personal issues with people I've just met."

The thought of meeting Devlin's family made Jillian's stomach clench. What little he'd told her made them sound less than accepting. Not that this mattered in her case, of course. She would simply be a houseguest, and only for a few days, until they sorted out this Sutton thing.

Trying to ignore the pain that rose with the thought of leaving Devlin and never seeing him again, Jillian stood and gave him a bright smile.

"Your aunt sent a couple of her strawberry tarts and a thermos of coffee. Would you like some?"

Devlin nodded. "Sure. Then we should see to settling in early. Grandda says the mover plans on arriving about seven tomorrow morning."

"All right." Jillian stacked his empty paper bowl on top of hers, then whisked away the plastic utensils and glasses.

"I'll get the tarts. Why don't you take the lantern over to the couch. It's getting chilly this far from the stove."

As she stood in the kitchen, arranging the tarts on paper plates and pouring coffee, she found herself glancing toward the black stove, where Devlin was busy loading more wood. It would probably be wiser to forgo sitting in front of the warm fire with that man, she told herself. It was altogether too cozy, too romantic.

But, damn it, romance was what she found herself craving. This might be so only because Devlin had pointed out that heretofore-ignored part of her personality, but she thought it had much more to do with the man himself. And dangerous as it was to walk down what looked like a hopeless path, romance—with Devlin Sinclair—was exactly what she wanted.

When she had everything arranged on a short length of board she'd found and put into service as a tray, she took it to the living area, where Devlin was sitting on the rug, leaning against the couch before the open stove door, gazing at the fire.

Jillian handed him a foam cup full of steaming coffee and his tart. Curling up on the opposite corner of the couch, she ate her dessert slowly. As she basked in the radiated warmth from the stove, she let herself imagine how lovely it would be to sit in a room like this, reading a book as the rain pattered on the roof.

Actually, things were just fine as they were right now, she thought. The silence, broken only by the soft snapping from the fire, was comfortable. The house seemed to surround them, enfold them, as if they belonged right there.

Jillian straightened. What a silly, dangerous thought. If she didn't watch it, she'd be fooling herself into imagining a future with Devlin, just as she had with Brett.

That thought sent a chill racing down her spine and dancing along her arms. Crossing them, she turned to Devlin and asked, "Why is it these places are so cold? I thought a fire like this would warm up the stones, which would then radiate heat into the room."

Devlin glanced at her. "Well, they do, but not enough to be truly efficient. The walls need insulating. My father had planned on doing that for Shaemus at one point, actually. He did install a solar hot-water heater. But that was back in the days when he liked to work with his hands."

Jillian was quiet for several moments. "I don't want to sound nosy, but since I'm going to be meeting your family tomorrow, would you mind telling me a little about them?"

She saw a quick frown drop over Devlin's eyes before he shrugged.

"Well, keep in mind, what I know is rather dated. My father used to spend several days a week in London managing the import-export business that's been in the family since Elizabethan times. He's also a landlord of sorts."

Devlin paused. His eyes shifted to gaze into the fire for a long moment, then returned to Jillian. "My mother immediately took to the role of country gentlewoman after we moved to Devon, so she's probably queen of the village garden club by now. And it seems that Colin went on to get his degree in archaeology, in spite of the pressures."

The vertical crease between Devlin's eyebrows deepened.

"Pressures?" Jillian asked softly.

Devlin placed his left hand over his right shoulder and began a kneading motion as he replied, "Well, before I departed, I signed a paper relinquishing any claim to the family business. It's to become Colin's now, but he has little training in business. I, on the other hand, was schooled to take over from the cradle. My father started training me for it before I even went to prep school, and he insisted I study finance at Oxford."

"Did you want to study something else?"

Jillian watched his features tighten as he shrugged. "I really don't think I cared one way or another. I was aware of what was expected of me—you know the British eldest-son thing—and I didn't give it much of a thought. Ironically, though, the business training did come in handy, once I reached America."

"When you set up your pubs?"

"Right. Although balancing books is not something I enjoy, having a head for business has allowed me to prosper and concentrate on what I really like."

"Which is?"

"The challenge of taking an old building that's facing the wrecking ball, restoring it and breathing life into it."

"Life?" Jillian asked. "I thought you said a building didn't have a life—or a soul."

Devlin glanced at her sharply. Slowly he shook his head. "That was just a figure of speech. It's not the building that has life. It's the builder. I find a great deal of satisfaction in working with my hands, and being able to see the results. Physical labor is a great antidote to working on the facts and figures required to run a business."

He paused and gave her a wry, wincing smile as he touched his right shoulder again. "Except when you overdo it."

"Did you hurt yourself?"

"I'm out of wood-chopping practice, apparently." Devlin got to his feet. "I'm going to see if that solar unit still works. A hot shower might loosen the muscle a bit."

After he left the room, Jillian bustled about, quickly putting the used paper and plastic items in a trash bag she'd found in the cooler, then washing up the pot that the stew had come in. She'd just finished when Devlin reentered the room, wearing jeans and a green hooded sweatshirt that zipped up the front.

"There appears to be plenty of hot water if you'd like to take a bath," he said. "Oh, and there were some towels way back in the cupboard. I left one for you."

The hot water was quite welcome, as far as it went. Jillian hadn't been able to fill the tub much past three inches, before it turned from hot to cold. She'd been hoping to immerse herself entirely in warm water and soak a bit, but the room was still steamy, so she stayed in until the porcelain began to cool the water down.

By that time, the room had grown cold, as well. She maintained a semblance of warmth by drying off vigorously, then quickly pulling on a fresh pair of leggings, warm socks and a tunic-length silk henley sweater that had the advantage of packing small yet retaining body heat, before making her way back to the living area.

When she walked through the arch, she saw Devlin sitting on the couch, kneading his shoulder again. She crossed the room to stand behind him.

"The shower didn't fix it?" she asked.

Devlin turned his head to glance over his shoulder. "Not quite."

"My gran taught me a little massage. I could see what I can do, if you'd like."

Devlin shrugged, then removed his hand from his shoulder. Jillian laid her right palm along the length of it, getting a feel for the muscle beneath the sweatshirt. Positioning her hand near his neck, she slowly applied pressure as she slid her hand down and across his shoulder, then reversed the motion.

Lifting her palm, she searched out a particular point near his neck, then placed her thumb there. "Does that hurt?" she asked.

"A little," he replied.

Jillian bent forward and angled around until she could see Devlin's face. "I'm going to press on this point for a moment. It's going to hurt, but I want you to try and relax. All right?"

His eyes met hers beneath a doubtful frown.

"I know what I'm doing," she said. "Promise."

"All right."

Jillian straightened to get the proper leverage, then pressed her thumb into the firm muscle, slow and hard. She heard Devlin's quick intake of breath, but she didn't remove the pressure for several moments.

When she did, she smiled at the sound of Devlin slowly releasing the air he'd drawn in. "Better?" she asked.

"Yeah. Now that you aren't pushing."

"Go ahead, test it."

Devlin moved his shoulder slowly, then raised his arm, and lowered it again. He turned to her. "It feels much better. Hardly stiff at all. What did you do?"

"Worked out a little knot of lactic acid. It's still stiff?"

"Just a bit."

"Here, let me massage it some more."

As Devlin faced forward again, Jillian curved her fingers over his broad shoulder and began to gently knead the muscle. When she was finished with the right side, she moved over to the left. As she worked on it, she could feel the tension ease out of Devlin's shoulder and neck, could see his head move gently as she pushed. A small smile curved her lips. Relaxed was a mood she hadn't experienced with this man. It felt good.

"Jillian." Devlin's hand closed over her left one as he spoke.

"Yes?"

"Thanks." He turned as he spoke. The expression on his face was nowhere near relaxed. She watched his frown tighten as he got to his feet, still holding her hand, and said, "Come around here and sit in front of the fire, while I go make up the beds."

Jillian tried to lighten the mood as she walked around the end of the couch to stop directly in front of him. "Oh," she said with a lift of her eyebrows, "so now it's your turn to get domestic, is it?"

Devlin was still holding her hand. His gaze held hers as he shook his head. "Not hardly. I just think it's time I put some distance between us."

Jillian blinked. "Well, that's certainly direct."

She tried to draw her hand back. Devlin's fingers tightened, trapping hers within them.

"I didn't say I wanted to. Just that I should."

Jillian's heart raced in response to the intense look in his eyes. "Why's that?" she breathed.

Devlin's eyes narrowed. He stared into her eyes a long moment, before he lowered his head and whispered, "I think you know."

A second later, his mouth claimed hers.

Jillian parted her lips to receive his kiss. Devlin took the silent invitation, touching her tongue with his. Hers touched back. When his hands slid around her waist, hers slipped up over his chest and shoulders to meet behind his neck.

She couldn't tell if Devlin was pulling her to his body, or if she was drawing him to hers. She only knew she couldn't seem to get close enough, couldn't feel all she wanted to feel. She was hot all over, from her toes to the top of her head. The portions of her body that touched Devlin's felt as if they were on fire. A strange heat settled low in her stomach, where Devlin's desire pressed. Her chest grew tense from lack of air, but her lips refused to leave Devlin's, clung to the promise of further pleasure found there.

Jillian didn't remember closing her eyes, but when the warmth of Devlin's lips suddenly left hers, she opened them to find herself staring into dark midnight blue eyes, shadowed by a deep frown.

Chapter 10

"You see, this is why we need that distance." Devlin spoke in a soft, husky voice. "I warned you that all the dangers you faced wouldn't be from someone following you."

Jillian stared at him for several moments. "Are you telling me that I'm in danger now?"

"Yes. It's been a long time since I last wanted anyone like this," he said. "In fact, I'm not sure I've ever wanted anyone the way I want you."

"I see." Jillian's breath caught in her throat. "And that's a problem?"

His scowl deepened. "Of course it's a problem. I'm not about to take advantage of your situation."

Jillian frowned. "Devlin, what makes you think I'm being taken advantage of? Do you think I'm kissing you, that I'm standing here wanting you, because I'm too emotionally distraught over the fiasco with Brett to know my own mind?"

Devlin gave his head a quick shake. "No, of course not. It's just that... I have nothing to offer you."

"Really?" She pressed her hips forward slightly, increasing the pressure of her hips against the bulge beneath the zipper of his jeans. "You could have fooled me."

Jillian watched Devlin's eyes open wide. She blinked at her own boldness. Never in her life had she said anything like this to a man. But then, never in her life had any man made her feel like Devlin did, truly desired.

"I'm not asking for any promises," she said. "And I'm not making any plans, if that's what you're thinking. I think the moment-to-moment stuff you've been telling me about is much nicer. Especially—" she leaned toward him "—moments like this."

Devlin's lips eased into a smile, but the frown remained, as well. "I don't have any protection," he said.

The tension in his voice brought a smile to Jillian's lips. "I do," she said. When Devlin raised his eyebrows, she hurried to explain. "The honeymoon, remember? Having a child nine months after the marriage was not on my agenda. The condoms were part of the stuff I transferred from my purse to the backpack. Girl Scout training."

Devlin's lips twitched. "I'll never make fun of your be-prepared approach to life again. Where are they?"

His voice held urgency in addition to tension. Jillian's smile became a grin as she replied, "In my backpack, with the bedding in the farthest of the two bedrooms."

She backed out of his arms as she said this. He grabbed her hand and pulled her around the end of the couch. Guiding her toward the hallway, he lifted the lantern from the table as they passed it.

The lamp found a place on the small table by the bed, while Jillian went to the corner, bent and unzipped her backpack. Behind her she heard the hiss of two more zippers, one long, the other short. A vision of Devlin removing his sweatshirt, then his jeans brought a hot blush to her cheeks as fumbling fingers touched the edge of a small round packet.

When she rose and turned, Devlin had lowered the lantern's flame, leaving the room lit by the softest of glows. His naked body was a bare shadow in front of her as Jillian crossed the room. His fingers gently brushed hers as he took the condom from her. He placed it on the edge of the mattress, then took her hand again and drew her to him for another long, searing kiss.

His hands slid up the smooth silk of her sweater, to cup her breasts, which grew warm beneath his touch, making her wish that the sweater was gone, that there was nothing between the palms of his hands and her tender skin. As if reading her mind, those warm, large hands of his slid downward, skimming her waist and her hips, to grab the hem of her sweater. He lifted his mouth from hers as he raised the fabric up, drawing it over her head. It hadn't even touched the ground before he was kissing her again, holding her to him, pulling her slowly down with him to the bare mattress.

It was cold beneath her back. Jillian gasped and arched up. Devlin groaned.

A cool rush of air brushed her skin as Devlin pulled away from her. Jillian opened her eyes, then her mouth. Before she could protest the lack of his body heat, he hooked his thumbs into the waistband of her leggings, slid the knit fabric quickly down to her ankles and tossed them aside.

He turned from her then, and reached toward the bedside table. She heard a crackling noise, then a snapping sound. A moment later, Devlin twisted back to her. Placing a hand on the mattress on either side of her shoulders, he lowered himself, stopping to rest on his elbows, his mouth inches away from hers.

"You're sure about this?" he asked.

His voice was gruff. She could feel the tension, the restraint in the body above hers. In that second of complete concern for her, any doubts Jillian might have had about this moment fled.

"Yes," she replied, then slid her hands up through the thick hair that covered the firm muscles of his chest. She smiled at his small gasp, then lifted her hands to bury her fingers in his hair and draw his head down to hers.

They kissed for what seemed like eternity. All the time their bodies were moving together, arching, swaying, until they were both too breathless to kiss any longer.

When Devlin lifted his head, Jillian gazed up at him. His eyes held hers.

She knew what he was asking. She gave him the barest of nods, then shifted her hips, welcoming him to her. A second later he was kissing her again as he moved within her. Her lips answered, as did her hips. Her entire body warmed, as if heat had spread from the contact between them to every muscle and pore. Pleasure flooded her senses, grew, deepened, localized into a searing, glorious need that melted and pulsed then splintered into pure ecstasy.

Wind whispered softly through the birch trees behind the cottage. Early-morning sunlight filtered through the lattice that formed the sides of the small potting shed attached to the rear of the house. Jillian sat within, on a worn wooden bench. Jeans-clad knees drawn up to her chin, arms wrapped around her legs, she gazed out at the soft blue, pink and yellow flowers swaying in the breeze.

All morning she'd been battling to gain some sort of equilibrium, and she desperately needed this island of quiet. A loud knocking at the front door had brought her and Devlin to instant wakefulness. After fighting with the blankets tangled around them, which Devlin had pulled over them before they fell asleep in each other's arms, they had dressed quickly and hurried out to admit the moving man.

Then, each time she had looked at Devlin, whether it was to glance his way as he and the dark-haired giant named

Ivan McGreggor lifted a piece of furniture, or over the Formica table as they all gulped down hard-boiled eggs and scones with warm coffee for breakfast, the air had become charged with a subtle electric force.

Now that she'd packed away the cooler and bedding as Shaemus had asked, and the two men were loading up the last of the boxes, she'd slipped out to find a few moments to come to terms with the past night.

Never, in all her dreaming of the future, had she dreamed of anything quite as wonderful as what had passed between her and Devlin, here in this simple little house. It was certainly something she would have never planned. If she had sat down ahead of time and considered making love to a man she'd only known four days, she would have sternly reminded herself of the humiliation of her recent almost-marriage. She would have told herself that surely nothing could come of a romance born of stress and fear and running.

And yet, she felt so very connected to this man, this virtual stranger. He knew about her past and hadn't once made her feel like a fool for having loved Brett, or at least thinking that she'd loved Brett. Instead he'd shared a painful story of his own, made her feel that being fooled wasn't all that unusual, or awful.

She was amazed that this man, who didn't like to talk about his past, would have done so with someone he'd just met. She found it further amazing that this man, who was so very obviously private, would be willing to have her along with him on this last, very personal, portion of his odyssey.

"We're all packed up."

Devlin's voice, and his sudden appearance at the opening of the small building, made Jillian jump.

"Sorry," he said with a smile. "Did I startle you?"

At first glance, his smile appeared to have an easy, casual tilt to it. At second glance, she noticed a slight tightness at the corners, hinting at an attempt at control. The intense, hungry gaze that had trapped hers at the breakfast table had all but disappeared, and had been replaced by a cautious warmth.

Jillian took this as a gentle reminder not to take the previous night seriously, to simply enjoy it for the special moment it was. Drawing a deep breath, she got to her feet.

"You did startle me, as a matter of fact," she replied. "I kind of got lost in all the little nature sounds. It's wonderfully serene out here."

Devlin turned to gaze at the flowers as she exited the potting shed.

"Yes, it is," he said. "It's a lot like the woman who tended it. My other grandmother is quite the gardener, too, but her creations are much more controlled, and unless the old woman has changed greatly, I doubt you'll find much serenity anywhere she happens to be. Anyway, you'll find out soon enough. Ivan wants to get going."

As he finished speaking, Devlin turned and started walking the path that would take them to the front of the house. Jillian matched her steps to his.

"You didn't tell me about your father's mother last night. She sounds a little frightening," she said.

Devlin glanced at her briefly. His smile took on a wry twist. "I believe the word is *indomitable,*" he said. "As my grandda likes to say, Vitality St. Clair thinks of herself as the woman God would have sit in for him, if he decided to take a vacation."

"Oh, my."

Jillian stopped walking as she said this. They'd reached the front corner of the house. Devlin stopped, too, and turned to gaze down at her. Doubt and insecurity both were reflected in the soft brown eyes looking up at him.

"Hey," he said gently, "Grandmother hasn't bitten anyone that I know of. She just has a rather fierce bark. And you have nothing to worry about. She'll be so busy tearing into me that she'll barely pay you any mind at all."

"Oh, well." Jillian shrugged. "In that case, I won't give her a second thought."

Devlin turned to start down the path again, but Jillian's gentle hand on the sleeve of his sweatshirt drew him to a stop. He turned slowly. The sober expression in her eyes told him that he wasn't going to escape some discussion of what had passed between them the night before.

"Devlin," she said quietly, "I want to thank you."

Her words surprised him.

"Thank me? For what?"

"For..." She hesitated a moment, a moment in which her face flushed a soft pink. "For *not* being the perfect gentleman last night. During the past four days I've felt like one rug after another has been pulled from beneath my feet. I'm not used to life being so capricious, and I really felt the need to have a say in what happened to me. To regain just a little bit of control."

Devlin stared into her warm, open gaze, nodding slowly. "I understand. Just so you understand that it's one thing to control yourself, and quite another to expect to control anyone else."

Her expression didn't change, but she seemed to stiffen ever so slightly as she shook her head. "Controlling anyone else was the furthest thing from my mind. I had no expectations last night, other than that I would receive exactly what I got."

"Which was?"

The pink of Jillian's face deepened, but she didn't take her eyes from his as she replied, "Amazing sex."

She turned then and began to walk along the house. Devlin followed her, aware that *his* cheeks had grown suddenly warm.

Damn. He wished that was all he'd gotten from the evening. *Amazing* was definitely the word for what had happened between them, but it had been far more to him than just sex. It had been like no coupling he'd ever experienced in his life. It had gone far deeper than the physical, touching him in some place he'd hidden from even himself.

Jillian's calm demeanor this morning, her simple thank-you-with-no-strings-attached attitude should make him feel at ease. It didn't. *She* might have no expectations, but he did.

Well, perhaps not expectations, but a very strong hope that he would taste those pleasures once again. Yet he knew it was dangerous for him to feel this way—moving into uncharted territory. When he'd left home all those years ago, he'd locked his emotions in some dark corner of his soul. Taking the lid off that Pandora's box now, when he had to face so many other things that he'd shut away, was worse than dangerous. It bordered on insane.

Yet he knew if he tried to keep Jillian out of his heart, whatever moments of passion they might share in the future would lack the depth, the soul-shattering pleasure he'd experienced last night.

Ironically, he'd been prepared to do just that, he reminded himself as he rounded the corner of the house. Jillian's simple, commonsense thank-you should have freed him to retreat from her as planned, but for some perverse reason, it made him want to get just that much closer to her.

So, as Ivan headed south on a two-lane, then moved onto a six-lane superhighway, where they sped along in excess of eighty miles an hour, Devlin found himself pointing out sights that might be of interest to Jillian. Each time he explained the history of a place, or described a great ruin in a city they passed, he could feel the wall he'd erected around his feelings for his homeland begin to crumble.

An hour and a half later, they left Exeter and turned onto another small highway, one that provided glimpses of the English Channel on their way east. As the lorry made its way down the left side of the road, Jillian watched the view out the driver's window. While she craned her neck, gazing at the tree-studded rolling green landscape, to catch even the briefest glimpse of the little villages perched on the sea, Devlin stared at the toes of his hiking boots.

Now it was time for *him* to regain a sense of control, he told himself. In perhaps three more hours, he'd be faced with sights far more evocative to him than the ones that had Jillian so enthralled.

Somehow, when he'd boarded that plane in San Francisco, he'd given little consideration to how he'd feel once he reached his home. Home. There was that word again. He couldn't allow himself to think of Blodwell Hall as home. It was never going to be his again. He couldn't let himself forget that—or that he alone had made the choice that made this be so.

"We're nearing Lyme Regis, sir."

Devlin turned to Ivan as the van slowed to pull off the highway. "Fine," he said. "Why don't you find a place in the village to stop and let us out. I know you have to get on to Southampton. Just drop us wherever it's convenient."

"Convenient" turned out to be a street on the edge of the harbor town. After thanking Ivan, and pulling their backpacks and coats from behind the seat, Devlin and Jillian waved goodbye, then turned to each other.

"What now?" Jillian asked.

Devlin glanced at his watch. It was almost noon. "Lunch, I think. The question is, where would you like to take it? There used to be a nice café at the top of the village."

Devlin looked up to find Jillian strapping her pack onto her back like a woman working in a dream. She wasn't paying any attention to him or to the pack. All of her attention was on the little fishing village snuggled within the arms of two tree-clad hills that sloped down to the sea.

Devlin didn't want to follow her gaze. He'd seen Lyme Regis with its color-washed Regency villas and stone houses topped with gray slate roofs a thousand times. Memories lurked around every corner—the sweetshop where he and Colin had spent their allowances, the tea shop with its pastries and huge, warming mugs of tea, the harbor where he and his brother had sailed those long-ago summers, and had almost lost their lives years later, courtesy of the Suttons.

If he could have things his way, he'd just turn and start toward Blodwell Hall. He was painfully aware that more memories waited him there, but he believed it was best to get unpleasant things over as soon as possible.

However, home was still several miles away, and breakfast had been hours ago.

As if she'd been reading his mind, Jillian turned to him and asked, "Could we eat somewhere down by the water?"

Devlin nodded. "Sure, I know just the place. At least, I think so. Things can change a lot in twelve years."

Actually, he found that things had changed little in this small town. The narrow street took them gradually toward the water, past a mixture of whitewashed and natural stone structures with window boxes dripping color. And The Wharf Rat was just as he'd remembered, a sparkling white building with its doors and many-paned windows painted dark blue. The familiar scent of malt ale and fried fish greeted him as he held the door open for Jillian, then led her to a booth next to a window that overlooked the boats riding at anchor in the small harbor.

"The fish and chips here were once the best in all of south England," he said. "Shall we see if they've stood the test of time?"

"Sure."

Devlin went to the bar to order their lunch, then returned with a glass of ale for both of them. Jillian turned from the window with a smile.

"This place is perfect," she said. "Thank you."

It was the sort of thing a bride might say to her groom after a night of newlywed lovemaking, Devlin imagined. And he found himself replying, "I'm glad you like it," as if he'd planned this out as part of a romantic honeymoon, as if the two of them weren't there because danger had dictated every step they'd taken since landing in England.

And yet, the words had come as naturally as the smile he found himself giving Jillian as she sipped her ale, and the memories he found himself spinning into words.

"This was once a regular stop of ours," Devlin said. "When Colin and I were kids, our parents would pull in here on the monthly trips we made to our grandparents' house, before my father inherited it. Father used to say he needed a meal and a stout mug of ale to get ready to visit his parents."

"You always say the most reassuring things," Jillian replied.

Devlin's lips twitched into a wry grin. He shifted his gaze, and stared out the window, recalling himself as a small lad, staring out at the same scene, wondering why they had to go to Blodwell Hall at all.

"I can't lie," he said. "I'm not sure what to expect myself, when we get home. When I was a child, the visits between my father and his father were mostly long stretches of silence, interrupted by my grandfather saying things like 'You can't go on ignoring tradition.'"

Devlin blinked, then gazed at a small blue sailboat bobbing in the water. How odd. His father had said those exact words to him on more than one occasion, and he'd never once recalled having heard them so many years before.

"You mentioned a hike," Jillian said softly. "Is it very far to your father's house?"

Devlin turned from the window.

"We have a five-mile hike down the South Devon Coast Path, going west. Then another couple of miles up a long, winding path that leads in from the cliffs."

Her eyes widened. "No regular road?"

He gave her a small smile. "Well, actually, Ivan drove past what is considered the road to Smeaton-on-Axe on the way here. It looked just as I remembered, a narrow thing paved only with gravel and bordered on each side with high, thick hedges. Deliveries usually come upriver from Axmouth. Small cars have a hard enough time getting up the track. Something large, like the moving lorry that brought us here, just can't cut it. I hope it's not too daunting for you, but since we have to walk, the back way into the village is the same distance as the road, and certainly more scenic."

"Oh, I don't mind the walk," she said quickly. She paused and glanced out the window. Her eyes narrowed slightly before she turned back to Devlin. "Hiking along the coast here was something I'd really wanted to do on this trip."

A cheery waitress wearing a dark blue apron over her T-shirt and jeans brought them their food just as Jillian finished speaking.

"It smells great," Devlin said as the girl left, "however, I'm going to have to ask you to hurry through the meal. I'm getting rather anxious to get this homecoming over with."

Jillian nodded. "Me, too, I guess. It suddenly occurred to me that my presence might not be very welcome. You haven't been home in years, and now you show up with a complete stranger."

Devlin stared at Jillian. Yes, his family would want to hear the story behind her presence, as well as many other things about him. Too bad. He couldn't even explain his relationship with Jillian to himself. He needed time to assimilate all the emotions that had built over the past several days. Emotions that had come flowing out of him the night before, intertwined so deeply with the rush of passion that he didn't know where one began and the other ended.

And time wasn't something he had at the moment.

Devlin forced a smile. "Oh, we'll have to tell them the whole convoluted story, I suppose. Then I can find out what they need, and move on. And speaking of moving on,

I think we need to do a little less talking and a little more eating. If I've got to face the music, I want to get it over with.''

Twenty minutes later, they stepped onto a path that ran along the edge of cliffs that overlooked the swirling sea to their left. The sun warmed Jillian's shoulders as she marched along next to Devlin. Waves crashed into the rocks below, sending up a spray of water that cooled the air, making for nearly perfect hiking weather.

They said little as they walked along. The path was rough in spots, so Jillian glanced down often. The rest of the time she was gazing at the ever-changing water, noting the line of fishing boats moving west, or watching the gulls float gracefully on currents of air above.

The sudden attack of nerves that had hit her in the waterside pub still sat uneasily in her chest. Devlin's homecoming was likely to be very personal. Hardly something to be witnessed by a stranger. Well, she thought with a frown. She wasn't quite a stranger, actually, especially after last night. But, certainly she was someone that none of his family had ever met. Their focus should be on him, free of any interference from an outsider like herself.

Devlin had mentioned a village. Perhaps she could stay there, instead of in the house, where she would be making everyone, especially herself, feel stiff and awkward.

''What's Smeaton-on-Axe like?'' she asked.

Devlin glanced over at her in surprise.

''Unspoiled,'' he said. ''At least it was. And having noticed that the road hadn't been widened, I would imagine it's much the same as when I left it. The town likes to bill itself as the Village That Time Forgot. It boasts a small bed-and-breakfast that caters to people who really want to escape from the more touristy places. But unlike some villages that are merely reproductions of past days, Smeaton-on-Axe has retained its agricultural-based economy.''

''It sounds lovely.''

Devlin's response was a brief nod, accompanied by an expression that could only be called morose. He missed the place desperately, Jillian realized with a rush.

For the next several minutes, she found herself reviewing everything he'd said about his home and his family and saw what had been staring her in the face all this time—Devlin had been suffering an acute case of homesickness. All his moving from city to city hadn't been due to restless energy, or need for the change he was always touting. It was because he'd lost his home and wouldn't risk the pain of falling in love with another place.

And he called *her* a romantic.

"All right. The easy part's over."

Jillian looked up to see that Devlin had stopped at a side path that rose to their right. She glanced at her watch and was stunned to see that they'd been walking for almost two hours.

"We head in from here," he said. "The path is quite steep in parts. You let me know if you need to stop at any point."

The rocky dirt track they stepped onto wound up from the coast to cross a stretch of soft green down before moving into a thick forest. There, the ground beneath the trees was damp in spots, making for slippery footing. The continuous climb soon had Jillian's legs protesting the unaccustomed vigorous exercise, but she marched gamely on, until the protest grew to a burning ache.

Jillian glanced at Devlin, who had come to a halt four feet in front of her. She was just about to ask him if they could take a brief rest, when he turned to her.

"Just a few more feet," he said.

He reached out to take her hand and help her up a last, rocky patch, then placed his hands on her shoulders and turned her, so that she was looking down the other side of the hill.

A green valley stretched out before Jillian, bordered on either side by thick woods that sloped down to a thin ribbon of blue. To her right, the spire of a church rose above the trees. Beyond them, she could see a clutch of buildings lining the banks of the river. Dark green hedges divided the land into a patchwork of different shades of green, several of which surrounded a house and outbuildings.

"Oh, it is lovely," she said, then glanced up at Devlin. "Can I see your father's house from here?"

Devlin gave her that lopsided smile she found so attractive. "Yes. But it's not down by the village. Blodwell Hall is over there."

He pointed to the right as he spoke. When Jillian turned in that direction, all she could see was trees. Slowly she realized that some of the green she was looking at belonged to another little valley, this one a bit higher than the other. Dead in the center of this, on a rise of bright green grass, she spied the corner of a brick building. Jillian shifted toward Devlin to get a clearer view, then stilled as the full stretch of house came into view.

A redbrick tower, octagonal in shape, rose three stories into the air. The square battlements that topped it were formed of gray granite, as were its numerous windows. Attached to the tower was a wide two-story stretch of house, also made of brick, with granite trimming the windows and the door.

Jillian stared at the structure for several minutes. She had been expecting to see a large English country manor, something with Elizabethan half timbering perhaps. Not this... this *castle*.

Slowly she turned to Devlin. "Pretty fancy digs," she managed. "The import-export business over here must really be something."

Devlin shrugged. "I told you that the business had been in the family for centuries. Well, the house came with it, along with an earldom."

Chapter 11

"An *earldom?*" Jillian demanded as she turned to Devlin. "Your father is an *earl?*"

Devlin nodded slowly. "I'm afraid so. The Earl of Axeleigh, to be precise."

Jillian glanced at the house, then looked at Devlin once again.

"Take me to the village."

He frowned. "The village?"

"Yes. You mentioned a bed-and-breakfast. I'll stay there."

"But why? As you might guess, there's plenty of room in the house, some thirty bedrooms, if I remember correctly."

Jillian shuddered. She had planned to tour several of the old houses restored by Britain's National Trust. But the idea of staying in such a place as a guest was mind-boggling. *She,* Jillian Gibson, living in such grandeur, eating with the family in some auditorium-size dining room, partaking of food delivered by the hands of servants?

To some this might sound like a wonderful dream. She saw it as a nightmare.

She'd been brought up well enough. She knew which fork to choose from even the most elaborate of place settings, but the idea of being waited upon by servants was completely foreign to her. And she most definitely lacked the sort of wardrobe a place like this demanded. In her dusty jeans, she was going to feel as out of place as Cinderella would have at the ball had her fairy godmother not transformed her rags into a lovely dress.

Somehow, she didn't think she was likely to find a fairy godmother.

"I don't care how many guest rooms there are, I'm not going to stay there," Jillian said. She turned to Devlin. "In fact, I don't even want to darken its doorstep. You have to see your family. I don't. I know nothing about dealing with aristocrats, and I can't remember the last time I tried to curtsy."

She was aware that her voice was edged with hysteria. It didn't help that deep crinkles were fanning out from the corners of Devlin's eyes, that his lips were twitching suspiciously. The thought of facing his family had been daunting enough before. Now it was terrorizing.

"Curtsying from guests is not expected," he said softly. "This isn't Victorian times. Not even my grandmother, who does like to be referred to by her full title of Dowager Countess of Axeleigh, wants anyone to curtsy to her."

Jillian supposed that Devlin's words and the lift of his eyebrows were meant to reassure her. They didn't. They made her angry.

"Devlin, look at me," she demanded. "I'm in jeans and hiking boots, nicely powdered with red dirt. I have no idea what my hair or face looks like. Not that it matters. Even if I had the clothes that Shaemus is forwarding, I wouldn't have anything I'd be comfortable wearing into a house like *that.*"

She pointed to the house as she finished. Devlin's eyebrows lowered to a frown.

"Jillian, *that* is just a house. Very oversize and quite old, true. But it's just stone and brick. And the people in it are just people. People with titles, I'll admit. So? You've been walking around in the company of a formerly titled fellow for the last four days, and you haven't come to any harm, have you?"

Jillian stared at him a moment. "Why didn't you tell me?"

"Tell you? What? That I turned my rights of ascendance over to my brother? That I was once Viscount Hambly, future tenth Earl of Axeleigh? Why? Would it have made you trust me earlier? Encouraged you to sleep with me sooner?"

Devlin's words and the scowl that had lowered over his eyes made Jillian take a step back. She stared at him for a puzzled moment, a moment in which she recalled him telling her about that woman—Prudence—who had broken their engagement. Because he'd been about to turn his back on—

She shifted her attention to the house. It was very impressive. She imagined that many women would covet such a home. Not her, though. She turned to Devlin, perfectly prepared to tell him just how insulted she was that he would think of her this way. But before she could say a word, he reached out and cupped her cheek with the palm of his hand.

"Hey, forget I said that. Please?"

The look in his dark eyes pleaded. When she nodded, he spoke again. "What I was trying to get at originally was that, even if I still had my former *exalted* position, you are quite aware that I am just another man. A title doesn't make me any different from any other fellow."

His former title might not make him any different, Jillian thought, but something certainly did. Something about that crooked smile of his, perhaps, or the light in his dark blue eyes whenever he gazed longingly over the countryside. Something about the way that first kiss had instantly healed her wounded heart.

"Hey, you all right?"

Jillian responded with a sigh, followed by a shrug.

"Look." Placing his hands on her shoulders, he turned her to face him. "No one in there is going to try to intimidate you," he said softly. "They'll be far too busy taking aim at me, I'm sure."

Jillian's nervousness faded the moment she heard the bitter note beneath his joking words. She couldn't miss the pain in his dark blue eyes as he shifted his gaze from her to the house.

Pretty thoughtless of her, she thought, to have made such a big deal about this, considering what she knew about what he faced. When he'd mentioned that he'd turned his back on family tradition, she'd figured he had been referring to the normal rebellious stage that many young men go through when facing their parents' expectations. When he'd said his father was a landlord, she'd automatically thought of someone letting out flats in London, or small suburban houses.

Now she knew. Lord of all he surveys—*that* kind of landlord. And the traditions Devlin had been talking about went back hundreds of years. That was a lot of titles under the bridge, a lot of traditions to live up to, which Devlin obviously felt he'd failed to do. If he wanted her by his side while he faced up to this, who was she to let a little self-consciousness about lack of breeding or proper wardrobe get in the way?

"All right," she said. "I'd be a fool to pass up the chance to stay in a place like this. Let's go."

Devlin turned to her with a smile. Taking her hand, he led her down the hill, picking out a path that he and his brother had worn over years of hiking to the coast. He had to stop from time to time, where vegetation had obliterated the way, but was always able to pick it up after a few seconds of searching.

As the two of them made their way, he realized that Jillian's decision had also helped him to avoid showing his face in the village just yet.

When he'd started out on this trip, he'd only thought of how he would deal with his family's reaction at seeing him again. He hadn't considered that he might run into old acquaintances, that he'd have to face curious stares and careful questions. He hadn't expected to feel a reluctance to meet these people's unspoken censure, and most of all, hadn't expected that anticipating this would hurt him like it suddenly did.

He also hadn't figured on being overwhelmed by nostalgia at every turn.

"See that old oak over there?" he asked.

They had reached more level ground, were walking beneath some huge, ancient beeches. Devlin drew Jillian toward a tree with an incredibly thick trunk, then around to the far side, where he peered closely at the rough bark.

"Look. There," he said. "You can make out the outline of an archway where the bark has healed over an old cut. Guess what Colin and I were trying to do."

Jillian stared at the tree for several moments, then shrugged. "Build a tree—" She stopped suddenly and turned to him. "No—you were trying to carve a door in the tree, to make an entrance to an underground house. Like the one Peter and the lost boys had in Neverland."

Devlin nodded. "Right. Fortunately, the gardener found us before we could cut deep enough to really hurt the tree. And, even more fortunately, we'd done this where my grandfather wasn't likely to see it."

"A bit strict, was he?" she said as Devlin stepped away from the tree and began guiding her toward a gravel road that led to the house.

"Yes. When we told the gardener what we'd been trying to do, Riggs said we'd better hope that Grandfather didn't ever learn about it, or he just might feed us to the crocodiles in the dungeon."

Devlin watched Jillian's eyes narrow in doubt as she turned to him. "I can believe that place has a dungeon. But crocs?"

He grinned. "Both are a bit of fiction, actually. My grandfather made up the dungeon story when my father was a boy, to keep him in line. When Colin and I came along, I guess he figured he needed more ammunition for the two of us, so he added the crocodiles."

"Your grandfather was either very cruel, or had a very sick sense of humor."

Devlin shook his head slowly. "I'm not sure which it was. I was only eight when he died. He was in his late sixties at the time we were visiting. Grandmother is much younger. She's only in her middle seventies now. Anyway, Colin and I were brought in to say hello to him, then sent off while the adults talked—or argued, actually."

They reached the road as he finished speaking, then turned toward the house. They walked in silence, Devlin barely aware of Jillian by his side until he heard her exclamation.

"Oh, look at this!"

He turned to find her standing on tiptoe, trying to see over a wrought-iron fence backed by a five-foot hedge. He joined her.

"This is the dowager countess's garden," he said quietly. "Rather different from my grandma's cottage plot, isn't it?"

Devlin saw Jillian nod, then turned to stare at the symmetrical gravel paths running past precisely spaced rosebushes and perfectly trimmed hedges to the white gazebo, situated in the center of the garden.

His grandmother used to take him there for tea on summer afternoons. Within her garden, and beneath that roof, her caustic personality would soften, and she would feed him stories of the St. Clair family's former glory along with his tea and biscuits.

The structure looked much as he remembered, except that some of the paint was chipping and several shingles were missing on the roof. He stared at the gaping hole a moment, then took Jillian's hand.

"You can visit the garden after we get settled," he said. "I want to get this over with now."

Several minutes later they mounted the wide stone steps and stood before the ten-foot-tall, five-foot-wide oak door. Their pull on the bell was answered by an older gentleman dressed in traditional butler's array. Wearing a crisp white shirt beneath black coat and tails, complete with a royal blue cummerbund trimmed in gold, the balding man looked down his nose, shifted his superior glance from Devlin to Jillian, then back to Devlin again.

"Hello, Franklin," Devlin said quietly. "You are looking well these days. Is my father about?"

The man stared at Devlin a second more. His eyes widened just the slightest bit before he gave a slow, deferential nod.

"Yes, Lord Devlin. He is, indeed. The family is taking high tea in the Yellow Room. Would you like to join them?"

"Of course."

Devlin drew Jillian through the huge door into the splendor of the two-story vestibule. Paneled in dark wood, the walls wore a collection of crossed swords and shields, along with banners worked in the same combination of dark blue and gold decorating Franklin's midsection.

While Jillian gazed up at the ornate ironwork candelabra above, Devlin removed his backpack then helped Jillian with hers. The butler took both items wordlessly, placed them in a closet disguised as one of the raised panels in the wall then turned to Devlin.

"Would you like me to announce you, sir?"

Devlin gave the man a dry grin. "I believe that might be advisable, Franklin. Please lead the way."

Franklin gave a small cough. "Might I have the name of your companion?"

"Oh, of course."

He turned to Jillian with a smile that he hoped would silently offer apology. The look of fear and intimidation that had colored her features when she first saw the house had returned. He reached out to take her cold hand into his and at her look of surprise, he gave her an even wider smile.

"I'm sorry, Jilly," he said softly. "Take a deep breath."

She frowned slightly but did as he asked, then gazed at him expectantly.

"Do it again," he said. After she complied he raised his voice a notch. "Franklin, this is my friend Jillian. Jillian, this is Franklin, who has been butler to both the eighth and ninth Earls of Axeleigh."

Jillian and the butler exchanged nods, then Franklin said, "If you will follow me, I will announce you, then see that additional refreshments are provided."

Devlin knew the way to the Yellow Room, as well as he knew his way across the Golden Gate Bridge, but following behind Franklin gave him a chance to reacquaint himself with the house.

Immediately he noted signs of neglect. The blue-and-gold hall runner beneath his feet was worn in patches, and a bench upholstered in dark green satin, sitting against one wall, showed signs of fading and the edge of one of the cushions was frayed.

The sound of voices echoing down the hall distracted him from his surroundings. The words were hardly the muffled, well-bred tones he recalled wafting through this house. They were angry and quite loud.

"Look, we all agree on the fact that Blodwell Hall should be preserved. I just don't think that the Larson Group can be trusted to do this. Their plans seem to completely ignore the area's ecological needs."

The second voice was more hoarse, accented with an aristocratic tone. "I must agree with Lucinda, for once, Andrew. I'm not happy with your suggestion that we sell to the National Trust, either. I find the idea of strangers wandering through these halls and my gardens absolutely horrid."

Devlin frowned as he followed Franklin toward the wide doorway. He knew the second speaker was his grandmother, but he could hardly believe that the first firm-toned voice had belonged to his mother. The sort of fuzzy-thinking woman he recalled had always been content to just do her thing, and let the older woman run the house that was so very important to her.

"Mother," a masculine voice was saying. "The way of life you wish to preserve is wasteful, not to mention completely outmoded. And Lucinda, the village must develop some economic diversity or rusticate out of existence."

Devlin reached the doorway just as his father finished speaking. He stared across the room, past the grand piano on his right and the fireplace with its ornate mantelpiece on his left, to the family tableau.

A sofa upholstered in deep gold stretched in front of a wide window framed in yellow satin. In the left corner of the couch sat his grandmother. Her hair was now pure white, but her posture was as rigidly erect as ever. Every line of her pale gray dress spoke of understated breeding, from its high collar to the pleats draping softly to the floor.

On the opposite side of the sofa, his mother looked comfortably casual in a loose, flower-print dress. Still fashion-model thin, her black hair was pulled into a loose tousle of curls atop her head. The only sign of visible aging was the streak of white above her left eyebrow, which had widened to a full three inches.

Two men sat in spindly Queen Anne chairs arranged at right angles to the couch. His father, on the right, wore a dark blue suit and maroon tie. Wings of gray filtered back from his temple to blend with light brown hair. Colin, sitting opposite the low table holding the silver tea set, appeared to have changed little. His hair was still a light brown, his face tan, but several shades lighter than the khaki jacket he wore over matching pants.

"Excuse me."

Franklin's words had an instant effect on the four people at the end of the room. They all turned at the same moment, just as the butler said, "Lord Devlin has arrived, with a guest, Miss Jillian."

Good old Franklin. Devlin couldn't keep from smiling at the way the man announced his return as if he'd only been gone on a two-week holiday.

"Well." His grandmother rose as she spoke. "I must say, your timing couldn't be better, boy. Andrew, I take back all those things I said about the incompetence of that detective agency you hired."

Devlin had started to step into the room as his grandmother spoke. Her words brought him to a dead stop. He turned to his father.

"Detectives?"

Andrew St. Clair got slowly to his feet. Devlin became aware that his mother and brother stood, also, but Devlin's attention was on his father's face, noticing that time had worn it more deeply than Devlin had first noticed.

"Yes," his father replied with a puzzled frown. "The ones I hired to look for you. I must admit, I'm almost as surprised as Mother to see you here, though. Just two days ago, the detectives informed me that they were having difficulty tracing your movements past your departure from Paris, twelve years ago. It appears they overcame that problem, however."

Devlin frowned. Before he could explain that his presence had nothing to do with detectives, Colin spoke up.

"Detectives? Why didn't you tell me you wanted to find Dev? I could have saved you the time and the money."

Andrew turned to his youngest son. "Do you mean to tell me that you've known all along where he was hiding?"

"No, he didn't." Devlin took another step into the room as he replied for his brother. "Colin knew what city I was in, and how to get a message to me, but not the name I was using. And I was *not* hiding."

His father's eyebrows met over his high, sharp nose. "Oh, really? Then would you mind telling me—"

"Not one word more."

Devlin blinked as his mother came around to stand next to his father. She scowled up at the man, then directed an equally quelling look at Colin before turning to Devlin.

"I don't care how he got here." She started across the room, her dark blue eyes holding his as she approached. "I'm just so very glad to see him, I think that I shall cry."

Devlin was stunned to see that her eyes were indeed shimmering. As she drew nearer, her arms reached out to him, and before he could stop himself, he reached out to her. As they held each other, he breathed in the fresh scent of the outdoors, awakening little-boy recollections of being folded in a similar welcoming embrace whenever he returned from school.

He felt the same odd tightness in his throat and chest that he'd felt on those occasions. And as before, where public displays of emotional expression just wouldn't do, when they broke apart and were facing each other again, he said, "Read any good books lately?" at the same moment as she.

They both laughed, then hugged again. When he released his mother this time, she blinked rapidly as she turned to Jillian.

"Hello, my dear. Please excuse all this ridiculous bickering. It's the way this family expresses emotion, I fear. Please, do come in, sit down and have some tea. Hopefully we shall be able to behave like the highly civilized people that the duchess likes to pretend we are."

At some point the butler had quietly slipped away, leaving Jillian standing alone next to Devlin. When she glanced up at him, he took her hand in one of his and his mother's in the other, then escorted them across the carpet patterned in shades of gold.

By the time they reached the low table, Colin and his father had drawn two more chairs forth. Jillian released a slow, tense breath of air as she took her seat. Up to that point, she'd been too fascinated by the emotionally charged scenes she'd witnessed to feel self-conscious. Now eight pairs of politely curious eyes were upon her.

"Here, let me pour you each a cup of tea, my dear." Devlin's grandmother leaned forward as she spoke. "Devlin, please fix your friend a plate of sandwiches and cakes, and of course, make the proper introductions."

Jillian smiled at each person as Devlin presented them. After he finished, the dowager countess handed her a delicate cup and saucer. As Jillian reached out with both hands, she noticed the woman's gray eyes rest on her left hand for a long moment.

Jillian followed the woman's gaze and stared at the gold band she'd placed there four days earlier. She met the older woman's eyes again, but before she could decide whether to rush in with an explanation, the countess said, "Please help yourself to cream and sugar, my dear," then turned to Devlin.

"So, if it wasn't the detectives, just what did bring you here?"

Out of the corner of her eye, Jillian saw Devlin take a long sip of tea before lowering his cup to the saucer and turning to his grandmother. As he explained the system he and Colin had set up, along with the message that had appeared in the San Francisco paper, Jillian became aware of a high-pitched voice echoing in the hallway.

The voice grew more distinct as Devlin finished speaking, only to be muted when Colin started speaking.

"Look, Devlin, there's a problem here. I didn't arrange for any—"

"Oh, I'm so sorry to be late," a female voice broke in.

Jillian turned to the doorway. A petite woman with dark red hair falling straight to the shoulders of her beige jacket-dress paused a second, then stepped toward them as she continued to talk.

"But I ran into Bradley Larson in the village, and he's come up with a..."

The woman stopped speaking and walking at the same time, to stare at Colin. Her smile faltered slightly, then brightened as she spoke again.

"Oh, Colin darling. You're here. I didn't expect you home for another week."

Colin stood, drawing Jillian's attention. He was a nice-looking man, his face more square than Devlin's, with eyes the steel gray of his grandmother's. He had rugged, weathered features, and deep lines at the corners of his eyes that creased as his lips twisted into a half smile that Jillian thought might express either shy pleasure or suppressed discomfort.

"Johnstone finished up with his research early, and took charge of the dig," he said as he approached his wife. "The foundation frowns on paying for two head archaeologists, so I came on home."

"Oh, really? How lovely. And surprising. You have been known to stay and work for nothing."

The reproach in the woman's voice was soft, her smile wide as she gazed up at Colin. He shrugged, then lowered his deep voice so that Jillian could barely hear his next words.

"I thought...well, that we needed some time together."

Apparently age hadn't diminished his grandmother's hearing, for those words had barely been uttered before she spoke up.

"Well, I don't care why Colin came home, only that he did, and at the perfect time. We need to get the question of succession settled. With both Colin and Devlin here, we can do so, then tackle those Larson people."

The woman standing next to Colin turned a blank stare to the older lady. Her gaze shifted, and her eyes widened as they settled on Devlin.

Jillian glanced his way and noted a certain tightness in his smile when he spoke.

"Hello there, Prudence."

Chapter 12

Prudence? Jillian thought. Devlin's I-can't-love-you-if-you-don't-have-a-title Prudence? Married to Devlin's *brother?*

Jillian gripped the delicate handle of her teacup as she watched Devlin turn to Colin. "Well," he said, "it seems that belated congratulations are in order."

No one spoke for several moments. Colin finally broke the silence. "Yes. We married eleven years ago."

"Well, Devlin," their grandmother said, "if I'd known that Colin had access to you, I would have insisted that he send you a wedding invitation."

Jillian watched Prudence closely, saw her china blue eyes widen and her face blush to a lovely shade of pink as she glanced from her mother-in-law, to her husband, to the man she'd once been engaged to.

"I'm afraid I would have been forced to decline," he said.

Prudence gave him a tight smile. "Then what brings you back now?"

"I have no idea."

Devlin turned to his brother. The two men stared at each other for a moment, then Colin shook his head.

"I was just about to tell you, when Prudence came in, that *I* didn't place any ad in the San Francisco paper."

"Well, someone did." Devlin's voice echoed with suspicion. "Did you tell anyone about our agreement?"

Colin's features tightened. "Yes. My solicitor. You remember Peter Sedgewicke? He joined the firm that handles the family business. Somewhere along the line it occurred to me that at least one other person should know, so I gave the information to Peter, with strict instructions for it to be kept a secret, unless something happened to me."

The two men glared at each other, until their mother said, "Come, boys, and have your tea. Colin, pull up a chair for your wife. There now, let's all sit down and work this out."

Jillian took another sip of tea. She had expected to be less than comfortable when meeting Devlin's family, but this went far beyond that. Tension filled the room like some invisible smoke cloud. She should probably be happy that she wasn't the focus of all the unpleasantness, but she was painfully aware that this encounter was not the sort that should be observed by someone who wasn't a member of the family.

"Now, Devlin," his mother said. "Tell us, did you have a nice trip over?"

Devlin glanced sharply at his mother. Her wide smile was a little too bright, her words a little too seemingly artless. And the look in eyes told him she was quite aware of what she was doing.

In that one second, years of hearing his mother use just that tone of voice spun through his mind, followed by incidence after incidence in which Lucinda St. Clair had effortlessly fooled the entire family into underestimating her, playing the part that had been expected of her, a somewhat muddleheaded former fashion model, when she'd been in charge of the situation all along.

The corners of his lips curved as he stared into his mother's blue eyes. He would have to be careful here. He'd noticed the attention his grandmother had paid to the bands that he and Jillian were wearing, and he suspected his mother had spied them, as well.

He had no idea how he wanted to explain Jillian's presence in his life. He'd grown oddly accustomed to the ring on his finger. It certainly complicated matters. Until he had time to figure that out, he decided he'd have to stay on his toes if he wanted to avoid a direct inquisition from either of them. Fortunately, he knew a subject that would definitely deflect interest from his personal life.

"Well, it was an interesting trip," he said. "For one thing, no sooner did I get off the plane than I was pushed into the path of an oncoming train in the airport underground. And for another, we've been followed constantly by two men who we now assume to be connected to the Suttons."

"The Suttons!"

Colin barely finished uttering these two words before he began choking on the tea cake he'd just bitten into. Prudence reached over to pat him on the back and spoke in a soothing tone.

"Nigel Sutton was released from prison a fortnight ago, Colin dear," she said. "I guess you've been too busy wherever you were in the wilds of Italy to read the London papers."

"Well, Pru," Devlin said. "I understand that *you* have had a run-in with our old friend, also."

Devlin watched the woman carefully. He saw her face pale beneath her makeup as he continued, "Jillian and I saw Grandda yesterday. He told us that Nigel had come into the pub, asking for Colin, and that when he called here to talk to him, you mentioned that you'd had your own encounter with the man."

Prudence straightened. She glanced at her husband quickly, before giving Devlin a pleasant smile. "Yes," she replied softly. "I did run into Nigel in the village—two days before Shaemus called. The man was most polite, and asked about both of you. When I said that Colin was out of town and that no one knew if Dev was still alive, he didn't get angry or anything, he just smiled at me."

She paused. Devlin watched a small frown form as she went on. "It was a very odd smile, now that I think about it."

"And did the man say anything after that?"

The sharp, autocratic tone to the dowager countess's question made Prudence start. "No." She lifted her chin and replied with soft dignity. "Except to ask me to tell Colin that he was sorry for everything."

Devlin's mother leaned forward. "And you didn't think fit to tell one of us about this?"

"I didn't want anyone to worry." Prudence shrugged. "The Suttons have left us alone all these years. Besides, Nigel mentioned he was planning to leave the country soon. I figured it might be best if nothing was made of it."

"Well, for once I agree with the girl."

The dowager countess's words drew everyone's attention. Having that, she turned to Andrew.

"The Sutton problem is in the past. We have more pressing matters to discuss now, such as the Larson Group and their plans for Blodwell Hall."

The earl gave his mother a tight smile. "You're probably right. Besides, although the thought of Nigel hanging about is less than comforting, I don't think he's behind the men who've been following Devlin and his friend."

"Excuse me," Prudence interjected. "But speaking of Devlin's friend, we have yet to be introduced."

Devlin watched the woman turn to Jillian as she spoke, saw her gaze travel slowly down to Jillian's dusty boots, all the time maintaining a painfully polite smile that made his jaw tighten and his eyes narrow. When her pale blue eyes shifted to him, he forced himself to smile and gave in to impulse.

"Excuse my poor manners," he said. "Jillian, this is Prudence, my sister-in-law. Prudence, this is Jillian—my wife."

He ignored the assorted gasps that followed his words as he turned to his father and asked, "All right, then, who *do* you think was following us?"

"The detectives I hired," Andrew replied. "You see, I was so disgusted with their lack of progress, that the last time they called I told them not to do so again until they had something concrete to report. Since I had informed my solicitors to cooperate fully, I think Peter must have revealed your little plan. Having that, they probably placed the ad you saw, then simply waited for you to arrive."

Devlin nodded slowly. "I suppose that's possible. And the fact that I came in using a different name might explain why the men just didn't approach me directly. But it still doesn't tell me why you wanted me home."

"And," Colin added, "why you didn't try to contact me about this."

"But I did." Lord St. Clair turned to his youngest son. "I had two telegrams sent to you. Despite technological advances, it seems you are still difficult to reach when you go on one of your digs."

"Well, one way or another," Devlin said, "you have us both here. Now, would someone please tell me who or what a Larson Group is?"

The dowager countess seemed more than anxious to answer that one. "They are a perfectly horrid bunch of people who want to purchase Blodwell Hall," she said. "They want to make the house into a hotel and use the land for an amusement park of sorts. They have plans to widen the road down to the highway to increase tourist access and bring people up the river from Axmouth on barges."

She shuddered as she finished speaking.

"Your ladyship. Really," Prudence said. "The Larson people simply want to bring the area into the twentieth century, before the rest of the world enters the twenty-first. Many people in town are quite pleased with that idea, you know."

Devlin turned to his mother. "Is this true?"

She frowned. "Only partially. Many others hate it. As do I. The Axe is prime breeding ground for several species of birds. The Larson's plan would put that in jeopardy."

"Well, I can see we have the makings of a mess here," Devlin said quietly, "but what's all this have to do with me?"

"Well," his father replied, "that piece of paper you and Colin drew up, handing the rights of firstborn son over to him, is not valid. You are still legally my heir, until *I* do something about it. Well, I'm ready to do that now. I'm no longer willing to battle with keeping this place running."

"He is not allowed to," his wife added. "His doctor's orders—and mine."

Devlin didn't miss the glances his parents exchanged. His mother's expression was firm, his father's resigned before he turned to Devlin and spoke again.

"You will find that Blodwell Hall is in a rather advanced state of disrepair. My father was struggling with this in his day, and things have grown worse over the years. The family import-export business is barely breaking even. Taxes and the price of running such a large house have risen drastically over the past years, eating into the relatively little cash I inherited from my father. This situation leaves the entire family in an uncomfortably precarious position, financially. If I were to die right now, the inheritance taxes would ruin all of you. One option is for me to pass on the title before my death."

Ah, the point at last. Devlin crossed his arms over his chest as he spoke.

"Leaving me to clean up the mess, should I take on the title, I suppose?" He paused and shook his head slowly. "Tell me, do I *look* like an insane man?"

His father's eyebrows lowered quickly over his gray eyes. "No, but I was hoping you had become a *man.*"

Andrew's words echoed off the high, molded ceiling. "I was hoping that you'd come to miss your home, perhaps learned to regret your rash decision, that you might be ready to come back and—"

"And, what?" Devlin interrupted. "Do the right thing? I did that once before, remember? And look what it got me. I lost several close friends, almost lost my life and I put you and everyone who lives here at risk. I made the right decision when I left twelve years ago. I see no reason to change it now."

"Devlin." His mother spoke softly but firmly as she got to her feet. "Do *not* shout at your father. He's given this a great deal of thought. I want you and Colin to go with Andrew to his study now, and discuss this out of our presence."

She paused as she turned to her mother-in-law. "Your ladyship, if I remember correctly, you planned on supervising the planting of those new roses. Prudence, I'm sure you can find something to amuse yourself, while I take poor Jillian here up to her room. She looks as if she's beginning to wilt."

Jillian glanced at Devlin. He was still frowning, but he gave her a small smile, accompanied by a brief nod.

"This way, my dear."

Jillian let Devlin's mother lead her down the hallway she'd traveled earlier, then up a set of polished wooden steps.

"Wilted" was exactly how she was feeling. The hike up to the house had sapped her body, and the pain she'd seen on Devlin's features as he confronted his father had sucked all the joy from her spirit, leaving her with barely enough energy to give more than a passing glance to the pictures on the walls, or to the statues set in niches in the hallway.

She understood her physical exhaustion, but not the shriveled feeling in her soul. She shouldn't care so deeply what happened to Devlin Sin—no, *St.* Clair. He'd made it more than clear he didn't want anyone caring for him, wanted only to be able to move through life as he pleased.

So why did she persist in thinking that he wasn't as happy with that life-style as he claimed to be?

Perhaps because he hadn't been able to disguise the pleasure he'd felt at showing her his home as they stood on the hill, nor his concern at seeing the hints of disrepair about the place.

Still, the fact that the man had discovered that he'd missed his home, in spite of himself, didn't mean he wanted to reclaim it. And, now that she had an idea of the work and financial struggle this might entail, how could she blame him?

"Here we are, Jillian."

Lady St. Clair pushed a door inward as she spoke. Jillian took one step forward, then came to a halt just on the other side of the threshold and stared.

The room ran more than thirty feet from side to side, and she figured there was at least twenty-five feet from the doorway to the two windows set in the opposite wall. They were wide, framed in dark blue velvet, and reached nearly to the top of the nine-foot ceiling. The same fabric covered the massive raised canopy bed located between them. A brown leather couch and two chairs were arranged in front of a large fireplace to her right, and, like the bed, these pieces were large and masculine looking.

Of course. This was probably Devlin's old room. Where else would a mother take the woman her son claimed to be married to?

"The bathroom is to your left."

Lady St. Clair's words broke into Jillian's thoughts. She turned to the smiling woman. It wasn't fair to deceive her, but she was Devlin's mother, it was his place to put her straight.

Besides, she was far too tired to deal with it at the moment.

"Thank you," she said. "I..." She glanced around. "I don't know what to say, your ladyship. It's very kind of you to—"

Lady St. Clair shook her head impatiently as she interrupted. "Don't be silly, love. And please, call me Lucinda. I'm not like Prudence, who insists on the use of *Lady.* I wonder what she'll do now that Andrew has made it clear that Colin never truly had a right to the title of viscount. Anyway, I've never really become comfortable with all the title nonsense." She paused to give Jillian a wide smile. "It comes of having my picture splashed through magazines wearing miniskirts that barely covered my sit-down, I suppose."

Jillian returned the woman's smile, but before she could say a word, Lucinda took her by the hand and led her toward the bed.

"You look to be very tired, my dear. And from what little Devlin said of your adventures in getting here, I'm not surprised. Of course, I am absolutely dying to hear your story, but that will have to wait for the dinner table. And although my mother-in-law would never make herself common, like me, and ask about it, I know she's seething with curiosity, as well. So, you rest up. I'm afraid what you saw at tea is only half as bad as this family can be when they get their aristocratic backs up."

By the time Lucinda had finished speaking, she'd pulled a small set of steps from beneath the bed, and drawn back the covers. After giving Jillian another smile, she walked toward the door, then turned.

"I forgot to ask. Did you leave your luggage with Franklin?"

Jillian forced her tired brain to function. "Well, what there is of it," she replied. "I left most of my stuff back in

Oxford. My suitcase would have made our hike today nearly impossible, so I only brought traveling clothes. Shaemus is sending the suitcase here by post, but until it arrives, all I have is my backpack, with some fresh jeans, a clean sweater and my makeup."

"Do you need any of that now, or would you rather just settle in and have me send it along in, say, an hour?"

Jillian glanced at the bed. It looked extremely inviting. Recalling the stairs and long hallway she'd just traversed, she figured it would be twenty minutes at least before someone arrived with her things, none of which was essential at the moment. Twenty minutes that she could spend sleeping.

"Later will be fine," she said.

"Wonderful. I'll send Amelia to wake you in time for you to freshen up for dinner. You'll want to be prepared. The duchess is a quite skillful inquisitor, and I've learned a fair number of tricks from her in my time, as well."

Just before she closed the door, Lucinda gave Jillian a quick wink that underlined the teasing note in her words, an expression very much like one she'd seen on Devlin's features more than once.

Jillian stared at the door a moment after it shut, then turned and walked toward the bed. She and Devlin were going to have to tell the family that she wasn't his wife. They deserved the truth. Besides, she thought as she removed her dusty clothes, it would avoid potentially embarrassing moments.

Like wrangling over sleeping arrangements.

Jillian stared at the huge bed in front of her. As she considered spending the night on that huge mattress with Devlin, her body grew suddenly hot, despite the fact that she was clad only in her bra and panties.

It wasn't just remembered, and anticipated, passion that brought the heat to her face and everywhere else, but wondering how to deal with all this. The night before had been wonderful, magical. And it had been so because there had been nothing planned about it.

But now would come the questions—what would it mean if they made love a second time? Were they moving toward a commitment? Were his feelings as deep as hers?

These queries swirled dizzily through Jillian's head. She shook them away. She was far too tired for this. Throwing back the covers, she mounted the little stairs, slid onto the soft sheets and pulled the covers over her.

She didn't remember her head hitting the pillow.

The study door closed with a loud snap. As Andrew St. Clair crossed to his desk near the window, Devlin noticed that the once-vibrant blue-and-gold carpet was faded in spots. He was also aware of the tension in the room. His father's back was stiff with it as he reached the edge of his desk, then turned around to face his two sons. They flanked the door. Devlin automatically glanced at Colin and saw that his brother had shifted his eyes toward his older brother. A very familiar feeling, this, like two young lads who'd been caught stealing sweets from the kitchen.

Once, along with the sidelong glances there would have been barely suppressed, nervous grins. Today the two men just calmly shifted their gazes back to their father as he spoke.

"Devlin, I want to start by offering you an apology."

It was more than just the words that stunned Devlin: it was the weariness in his father's voice, the paleness of his face, and the drawn look about his eyes.

"I am quite aware that I sounded very much like my own father out there, harsh and unbending. I've had many a year to rethink the way I brought you up—you and your brother. And I see that I made some grave mistakes. I don't wish to repeat them. If you truly prefer that I sell this place rather than deed it over to you, you shall have that choice without any further comment from me."

When Devlin opened his mouth to respond, his father held up a restraining hand. "Wait. I want to explain what is going on. Your mother insists that both of you know everything that has gone into my decision. I came down ill last year, and after numerous trips to the physician, I was finally diagnosed with hepatitis B. Right now, I am doing fairly well, but the main treatment for this seems to be rest, and a relative freedom from stress."

A full minute of silence followed Andrew's words before Colin spoke. "Good Lord, Father. Why didn't you tell me? I would have been more than happy to help out."

Andrew gave his younger son a weak smile as he shook his head. "I know. But I couldn't do that to you. I know how much you love your work. I once had something I loved as well, my music. I deserted it because my father convinced me that tradition dictated I concentrate on being a good and proper earl, like all the first sons before me. And because my heart wasn't in it, I have led the family down the path of financial ruin."

He paused and turned to Devlin. "I knew from the beginning all about the scheme the two of you cooked up, to pass your rights onto Colin. I also knew the paper you'd signed was worthless, but I said nothing because I was so sure that you'd come home after a few years. I was convinced that you had strong feelings for Blodwell Hall and that these feelings would bring you home, eventually."

Devlin said nothing. His father was right. He loved the old place. Each moment he'd been here had been painful, like visiting an unforgotten love and pretending it didn't hurt to see her in the arms of another.

But he wasn't about to admit that. Not now. Stunned as he was by his father's warm manner, reminding him so sharply of the man he'd known as a young child, he had spent too much time convincing himself that he could never have the home he'd once loved to believe that this could be suddenly and easily reversed.

"Perhaps you've changed over the years," his father said softly. He straightened from his desk and approached his sons. "I don't expect an answer from you immediately. Look around the place. Think about it. You, too, Colin. If Devlin decides he doesn't want the place, I shall offer it to you before I consider the Larson offer."

Passing between the two boys, he clapped them each on the shoulder once, then opened the door and stepped out of the room, leaving Devlin staring at the framed country scene that filled the wall behind his father's desk.

"I suppose this is my fault," Colin said softly.

Devlin turned to his brother. "Hardly. I was the one who raised the Suttons' ire, if you recall."

Colin's gray eyes met Devlin's. "Yes, but most likely a few years out of the country would have been enough to calm those troubled waters. You would have never turned your inheritance over to me if I hadn't insisted that I would do such a good job of managing the place."

"Well, as you haven't had a chance to try, how do you know that you wouldn't?"

Colin gave him a tight smile. "I know. Both my secretary and my wife will tell you I am hopeless with details, financial or otherwise, unless they involve civilizations that are at least five hundred years old. I probably knew deep down that, given my passion for archaeology, I wouldn't make a great landowner, or import-exporter. Shows you what a healthy dose of sibling rivalry will do to a second son."

After Colin finished speaking, Devlin stared at him silently for several moments, weighing the words he wanted to say before he spoke.

"Speaking of sibling rivalry, I have to ask. Did you want Prudence even before she broke it off with me?"

Colin's tanned face grew several shades darker as he returned his brother's gaze. Finally he nodded.

"Yes. I fell in love with her the moment I met her, which was prior to the party in which the two of you were introduced."

"Odd." Devlin shook his head. "I always knew you sometimes envied my position as eldest son, but I had no idea how you felt about Pru."

Colin shrugged. "Well, they are two different things, now, aren't they? It's one thing to covet a house, another thing all together to covet a fiancée."

Devlin nodded slowly, then turned and stepped to the door. He placed his hand on the brass knob, then pivoted back toward his brother.

"Did she ever tell you why she refused to leave with me?"

"No." Colin took a deep breath and released it. "But I'm not a fool. I know the reason she turned to me was partially because of that paper we drew up. She thought our marriage would gain her a title. That didn't matter to me then. It doesn't matter now. She and I have drifted apart these last couple of years, but I know how to rectify that. If you don't let Father deed Blodwell Hall to you, I shall take it on. That and the title."

Devlin lifted his eyebrows. "I see. And what will you do to save your marriage if I decide I want the old place after all?"

"Work things out another way," Colin replied with a tight smile. "Prudence has often complained about how far we are from the London social scene down here. I've a standing offer to work at a museum in the city. Taking that job, and a nice Mayfair flat, will go a long way to soothing her. It's time I stopped gallivanting around, and concentrated on us, anyway."

Devlin shrugged as he opened the door. He had his doubts that anything short of a title and all that went with it would make Prudence happy. But time might have changed all that. Besides, he had no right to offer his opinion where it was so obviously not wanted.

"Devlin?"

The urgency in Colin's voice caught him as he stepped out into the hall. When he turned to his brother, Colin opened his mouth to speak, then as if he'd thought better of it, shook his head and said simply, "Dinner is at seven. Grandmother still insists on absolute punctuality."

"Or no dessert?"

Devlin managed a small smile as he asked the question. He waited until Colin's lips twitched slightly, before turning and making for the stairs.

As he mounted them, he determinedly turned his thoughts from the encounter with his father and brother, and concentrated on the shower he'd take once he got to his room. He ran into his mother as he turned the first landing. She informed him that his things had been placed temporarily in the bedroom next to his, since his wife was taking a much-needed nap.

A loud knock woke Jillian from a deep sleep. She blinked several times before she could even remember where she was. Once that information surfaced, she recalled that someone named Amelia would be coming to bring her backpack.

Jillian turned quickly to get out of bed, forgetting until she was in midair that this bed was several inches higher than the one at home. Her feet hit the floor with a thud, and she only kept from falling by grasping the sheet she'd been holding. Picking up her long sweater from the floor, she threw it on, crossed the room in stocking feet and opened the door. A woman with short gray hair, wearing a white apron over a dark blue dress, smiled at her.

"Hello, miss. Her ladyship said to bring you these."

Jillian recognized the backpack the woman handed her, but frowned at the yellow flower-print dress draped over the woman's arm.

"Her ladyship hopes you won't be offended by this," Amelia said as she held the dress out. "She sent along a pair of soft little shoes, as well, but said you shouldn't feel you have to wear any of this if you'd be more comfortable in your own clothes."

Jillian smiled at this example of legendary British politeness as she took the dress and beige shoes.

"There should be plenty of towels in the bathroom," Amelia said. "Mind, now, you must let the water run ever so long before it gets hot. Is there something I might bring you? A cup of tea, perhaps, for after your bath?"

The offer made Jillian feel less than comfortable. She knew that waiting on others was this woman's job, but being the waitee felt very awkward after a lifetime of seeing to her own needs.

"I don't think so," she replied.

"Well, just pull the cord by the bed if you change your mind. Ruth or I will be up as soon as possible, if you should find you need anything at all."

Jillian thanked the departing woman with a smile, then closed the door. She was more than capable of seeing to her own needs, starting with that bath the woman had mentioned.

The bathtub was huge. Set within a pink marble enclosure, it was some seven feet long and three feet deep. And after the requisite wait, there was more than enough hot water to make for a bone-melting soak.

After a full, luxurious half hour in the water, Jillian emerged from the water to dry her hair and get dressed. She'd just finished lining her eyes and applying a hint of blush when there was another knock at the door. The long, flowing dress brushed her legs as she crossed the room. She opened the door, half expecting to find Amelia bearing tea, and saw, instead, Devlin's smiling face.

Chapter 13

After gazing into the blend of confusion and banked anger in Devlin's midnight blue eyes, Jillian decided that his smile was definitely forced.

Other than that, he looked great. He'd changed into a crisp blue shirt and clean jeans. His jaw had that slightly shiny look that came from a recent close shave, and his still-damp hair fell onto his forehead in dark waves that made her fingers itch with the desire to touch them.

A desire that reminded her sharply that it was his room he was so politely waiting outside of.

"Come in, please," she said.

Devlin nodded. Once inside, he let the door close behind him. Jillian stepped back, expecting him to examine the room that he'd grown up in, but he seemed more interested in the filmy dress that skimmed over her breasts to flow softly to the ground.

"Your mother lent me the dress," she said.

Devlin lifted his eyes to hers. They seemed to darken as the corners crinkled. "It suits you well."

Jillian turned as heat rose to her face, and crossed to stand by the window to the left of the bed. She was aware that Devlin had followed her. The slightly cooler air near the many panes of glass removed some of the heat from her cheeks.

Still she was suddenly very aware of the fact that the bed she'd so recently risen from had once been his. She felt it was somewhat silly to be experiencing such shyness, given what had passed between them the night before. But perhaps that was the point. Those moments had been between the two of them only. There hadn't been a household of people around, thinking that they were married.

"Devlin?"

When she looked up, he was exactly where she'd sensed him, standing in front of the window, even with her, two feet away.

"Yes," he replied. The look in his eyes was cautious.

"Why did you introduce me as your wife?"

The wariness in his eyes receded, replaced by a glint of mischief.

"Shock value, I suppose. It seemed the thing to do at the time."

His lips twisted into a wry smile, which slowly faded as a frown formed above his eyes.

"I'm sorry, Jillian. This puts you in a sticky situation, I know. But it's not that big a deal. My stuff is already in the room next door. I'll just tell my mother we'll be using both rooms. Perhaps one of us is coming down with a cold, or something."

"More lies?" Jillian asked softly.

Devlin's frown deepened. He turned to stare out at the darkening sky above the trees on the horizon, sighed loudly, then turned back to her.

"Yeah. For the time being, anyway. I'm sorry, but I don't have the energy at the moment to face explaining how we actually met, let alone why I made that last bit up."

Jillian gazed into his eyes, seeing an emptiness she'd never noticed there before. Slowly she nodded.

"Rough time with your father and brother?"

Again his broad shoulders rose and fell with a sigh before he replied, "Not really. But things are more complicated than I thought."

"All right, then." Jillian reached out to take his hand. "We shall continue with our honeymoon, for the time being. But, you need to know that your mother warned me that she and your grandmother would be lying in wait, prepared to grill us on our relationship. Maybe we should work out a story for them."

Devlin's smile built slowly. The gleam returned to his dark eyes as he shook his head. "We don't have time. Dinner is served in five minutes, and it'll take us that long to get to the dining room."

His fingers tightened over hers as he turned and drew her with him toward the door. He held it open for her, and as she passed in front of him, he winked and said, "We'll just wing it."

Behind Jillian, a fire burned in the grate set within a marble hearth bracketed by five-foot-tall Doric columns. Just as she had imagined, dinner was served in a room nearly large enough to house an Olympic-size swimming pool. There was no one sitting on Jillian's left. That end of the table, at least ten place settings on each side, was empty, leaving seven people huddled at one end of the long table.

As promised, Devlin's mother peppered her son with questions about his marriage during the meal. Devlin kept his answers close to the truth, and Jillian followed his lead, including hints about the con man who'd left her at the altar, and making Devlin into the hero of the piece.

By the time the servants had cleared away the dishes that had contained ripe strawberries topped with thick Devon cream, however, Jillian was growing weary of the game, and nervous that she or Devlin would say something that would trip the other one up. She was more than relieved when Devlin turned to his mother and spoke.

"Lovely dinner, Mother." He continued to speak as he got to his feet. "Please tell Cook we enjoyed it. If you don't mind, I'm going to take Jillian on a brief tour of the house before we turn in for the night."

He waited impatiently as Jillian stood, then took her hand and led her from the room. When the door shut behind him, he released a slow breath.

"You were very good back there," Jillian said.

Devlin glanced down at Jillian's smiling face as she went on.

"I'd give you a standing ovation for that role of devoted newlywed, if I weren't already on my feet."

"Well, what can I say?" He lifted his shoulders. "Practice makes perfect. Actually, we've both gotten pretty good at pulling off this honeymoon thing, haven't we?"

Jillian's smile seemed to fade ever so slightly as she nodded.

And rightly so, Devlin thought. What had started out as a simple lark, a way to satisfy her need for money and his need for a plane trip, had evolved into something far more complex.

Somehow he'd imagined that once he reached his home and had to deal with the realities of what awaited him here, he would forget the fantasies that danced through his mind when in the company of Miss Jillian Gibson.

It wasn't happening that way. The fantasies seemed to assail him more frequently, like now, when the way her nearly shapeless dress skimmed her slender body made him acutely aware of the curves beneath.

Memories of that body melting to his brought a sudden surge of blood through his veins. At the same time, the feel of Jillian's hand within his sent a surge of electricity in its wake, and suddenly the only part of the house he wanted to show her was the room he'd grown up in—concentrating on the bed.

Again, not the time or the place, he told himself. His life was too complicated for that now. He couldn't allow himself to remember what it had felt like to lie with her, to join with her. Not when he had so many other things demanding his attention.

"Where are you going to take me?"

Jillian's question made Devlin blink. After a second's delay, he recalled the house tour he'd promised.

"To the tower section," he replied, then took her hand and led her down the hallway to their left. "The upper portions of the tower were in poor repair even before I left, so I've no doubt they're even worse now. But the ground floor houses the ballroom, which should still be in good shape. My grandparents used to hold a Christmas ball down here, once a year. They invited the usual complements of titled folk from their set in London, and the entire village of Smeaton-on-Axe."

"The entire village? The room must be huge."

"It is that. Large enough for all four hundred and forty-two villagers to rub shoulders with their *betters*—" Devlin turned to Jillian on this word and rolled his eyes "—with room to spare. The ballroom was the crowning glory of the copycat castle, created by Sir Philip Blodwell-St. Clair, fifth Earl of Axeleigh."

Devlin guided Jillian around a corner, as he continued, "The place wasn't that large, compared to some country homes, but large enough and authentically castlelike to be quite drafty. History records that Eustacia Blodwell-St. Clair died three months after the place was finished, of pneumonia."

Jillian glanced up at him. "How sad."

Devlin purposely lifted his shoulders in a nonchalant shrug. "Not really. She'd already provided her husband with a male heir."

His lips twitched at Jillian's shocked expression.

"That's a joke," he said. "Though, admittedly a bad one. However, dying of pneumonia was quite common for those times, even in normal houses. Not that Sir Philip, or anything connected to him, could be called *normal* in any way."

"How's that?"

Devlin stopped before a large oak door, his hand on a metal latch, and gave her a tiny smile.

"Wait till I show you his picture," he said. "It's in here."

Carefully watching Jillian's face, he pushed open the door to the ballroom, reached in to flick the switch. Once he saw her jaw slowly go slack and her eyes widen appropriately, he turned to share in her appreciation of the room.

It was just as he remembered. A thousand tiny lights glimmered from the huge chandelier hanging from the twenty-foot ceiling. Beneath this stretched an empty chamber large enough to house a game of soccer, though of course, the polished marble parquet floor pieced together in tones of blue, cream and gold would make for a rather dangerous surface to play on.

And combined with the gray stone walls, it made for a very cold room.

He glanced down at Jillian to see her cross her arms and shiver. Her action emphasized the tightening of her breasts, revealed the taut nipples straining at the thin fabric of her dress, and suddenly Devlin found that the room didn't feel half cool enough.

"I promise we won't stay in here long," he said, then paused to clear a voice that seemed to be having difficulty squeezing past the desire tightening his throat.

When Jillian glanced up at him, he tugged on her hand and spoke again. "Philip's picture is just down the way."

As they walked toward the center of the room, passing portrait after portrait of gone-but-never-quite-forgotten St. Clairs, Devlin gazed up at their familiar faces, then pointed to one.

"That's my grandfather. Reginald St. Clair."

As he came to a stop to stare up at the paunchy, gray-haired man, Jillian asked, "What happened to the Blodwell part of the name?"

Again he looked down at her with a half smile that was purposely enigmatic. "Well, that's part of Philip's story. Have patience." Pausing, he stepped to his right, drawing Jillian with him another ten feet, then said, "And here he is."

Devlin stopped in front of the largest of all the paintings. High above him loomed a life-size figure of a man in a tightly buckled black jacket over an elaborately ruffled white shirt. The jacket's peplum ended at the top of his tightly fitting black leggings and knee-high black boots. A slender scabbard hung from his belt, and his left hand rested on the curved handle of the sword within.

The man's pale face, framed in shoulder-length black curls, seemed to smile contemptuously as he scowled down from beneath a broad-brimmed black hat that sported a large, royal blue ostrich plume.

Devlin felt his own lips begin to curve as he stared at the picture and recalled playing pirate in this room with his brother. He could almost hear the clashing of tin swords and the boyish shouts of "En garde!" and "Avast ye, ye beggar!" echo in the long-unused room.

Decidedly preferable to the verbal sword fight the two of them had just shared in his father's study.

"*That's* Sir Philip?"

Jillian's question banished fading echoes of boyhood mock battles, and the more recent ring of angry words. Devlin turned to her as she spoke again.

"The man looks like a pirate."

"He was."

Her surprised glance brought a smile to Devlin's lips, in spite of the emotions tightening his stomach.

"His piracy was the legal sort, however. Philip Blodwell did quite a bit of work for Queen Elizabeth, scuttling

Spanish ships and relieving them of their plunder. For this, he was knighted and awarded an import-export business."

"Well, that explains the Blodwell part of the name. I take it the St. Clair portion came through marriage?"

"Right. His wife, Eustacia, was the only daughter of the Earl of Axeleigh. I'm sure that you're aware that in most English families, the title can be passed only to a male heir. A remote male cousin would inherit before a daughter, for example. But in a few families, the title can be passed through a daughter, to her male offspring."

"Well." Jillian lifted her eyebrows. "How very egalitarian. That is, if one overlooks the fact that this makes the woman into some kind of carrier of a recessive gene, like baldness."

Devlin stared at the scowl on Jillian's very serious face. When he started laughing, she turned a puzzled, almost hurt, expression to him.

"What's so funny?"

"You. You have just managed to cut through centuries of pomp and tradition to see things exactly as they are."

Jillian wrinkled up her nose. "It's that practical thing I keep telling you about. It tends to come to the fore at the oddest moments."

She paused, then shivered. "Like when I'm in danger of freezing to death. Devlin, I would really like to see more of your family, but this dress is absolutely no help in keeping me warm."

She saw Devlin's attention slip from hers, to travel down her form. Following his gaze, she frowned, until she saw the way her breasts were swelling against the filmy fabric of her dress.

The blush that heated her body almost made up for the icebox atmosphere of the room.

"I must say," Devlin whispered. "Something about that dress is doing a fair job of keeping *my* blood flowing."

Jillian's head came up with a jerk. Amusement curved Devlin's lips. She saw that same emotion, along with something deeper, smoldering in his eyes as he bent his head toward hers, to caress her lips with his.

The kiss ignited all the desire that had drawn them together the night before. His arms slid around her, pulling her to him as he kissed her more deeply. Her lips parted to release a moan. He answered with a groan that rumbled in his chest.

A sharp click announced the unlatching of the door.

Jillian realized she'd jumped and pulled back from the kiss before she recalled that whoever was entering would only come upon what they thought were two newlyweds acting just like newlyweds should.

The intruder was Colin, who glanced from her face, which she was certain was bright red, to his brother's.

"Excuse me," he said. "Father sent me to tell you that Bradley Larson has called and wishes all of us to meet with him at the pub for lunch tomorrow."

"All right."

Jillian heard the strain in Devlin's voice, and she didn't think it was all connected to the kiss they'd just shared. She was convinced of this when he released her from his arms and took her hand, holding it just a little too tightly as he started toward his brother.

"Showing her the illustrious ancestors?" Colin asked as they reached him.

"Right." Devlin drew Jillian into the hallway with him. "I'm saving the less-than-illustrious ones for later."

"Good move." Colin smiled at Jillian. "No need to frighten her too early."

"Oh, that's hardly a consideration here. Jillian knows she's safe."

Jillian was aware of an odd undercurrent beneath the brothers' banter, saw the tight smiles that they gave each other several minutes later when they reached the stairway, before Colin headed in the direction of the Yellow Room, and Devlin led her upstairs.

The trip up the stairs and down the hall to Devlin's bedroom was silent. Still holding her hand, he drew her in with him, and across to the large window again. Releasing her hand at last, he lifted a lever in the center of the window, then with a push sent each half out to open on either side, letting in the night air along with a soft, tinkling sound.

Jillian lowered herself to the cushioned window seat, leaned forward and looked out to see the light from the full moon kissing the rosebushes in the dowager countess's garden over by the far wall. Closer to the house, she noticed irregular beds, bisected by curving gravel paths.

"That's my mother's herb and vegetable patch," Devlin said quietly. "The tinkling sound you hear is made by little chimes. My mother insists, however, it's the sound of the fairies as they hurry about, comparing notes about the flowers in their charge."

Jillian glanced at Devlin. He had joined her on the cushion, drawn his feet up and was resting back against the wall inset.

"I like your mother," she said. "Your tone tells me that you doubt what she says."

He gave her one of his half smiles. "Well, in all the years I lived here, I never saw a fairy once. Did you see any at your grandmother's house?"

"No," she said softly. "But Devlin, seeing isn't always believing. Sometimes it's the other way around."

Devlin lifted his eyebrows a notch. "You sound very certain of that. Especially considering what placing your faith in Brett Turner did to your life."

Silence, accented with the soft *eek...eek* of a lonely cricket and the almost inaudible tinkling, filled the moment as Jillian stared at him. Pain twisted in her chest.

"My mistake there," she said at last, "was believing too much in him, and not enough in myself. I won't make that one again."

It was Devlin's turn to be silent.

He took a deep breath, drawing in the faint pungent scent of the plants below. Believing. Is that all it took? It had been a long time since he'd placed any of his faith in anyone or anything, other than his own abilities.

"I'm sorry." He reached over and put his hand on Jillian's arm. "I'm not normally mean on purpose."

Jillian blinked and then shrugged. "It's all right. I'm not normally so fanciful. At least I wasn't until someone pointed out my latent romantic side."

She turned slowly to him, surprising him with a wide smile. "Of course, you do know that they say it takes one to know one."

Devlin stared at her a moment before a chuckle escaped his chest as he shook his head.

"You could be right. Believe it or not, I actually find myself wanting to take this old place on."

"Really? Then the meeting with your father went well?"

"I wouldn't go that far," he said quietly. Turning, he gazed out at the moon. "But it did give me a lot to think about."

"Care to talk about it?"

Jillian's soft words brought a small smile to Devlin's lips. The tone had been just right, encouraging without being demanding—perfectly natural and honest.

He'd found himself wanting to unburden himself to Jillian off and on since the moment he'd come to get her for dinner. This wasn't like him at all. He had been accustomed for so very long to keeping everything to himself. And maybe that fact was all that was behind his sudden desire to share, to compare notes—just a buried need too long denied.

"It's odd," he started slowly. "Everything is very much the same as the day I left, and yet completely different."

"Really? How?"

"Well, for one thing, my mother is so much more—*in tune* than I remember, so much more forceful. No longer under my grandmother's thumb."

"She might have been intimidated by the woman back then. I know, I might feel a little daunted with a mother-in-law like that."

Devlin shrugged. "That could be. But Mum's not the only one who's changed. Father is completely different. We argued in his study, but for the first time I was able to catch a glimpse of the man I remember when I was younger, enthusiastic, excited. I wouldn't be surprised to learn that he's started playing the piano again. It's funny. . . ."

Devlin paused for several minutes before he continued. "All the time that I was moving from one place to another, learning from new experiences, I always pictured my parents staying exactly as I'd left them. Instead, they've been changing, too. I guess even more so, recently. Twelve years ago, my father would never have given a second thought to these Larson people, would have defended St. Clair tradition with his last farthing."

"He's really serious about selling Blodwell Hall to them?"

"He hasn't decided yet. But whether I agree to take on the title or not, he says he'd like my thoughts on the matter. I haven't told him, but I suddenly find the idea of selling the old place unthinkable, despite the fact that I believe the outmoded life-style of a huge country house is wasteful. However, I do agree with my grandmother, that Blodwell Hall should be preserved somehow, other than selling it to the National Trust and having it made into a museum."

There was a long pause before Jillian said, "I understand that some places rent part of the house out for business conventions."

Devlin shrugged, then turned to her.

"I know. But that sounds too cold. Almost an insult to the place. It's been a family home for years, not a showplace like Arundel or some of the other large old houses."

He watched Jillian's lips curve into a slow smile before she spoke.

"Oh. I see. The soul of the house would be offended by that plan."

Before Devlin could explain away his words, she hurried to complete her thought. "How about reviving the spirit of the country house, then? I've read about the wonderful amusements enjoyed in earlier ages, when people came to these places to escape the London summer. Groups of people could come down for Friday, Saturday and Sunday, say. Servants would wait on them, horses would be available for rides and garden picnics provided. The other four days of the week, Blodwell Hall would just be a family home."

Devlin stared at Jillian a moment, before nodding slowly. "We could arrange shooting parties, as well, I suppose. Of course, given my mother's love of birds, the targets would have to be restricted to clay pigeons. And you know, once my grandmother got used to the idea, she might decide to join in—it would give her a chance to play the role of Dowager Countess of Axeleigh to the hilt."

"You think it's a good idea, then?"

Devlin hesitated before he replied, "Perhaps, but..."

"But what?"

"But... a million things. My father was brutally honest about the poor state of the family finances, especially the import-export business we've relied on for our income the past several hundred years. Everywhere I looked today I saw signs of decay, of the need for very expensive repairs. And that was just a first glance."

"Oh," Jillian said. The single syllable expressed paragraphs of regret. "Money."

Devlin shook his head as he watched her turn to stare at the moon again. He should leave her to her assumptions. But to do so would mean he'd have to end the conversation, abort the decision-making process she seemed so adept at aiding.

"Actually, money might be the least of my problems."

He smiled when Jillian turned to him again.

"What do you mean, the least of your problems?"

"Well, I have half interest in eight very profitable pubs in America. Selling out would net me some very decent cash."

"Well, then, what's stopping you?"

He gazed down into her puzzled eyes, then stared out the window as his chest tightened. "The sheer impossibility of it all. If I sell those pubs, and sink all my money into some fantasy weekend hotel, there is no guarantee the plan will work, that people will come. Besides—" he turned to her slowly "—I wouldn't have the first idea where to start."

"Well, that's simple enough," she said. "All you need is a plan."

Even in the dim light Devlin could see Jillian's satisfied smile as she shrugged. "*Or,* you could do what you've been advising me to do since we met, not look down the road too far. Just start someplace and work from there. Go with what you feel."

Devlin stared at her for several moments. He got to his feet, slowly letting his lips curve into smile as he took her hand and drew her up from the cushion to stand in front of him.

"Go with what I feel?"

He placed his hands on her arms as he spoke, then gently drew her toward him.

"I was talking about the house," she said.

She was now standing a mere inch from him. The expression in her eyes was wary, but she made no attempt to pull back. Her gaze never wavered from his as Devlin bent toward her, brought his lips to within a breath of hers.

Softly he whispered, "Oh, my mistake," then kissed her.

The contact was electric, magnetic. He didn't want the kiss to end. He knew this was insane. He'd tried, all day long, to control his responses, both to Jillian and to the home he'd returned to. But he'd been fighting a losing battle on both fronts.

Especially where Jillian was concerned. He reacted to her in a way he'd reacted to no other woman. Perhaps because, for the first time in more years than he cared to remember, there were no secrets between him and the person he was holding in his arms.

Or, more likely, because that person was Jillian Gibson.

He didn't understand how he could feel this way about a woman he'd known for so short a time, but he couldn't ignore the soul-deep sense that they were made for each other. Not just because her buttocks fit perfectly into his hands as he cupped them and pressed her hips to his. Or because her mouth moved in silent communion with his. Or because her body swayed evocatively in perfect time with his.

Their minds fit, as well. He could read her emotions, and she seemed to understand him when even he didn't.

Like now.

While his hands were busy undoing each tiny button down the back of her dress, hers were working on the buttons of his shirt. They simultaneously stepped back, he to remove the shirt, she to allow the dress to slide down over her breasts and hips to pool on the floor. While she unhooked her bra, he unbuttoned and unzipped his pants and let them joined the dress at their feet.

He stared at her in the moonlight, all glimmering pale, except for the white bikini panties at her hips. Bringing his gaze up to her eyes, he reached for her, she for him. Their lips met again, their bodies melded together, hot skin against hot skin.

There was no need for words. Jillian relaxed against him as he lifted her to place her on the bed. She arched to him as he joined her to cover her body with his, moaned in response to his low groan. When he tugged on the silken panties, she lifted her hips so that he could pull them off. She parted her legs in invitation as he moved against her, sighed as he entered her, then rocked in perfect, building rhythm, until each pulse of her release matched his.

Chapter 14

Jillian awoke to a gentle rocking motion.

For one panicky moment she thought she was back in San Francisco, and that the earth there had once again decided to give the place a good shaking.

When she opened her eyes, however, she immediately recognized the huge window in Devlin's room. Bright sunlight streamed in, glowing yellow on the sapphire comforter covering her.

The bed moved again. Jillian lifted her head from the pillow, and turned to find Devlin, fully dressed, bending over the other side of the bed, pressing on the mattress.

"Awake finally, sleepyhead?" He grinned. "I've been up over an hour. I have breakfast waiting for you."

Jillian glanced at the sofa and chairs. A dome-covered tray sat on the low table in the center, and a fire blazed on the hearth beyond. A tempting, cozy sight, but she couldn't help being aware that she was completely naked beneath the sheets.

Considering that the man now standing at the foot of the

bed, gazing at her, knew every inch of her body intimately, she really shouldn't feel such shyness, but there was no changing that.

Slowly she sat up, holding the sheet to her breasts, aware that Devlin was watching her every move. She saw him smile, turn to cross the room and draw open the huge armoire. He returned to her, holding out a large brown robe.

"Here," he said. "The chill isn't off the room yet."

In a matter of minutes Jillian had the robe on and had slid from the bed to tie the belt around her waist. She followed Devlin to the table and watched as he lifted a huge stainless-steel dome from the tray to reveal a dizzying array of scrambled eggs, sausages, something she was sure must be kippers, four pieces of toast, a small bowl containing jelly, two croissants and a plate of chopped and fried potatoes. A thermos bottle occupied the center of the tray, flanked by two thick white mugs.

"Coffee, I hope," she said as she pointed to the thermos.

Devlin nodded. "That was the only thing I had to ask the cook for. The rest I unceremoniously pinched from the sideboard, before anyone could come down and question me."

His lips had twitched into a smile as he handed Jillian a plate. She took a little of each offering, filled a cup with coffee then took food and drink to the overstuffed chair nearest the fire, while Devlin lowered himself to the sofa and began eating his own plateful.

After a few bites had silenced the growling in her stomach, Jillian asked, "So, what got you up so early?"

Devlin glanced up. "You," he said.

"Me? What did I do? Don't tell me I snored?"

"No. It was something you said—last night—about this place presenting endless challenges. I've been thinking of the possibilities, and I'm anxious to check some things out."

He paused to take a sip of coffee, then a few bites of food before he asked, "Would you like to join me on my inspection tour?"

Jillian could think of nothing she'd like better. Finishing her breakfast quickly, she removed her clean jeans and white turtleneck from where someone, Amelia she supposed, had hung them in the armoire.

It took her only minutes to dress and brush the sleep tangles out of her hair, then join Devlin by the door. When he glanced questioningly at the zippered day book in her hand, she smiled.

"To take notes. You *are* serious about this, aren't you?"

He was. Jillian followed him to the kitchen, where the cook took a few moments to explain which equipment needed replacing, then outside to inspect the structures that would be used to house the garden parties that would be part of the package. As they walked through the various areas, visiting a hidden pond and the nearby dilapidated gazebo that would need replacement, Jillian watched Devlin express a cautious optimism she'd never seen before.

As they reentered their room, to freshen up for their meeting with Larson, it suddenly hit Jillian that what had appeared on the surface as a devil-may-care attitude had really been a facade, Devlin's way of hiding a cynicism born of past hurts. Now, the controlled excitement that lit his eyes and eased the lines from his features made him even more attractive, if that was possible.

It was possible, she thought as he turned from the armoire, holding a blue school blazer he'd probably outgrown at the age of fourteen, that he'd promised to lend her to spruce up her jeans and turtleneck for the coming meeting. Taking the blazer from his hand, she tossed it to the end of the bed. When Devlin looked at her in surprise, she raised herself on tiptoe, allowing her breasts to brush his chest as she did so, reached up to tunnel her fingers into his thick hair, then pulled his head down so that she could kiss him long and deep.

When the kiss ended, Devlin lifted his head, gazed into her eyes and asked, "Are you trying to distract me? Because, if so, you're doing a very good job of it."

Jillian shook her head. "No. Just responding to the moment."

He gave her a slow smile. "Well, this is one of those moments that require a choice. If we don't get downstairs soon, my family will assume I'm not interested in the old place and leave for the meeting with Larson without me."

"How soon, exactly?"

Devlin glanced at his watch. "About thirty minutes."

When his eyes shifted back to hers, Jillian smiled and pressed herself against him as she murmured, "I think we have time to spare."

Jillian sat next to Devlin in the back of the family's black Rolls-Royce, her face still warm from the quick, passionate moments she'd shared with him, followed by the rush to make themselves presentable for the meeting.

Lucinda shared the seat with them, facing the one occupied by Lord St. Clair, Prudence and Colin. The countess had her own spot in the front with Lawrence, the elderly gentleman who had been the family chauffeur for forty-five years.

The road led down toward the river. As they neared the water, the car slowed, then took a quick turn to the left. This brought Jillian's side of the car within four feet of a waist-high rock wall, giving her a stunning view of the river, some twenty feet below.

"That's quite a drop there, isn't it?"

She turned to Devlin. His eyes narrowed as he gazed out over the water.

"It is. That's the spot my car was headed for when the brakes stopped working. It's just lucky that Father managed to pull on the hand brake and turn the wheel just right, or he wouldn't be here at all."

"Luck had nothing to do with it."

The earl's words drew Jillian's attention. His smile eased some of the weary lines from his face, gave him an almost youthful appearance as he spoke again.

"That was a trick I learned in my dissolute youth, hanging out with race car drivers."

"Race car drivers?"

Devlin and Colin asked the question simultaneously as they turned to their father. The earl gave his wife a sheepish, sideways glance.

"Well, your mother and I agreed we wouldn't tell you boys about that until you were older. I guess you qualify now. I met your mother at a racetrack, you see. She was the fancy London model sent out to give the winner his cup and a kiss. I almost killed myself that day trying to get that checkered flag."

"After that kiss," Lucinda said, carrying on with the story, "I felt compelled to date him, but when it came to marriage, I balked at committing to someone who was involved in such a dangerous hobby. I didn't want any part of being a young widow. Fortunately, music was Andrew's first love, so giving up the racetrack for me was acceptable to him."

Jillian relaxed against the luxurious leather seats as Lucinda and her husband traded stories of their life B.C.—before children—during the rest of the short ride down the narrow, gently sloping road. When they entered the village, Devlin took over, pointing out to her the various shops that lined the main street, including a long, low thatched building painted a pale pink color with a sign that proclaimed it, appropriately, Rose Cottage.

A few feet past the bed-and-breakfast, the car pulled to a stop in front of a two-storied cream-and-dark-wood building. After the family had exited the car, they headed for the door beneath a weathered sign, carved with the words *The Flying Pig*.

Devlin continued to hold her hand as they followed the rest of the St. Clairs inside. The interior of the pub was very similar to The Leaf and Fig back in Oxford, but much more crowded than Shaemus's place had been.

In the center of the bar that ran across the rear, a knot of people turned from their conversations when Devlin and his family entered. A man with thin blond hair broke away and strode forward, a welcoming smile on his face.

He looked familiar, somehow, but it wasn't until he was a few feet away that Jillian recognized the slight man with the glasses as the fellow Devlin had spotted at the airport, that first day in London.

She glanced at Devlin, saw the way he watched the man carefully as he greeted his mother, father and grandmother. Then Jerome Sedgewicke turned to him, eyes wide in surprise.

"Devlin—it *is* you. I'd heard rumors that you were back, but frankly, I didn't believe them."

"Really?" Devlin took the man's outstretched hand and shook it briefly. "I saw you the first day I arrived—at Heathrow."

"You did? Why didn't you say something?"

"Well, you were standing right behind me, and didn't seem to recognize me, so I wasn't certain if it was really you."

"Oh, Lord." Jerome shook his head. "I've been rather distracted lately, I'm afraid. I sold the family business six months ago to take a position with Bradley Larson, you see, and he has me running here and there constantly. Great job, really, though one of these days I'm afraid I'll walk into the airport and run into myself leaving... but tell me about you. Where've you been keeping yourself all these years?"

Devlin seemed to hesitate. In that silence a deep voice boomed out.

"America, the old sod. And without a word to any of his old chums."

Jillian turned, looking for the source of the hearty voice. Standing behind her were two uniformed police officers.

One was about five foot ten and so thin that his uniform hung on him as loosely as it might on a hanger. He had a narrow, well-lined face and gray sideburns beneath his tall policeman's hat. The second fellow looked to be in his early thirties. He was a few inches taller than the other man, with a burly build and a freckled face.

"Evan, is that you?"

Devlin stepped toward the larger man as he spoke. When the freckled face broke into a grin, the two men shook hands, then Devlin turned to Jillian.

"I'm sorry," he said. "I'm being rude. Jillian, this is Evan Smithers. We attended school together here in the village."

"Until his lordship was sent away to Eton," the officer added.

Devlin made a face, then went on as he moved toward the older man. "And this is Albert Hornsby, who has been keeping the peace in the village for over thirty years. How are you, Hornsby?"

The older officer took his dark brown eyes off Jillian for a moment to turn to Devlin and nod as they shook hands. A moment later the officer was once again looking at Jillian from beneath a small frown. She found his intent gaze disconcerting, so when Devlin spoke again, she was grateful for the chance to turn to the man Devlin was introducing.

"And this is Jerome Sedgewicke, the future Earl of Cuppingham. Colin and I went to Oxford with Jerome and his brother, Peter."

Devlin paused, then turned to her and said, "Gentlemen, this is my wife, Jillian."

A shiver slid down Jillian's spine. There hadn't been a moment's hesitation before he'd said the word *wife*. That might be fine if it were the truth, but the word was beginning to sound like a mockery, reduced to a simple in-joke between the two of them.

This was not the place to get into this, however, so Jillian dredged up a smile, then nodded to each of the men she'd been introduced to. Jerome smiled widely in return and bowed slightly, as did Evan. Albert gave her only the briefest nod. He opened his mouth to say something, but before he could do so, Jerome spoke up.

"Bradley, there you are."

Jillian turned to the man that had stepped forward. As Sedgewicke went through the introductions again, Jillian studied the fellow that had offered to buy Blodwell Hall.

Of average height, Bradley Larson carried himself with the air of a man who knew what he wanted, and how to get it. His perfectly styled, gold brown hair gleamed in the dim light, his teeth glittered as he nodded to each man as they were introduced. His dark brown eyes narrowed ever so slightly as he took Devlin's measure then started to describe his plans for Blodwell Hall.

Before he could say more than three sentences, a loud voice called out, "Devlin St. Clair. I do not believe my eyes."

Jillian turned to the booming voice, watched a tall man with curly brown hair dressed in a tweed vest over a white shirt round the end of the bar and stride toward them, speaking loudly again.

"Where have you been keeping yourself?"

Devlin's tight features relaxed as he turned to greet the man.

"Josh Woolsey. Are you still hangin' about?"

"That I am," Josh said. "I took this place over from my dad this January last." He paused. "So what brings you down here?"

Devlin nodded toward Bradley. "This man. He's asked my family in to discuss some business."

Josh nodded. "Ah, yes. Well, the tables you requested are ready, Mr. Larson."

Jillian thought she detected a hint of coldness beneath the proprietor's polite tone. But his smile never wavered as he led Bradley and Devlin toward a large table in the corner.

As she followed Devlin, Jillian was surprised to see that his father was sitting with his wife and mother in a nearby booth, and that Jerome Sedgewicke had drawn Colin and Prudence to a table for three situated between the corner table and the bar.

Once Jillian was seated to Devlin's right, with Bradley Larson to his left, Officer Evan Smithers pulled up a chair.

"Where's Albert?" Devlin asked as Josh brought over a tray of ales.

The young officer frowned. "He went back to the office. Said something about a fax he needed to check on."

"A fax? We have a fax machine in Smeaton-on-Axe?"

"That we do." Evan lifted his mug. "Not that it gets much use. Just an excuse for some administration bloke to send out new rules to all the constables. Rules that have little to do with our life down here, of course."

The officer's words seemed a cue of some sort, for during the entire lunch, Devlin was approached by one person after another who wanted to talk about the future of the village, and to present what they considered the true wishes of the villagers.

Jillian listened with half an ear as she ate the delicious lamb stew that had been placed before her. She fought a grin as she watched frustration tighten Bradley Larson's smile each time he started to offer his proposal, only to be interrupted by yet another person who sat down to talk "for just a moment."

As one gentleman left, after telling Devlin that the town didn't need any strangers coming in to "muck things up," Jillian noticed a couple standing at the bar, who seemed to be very interested in what was going on at Devlin's table. The woman, wearing a beige coat, had chin-length, mouse brown hair and wore glasses. The man was dressed in a brown suit and had short, rust-colored hair. His features, ruddy and covered in freckles, were tight with concentration.

The object of his intense gaze seemed to be Devlin himself. Jillian watched them step away from the bar and start across the room. Just as they reached the center, Jerome Sedgewicke met them. The smaller man gave them a tight smile and spoke to the man, and shrugged. The couple glanced at each other, then at Devlin as Jerome placed his hand on the man's sleeve and spoke again.

The man and the woman turned and left the pub just as a Mrs. Leeds stepped up to the table, introduced herself as the owner of Rose Cottage, and explained she hoped that the St. Clairs' plans for the future included some ways to increase tourist trade in the village.

Devlin sighed as the woman departed. He'd grown more uncomfortable by the moment, between listening to Bradley Larson's plans to turn Blodwell Hall into an elaborate four-star hotel and a growing awareness that the villagers were looking to the St. Clair family to save the unique qualities of the area and at the same time revive a stagnant economy.

It hadn't escaped him, either, that his parents and his grandmother were politely left alone, as if they weren't part of the equation at all.

And if he were to become the earl, he realized, that was how he'd be treated, as well.

The villagers felt comfortable speaking to him now, for he'd grown up with many of them. His mother had made certain that he went to school with the local children, had them up to the house, encouraged Devlin and Colin to play on the village green.

But the moment he stepped into his father's shoes, he would become the earl. His lordship. Sir.

There would be no more cozy evenings at the pub. There would only be the work of restoring a huge old drafty house, as well as the burden of the futures of all the fine people who made Smeaton-on-Axe home and who, faced with the proposition of turning over their futures to a nameless corporation, were desperate to find a more personal savior.

Him. The future Earl of Axeleigh, if he should choose to accept the assignment.

"I want to hear more about these pubs you've set up in the States," Josh was saying.

Devlin turned his attention to the man and forced a smile as he replied. "I'm always happy to chat that up. But just now, I think it's time I got together with the family so we can discuss everything we heard today."

He was silent in the car on the way home, as was everyone else. Waiting for him to speak first, probably. Devlin fought off a shudder. He wasn't ready to speak. All the enthusiasm he'd woken up with had been drained from his soul as he listened to the divergent points of view he'd been force-fed at the pub.

The car had barely pulled up in the driveway before Devlin had the door open and was standing on the driveway. The gravel crunched beneath his feet as he strode away, making for the woods. He heard his father call to him, heard his grandmother say something about tea, but he didn't look back.

Within minutes he slipped into the dark of the woods rising behind the house. Beneath the rustling of the leaves, words echoed through his mind, "Something must be done to preserve our way of life." "Without progress, and more outside access, the village will die." "Blodwell Hall has always served Smeaton-On-Axe well. I hope it doesn't fail us now."

Finally the strenuous climb and the voices in his head had his heart racing so fast that he had to stop walking. He turned. Through the woods he could catch just a glimpse of the tower. A castle, Jillian had called Blodwell Hall, her voice filled with awe.

Castle, hell. It was a trap. An illusion from a past age that caught families and bound them to a useless, outmoded life-style.

He'd forgotten, in the emotional rush of homecoming, what it had represented to him all those years ago. It had been the house and the title that came with it that had attracted the likes of Nigel Sutton and Prudence Merryweather.

Well, he didn't need friends like that. Didn't need people hanging on to him. He could barely make his own way in life. He certainly didn't want to be responsible for a crumbling relic, as well as an entire village of people.

A twig snapped loudly in the relative silence.

Turning, Devlin saw Jillian standing ten feet away. "Your family is worried about you," she said.

Her words were spoken with no hint of recrimination, yet Jillian's soft tone only added to his irritation.

"Oh?" he said. "Why is that?"

Jillian gave him a small smile. "Well, your mother said something about your temper," she said lightly. "Prudence said something about dark moods, and—"

"Oh, let me guess," Devlin interrupted. "My father is concerned that I won't take on the title. My brother is torn between wanting the place to please his wife and a desire to continue digging into the past, while my grandmother bemoaned a way of life that might be destroyed if I don't agree to take this place on." He paused. "No doubt my mother is concerned that I might, once again, disappoint everyone."

He saw a frown form over Jillian's eyes, knew he should apologize, if not for his words then his tone of voice. But he couldn't. Not when the forest continued to feel as if it were folding in on him, trapping him.

"Actually, it was just the opposite," she replied. "They think your plans are great. They wondered—"

"You told them about the weekend parties?"

He'd stepped toward Jillian as he spoke. She took a step back, her frown more pronounced. "Well, yes. They all seemed so overwhelmed by the Larson Group's plan. They were saying how sad it was that the village might end up like so many fear, overrun by people in search of an English version of EPCOT Center, mindless of the history of the area and the fact that people were trying to have lives here."

"*Antiquated* lives," Devlin snarled. "Did any of them mention that? Certainly not my grandmother. And probably not my father or Colin, either. They won't mention a thing that might discourage me from lifting this burden from their shoulders. Both of them would only be to glad to see me chain myself to this rapidly failing wreck of a place. Lovely, won't it be, for all of them to be free to live the lives they want? Lovely for everyone but me, stuck with a place that is falling apart at the seams."

"Devlin," she said quietly. "That isn't true. Yes, the place needs repairs. But you told me you have the income. Of course, you can't do everything at once, but with a plan and some faith—"

"Oh, a plan. Your answer to everything—that and believing. What a crock. Look what believing got you. Look what believing in others got me, years ago. And as to this place, well, it isn't like believing in fairies, my girl. It will take a whole lot more than clapping some hands and believing to revive this money pit." He paused. His mouth tightened as he continued, "Besides, what if my grand plan fails? Everyone will be worse off than they are now. At least the Larson people know what they're doing."

Jillian saw the pain in his eyes, the self-doubt and anger that twisted his features, so completely different from the expression of excitement she'd seen earlier. She took a step toward him.

"Devlin, what happened? This morning you were brimming with ideas. I thought that—"

"You thought that I would settle down, leave off my wandering ways," Devlin interrupted. His eyes narrowed.

"Perhaps you even thought I'd ask you to marry me, that you'd found your little piece of Neverland here in the Village That Time Forgot."

Jillian grew very still. In the past few moments, she'd gone from sympathetically concerned to bewildered. Now she was angry.

"That is ridiculous."

"Are you going to deny that you didn't see yourself as a part of the plan I laid out this morning?"

"That's exactly what I'm going to tell you."

"Oh, then. All our little cozy scenes were just sex, then. A way for you to regain a sense of control, so that you could go back to your little, carefully planned life?"

Jillian stared at him.

"No, that wasn't it at all. It was all about learning how to take life as it comes, which oddly enough, I learned from you. It was also about falling in love with you."

She paused as the words echoed softly in the trees. Devlin's expression didn't change a bit, except to perhaps grow more wooden.

"Silly me," she said quietly. "It's pretty obvious that you were just spouting nonsense. You haven't been seizing the day, you've been running, all this time. And not just from the Suttons. From some fear of failure. And look—you've found the answer. If you don't invest too much of yourself, you can't be hurt."

She turned from him, took two steps down the hill then pivoted back to him.

"I just realized something else. You're not all that different from Brett Turner. He was an expert at fooling other people, but you're far better than that. You've learned to fool yourself. Well, the one thing that I've learned in all this, is that if you can't believe in yourself, you can't believe in anything. Goodbye, Devlin."

Jillian turned on her heel, then walked down the hill as fast as she could, trying to outdistance the knot in her stomach, the ache in her chest.

They were still with her when she reached the bedroom she'd shared with Devlin. Any hope for a private moment, in which to shed a few tears and release the burning pressure behind her eyes, was dashed when she opened the door and stepped in to find Prudence standing by the window.

"Oh, there you are," the woman said as she turned. "I was hoping you hadn't gotten lost. I thought perhaps you and I could take a walk in the garden, become better acquainted."

"No, thank you."

Jillian could barely speak, her throat was so clogged with pain and anger. Prudence stepped toward her, her forehead tightening in concern.

"Did that new husband of yours do something to upset you?" she asked.

"He's not my husband."

Prudence's pale blue eyes widened. "But he said—"

"I know what he said," Jillian interrupted as she walked toward the armoire. "But it was a lie. He can explain it to you. I'm leaving."

Taking her backpack from the floor of the closet, she grabbed the now-cleaned pants and shirt she'd worn the day before, took them to the bed and began stuffing the clothes into the canvas bag. As she turned to the bathroom to collect her brush and makeup, Prudence's soft words stopped her.

"I'm glad you told me the truth about the two of you."

Something about the woman's soft, musing tone made Jillian look up sharply to find Prudence gazing out the window. As if aware of Jillian's attention, she turned to meet Jillian's gaze and give her a small smile before speaking again.

"I just think that things are much better when the truth is on the table, don't you?"

Jillian gave the woman a quick, noncommittal shrug then walked into the bathroom. When she returned, Prudence was standing right next to the bed.

"I'm sorry to see you so distraught. Devlin was always less than sensitive. Is there anything I can do for you?"

Jillian started to shake her head, then stopped. "Yes, there is. Devlin's grandfather, Shaemus, was sending the rest of my luggage along by post. If I leave you my address in San Francisco, would you have it forwarded to me?"

"Certainly. Anything else?"

"Please give Devlin's family my apologies for my sudden departure. It's rude, I know, but I want to make it to the village and get a room at the bed-and-breakfast before it gets dark."

"Well, if you like, I could drive you. I'd offer to have Lawrence do so, but I just sent him off to Lyme Regis in the Bentley to run some errands."

Jillian shook her head. "I can use the walk. It's only about three miles, right? The time on the road will do my emotions a world of good."

Prudence accompanied Jillian to the door, then into the hall. When they reached the stairway, she placed a hand on Jillian's arm and spoke softly.

"I'm sorry, Jillian. We don't know each other at all well, I know, and I'm sure that Devlin hasn't told you anything but horrid things about me, so I understand you not wishing to confide in me. Just know that, whatever has happened between the two of you, it's best that it happened now. Devlin is, I'm afraid, not much more stable than that Brett Turner person that you almost married."

Jillian managed a nod in reply. Her throat was too tight to do anything more.

It had cleared a little by the time they reached the front door. Jillian turned from the front step to the slender woman who stood just inside the partially opened door, and managed to say thank you before walking down the steps and starting toward the village.

She reached Rose Cottage just after four, warm with the exertion of her walk, and emotionally drained. Her knock on the bright pink door of the bed-and-breakfast was answered by Mrs. Leeds. The white-haired woman Jillian recognized from the pub gazed at her through wire-framed glasses for several moments before she spoke.

"Can I help you, miss?"

"Yes. I would like to book a room for the night, if I may."

The older woman blinked one time, then stepped back to let Jillian enter. "Certainly," she said. "I have several to choose from, being as there is only one other room occupied at the time. The best offer has a nice entry onto the garden. How does that sound?"

Jillian managed a tight smile. She doubted she'd be staying long enough to walk among the flowers, let alone feel like doing such a romantic thing. Yesterday someone had mentioned a bus that made a loop between Exeter and Lyme Regis, which could only be caught at the highway. She would find out what time it passed on the way to Exeter, and make that long walk tomorrow. From Exeter, her BritRail pass would get her to London, where she could take the underground to the airport.

Her stay in England had been a lovely spell of fantasy. But it was over now. The sooner she returned to San Francisco, where she knew who she was, the better she was going to like it.

"I do serve a small tea, by the way. It only adds a pound to the price of your stay. We were just sittin' down to it when you knocked. Would you like to join us?"

Jillian was aware that she was near starving, so she nodded, then followed the woman out the back door to a small flagstone patio where four white iron tables sat under lacy umbrellas.

"Such a nice day," the woman was saying. "I love to take advantage of the pleasant weather when we have it. And it's even better when I have company."

With a sweep of her arm, the landlady drew Jillian's attention to the couple seated at the farthest table. She recognized the man and woman who'd been staring at her in the pub earlier in the day just as Mrs. Leeds said, "Come over with me and meet Mirabell and Nigel Sutton."

Chapter 15

Devlin never made it to tea.

After Jillian had stomped away, he'd turned and walked deeper into the woods, following the meandering path of a tiny stream. But no matter how fast and how far he walked, he couldn't get her words out of his head, what with the leaves above whispering the words she had not said but certainly had meant.

He was a coward.

At first he argued with the harsh rustling. All those years ago he had been right to leave Blodwell Hall. How could anyone call it cowardice, when he'd given up his birthright in order to keep his family safe from the threat of the Suttons?

But that was only half of the story. It was just as true that the crisis brought about by Robbie Sutton's attempt at revenge had enabled Devlin to escape his father's fate—Blodwell Hall and all the responsibility it represented.

This realization hit Devlin like a blow to the stomach.

His feet came to an instant halt in a clearing near the top

of the hill. He turned toward the house, drawn like the needle of a compass. The valley below was a blur of green. In the murmur of the brook to his right he heard another truth—Jillian's words again—that he'd been running all this time.

Suddenly what had seemed like a life of searching out new challenges looked like just one escape after another. Over and over he'd put all his energy into his newest pub, lovingly restoring an old building, searching out just the right antiques to bring the ambience alive, only to turn the finished project over to someone else's care. Good business, he'd told himself at the time, always ignoring the tug he felt at leaving another little piece of himself behind when he moved on.

Devlin blinked, then lowered his gaze and focused on the heap of granite and brick below.

Blodwell Hall, even in its faded state, represented far more than simply a little piece of his heart. It was a monument to the lives and loves of the generation after generation of men and women who'd lived there before him, people whose blood ran in his veins. People whose spirits would most definitely be diminished if Blodwell Hall stopped being home to the St. Clairs, no matter how well the new owners preserved it and cared for it.

This ideal sobered him far more than any of the words Jillian had thrown at him. But he wasn't sure if this new perspective changed anything. The thought of all that needed repairing remained as daunting as ever. He still wasn't sure that he possessed the stick-to-itiveness that restoring this place would require, nor was he convinced that the town wouldn't be far better served by the plan that Larson had put forth.

Devlin shook his head as he slowly made his way down the hill. His mind told him it was good business to sell to the Larson Group, but he had no doubt that the tightness in his chest was his heart rebelling at the idea of his home, the home of his ancestors, becoming an impersonal hotel.

His mind and his heart warred all the way to the room. He didn't want to go down to dinner. He dreaded the sidelong looks from his family, the silent anticipation of his decision, the decision he couldn't bring himself to make.

Devlin stood before the room he had shared with Jillian for several moments before knocking. When there was no answer, he entered. Finding it empty, he glanced at his watch and realized that he had even more to worry about. He was going to be late to dinner. And as he feared, when he entered the dining room, he found everyone else already in their seats. Everyone but Jillian and Colin.

Devlin avoided looking at his grandmother as he took a seat opposite his sister-in-law. A moment later, a servant ladled a wonderful-smelling consommé into his soup bowl. When the serving girl left, he turned to his mother.

"Where's Jillian?"

The expression shadowing Lucinda's eyes reflected a combination of weariness and suppressed emotion. "Prudence tells me that Jillian walked into the village before teatime," she said.

Stunned, Devlin stared into his mother's shadowed eyes a moment longer, then forced his attention to the clear brown broth in the bowl before him. He'd taken three spoonfuls before he realized it had no taste to it, at least none that he could detect.

Damn. He laid his spoon on the saucer beneath the bowl. He hadn't meant for Jillian to leave. In fact, he hadn't meant to say half the things he'd said to her. That was what comes, he thought, of getting to know someone so very quickly. Everything else moves just as fast. Into your life and out again, in a flash.

And what do you *care, Mr. Live-for-the-Moment?*

He could almost hear Jillian's taunting voice and the teasing lilt she'd used when calling him that, what, three days before.

How quickly teasing had become serious. And how quickly he'd turned and run when he realized just how serious. No wonder she'd compared him to Brett. No wonder she'd walked out of his life.

"Prudence, would Colin like some food sent up to him?"

Devlin glanced up at this. "Is Colin ill?"

Prudence shook her head as she dabbed a square of linen at the corner of her mouth. "No. It's Professor Johnstone who is sick. I received a call from the dig, requesting that Colin hurry back to oversee things there. Colin is up packing, and plans on leaving for London this evening, so he can make an early morning flight tomorrow."

Devlin nodded, then turned his attention to the meal before him. There was little more conversation as the meal went on, though Devlin was quite conscious of the tension in the room, the furtive looks that often flashed his way. He ignored them.

He had to speak to Jillian. As soon as dinner was over, he'd take one of the cars down to the village. He hadn't the foggiest idea what he was going to say to her. Apologize, certainly, for that remark about her making love to him in order to control his life. Beyond that, he didn't know. He could hardly make any promises about a future that seemed so uncertain.

"Devlin?"

Prudence's query came just as he was getting ready to rise from the table. When he glanced at her, she gave him a small smile.

"Colin needs a ride to Exeter," she said. "So he can take the night train to London. Lawrence may not be home for several hours, and I hate driving the Rolls, especially at night. Would you mind doing it for me?"

Jillian couldn't believe what she was doing. The constables were certain to think that she was insane.

The sun had dipped behind the western slope. Shadows spilled onto the narrow village street as she and her two companions approached the police station.

"We're going to have trouble getting them to believe us."

Jillian glanced at Nigel Sutton. He was right. *She'd* had trouble believing that his family hadn't hired the men who'd been following her and Devlin.

If not for Nigel's wife, Mirabell, she might never have listened to his story and realized that Devlin was in danger. Theirs was an oddly romantic tale. Mirabell had begun writing to Nigel in prison, in an attempt to "save his soul." They'd fallen in love, and through the woman's strong faith, Nigel had come to see the devastation his family had caused. Mirabell had made him promise that, if she married him when he was released from prison, they'd leave the country to escape his family's influence.

Jillian couldn't help thinking about what Devlin had said about the Suttons and their fondness for B movies. Part of her wanted to laugh Nigel's story off, but that would mean discounting the other things he'd told her, things that had made her aware of the possible threat to Devlin's life. She just hoped that she could convince the officers she'd met earlier in the day to keep an open mind and check the matter out.

The constables in question were coming out their office door just as Jillian, Nigel and Mirabell came up the steps. Evan stared silently at them, his freckled face an immobile mask. He glanced at Albert briefly before he turned his attention to Nigel.

"Well, Nigel Sutton, as I live and breathe," he said. "I thought I spied you in the pub earlier. You left a week ago, if I recall. When did you sneak back into town?"

Nigel returned Evan's level gaze as he replied. "This morning, Officer Smithers. And I didn't sneak, I was asked back. By Prudence St. Clair."

"Yes." Jillian stepped forward. There wasn't any time for this sort of sparring. "And it's because of Prudence that we've come to you. I have reason to believe that she plans on harming Devlin in some way. And possibly Colin."

The word *incredulous* was far too tame to describe the astonishment that raised Evan's eyebrows, or *disbelief* to describe his tone of voice as he said, "Oh, that's most interesting. I think perhaps we should go into the office, so Albert and I can give this a proper listening to."

Jillian started talking again the moment they were inside the door.

"Look, I know what I'm about to tell you will sound crazy. And I'm willing to admit that I have no proof. I'm not even positive *myself* that Devlin is in danger, but I have grave suspicions."

Evan and the still-silent Albert turned in unison as they reached the large desk in the center of the room. Simultaneously they leaned against it, crossed their arms over their chests and trained their eyes on Jillian.

"And these suspicions would be?" Evan asked.

"That Prudence lured Devlin back to Blodwell Hall so that she could kill him, or at least have him killed."

No eyebrows lifted this time. The two men just nodded ever so slightly as Evan said, "I see. And what would lead you to believe this?"

Jillian shook her head. She knew this was going to sound crazy. But she had to get it all out without allowing these men to waste a lot of time asking questions.

"Devlin came home in response to a message he read in the *San Francisco Chronicle,* assuming that Colin had placed it to alert him of an emergency at home. When Devlin and I arrived in London, the first person we saw was Jerome Sedgewicke, who, I've learned, has been spending quite a bit of time with Prudence since this Larson thing started. Anyway, not twenty minutes after seeing Jerome, Devlin was pushed off the platform as we waited for the underground. If not for a fast-thinking bystander, he could have been killed by the approaching train. Then we were followed around London by two men."

When Jillian paused to take a breath, Nigel took over. "Because I'd been asking about Dev and Colin, Devlin and

Jillian assumed that I had somehow lured him into the country, and that members of my family were lying in wait to get revenge for Devlin's having testified against me. However, that is not the case. I came looking for them to apologize for anything my family might have done in the past, and to assure them that there would be no more of that in the future."

Evan frowned. "Well, that's quite lovely, now isn't it? But what's it all got to do with some threat to Dev's life? More important, why suspect Lady Prudence of being involved?"

Jillian rushed into this opening.

"Just before I left, Prudence referred to the man I'd been engaged to by both his first and last names. I had mentioned Brett's first name, but never his last. However, at the airport, where Devlin was using my former fiancé's name and identification, Jerome Sedgewicke went through customs right behind us, apparently without recognizing Devlin. When we arrived at Blodwell Hall, Colin insisted he never placed that ad, but he did admit that he'd told his solicitor how to contact Devlin. And that solicitor just happens to be Jerome's brother. I think that Jerome learned of this, then once he and Prudence placed the properly worded ad, he watched for Devlin to arrive, then pushed him, hoping Devlin would have what looked like an unfortunate accident."

Evan's sandy eyebrows had dropped to a frown. Every freckle on his face expressed confusion. Jillian shook her head in frustration.

"Look, I know this sounds mad. But I don't think it's any secret that Prudence married Colin thinking that he would eventually become the Earl of Axeleigh. She learned that their father wanted Devlin to have another opportunity to take on his birthright. This would put an end to any chance of Prudence having any title. To make things worse, Colin really doesn't want the position, either. Jerome Sedgewicke is going to be the next Earl of Cuppingham. If she can get rid of Colin and Devlin, Prudence will inherit Colin's part of the St. Clair money, which, with the sale of Blodwell Hall, stands to be signifigant. Then she can bring her wealth to the Sedgewickes in return for the title of Countess of Cuppingham."

"Look," Nigel said, "Pru once told me that her family is descended from Henry the Eighth, on the wrong side of the blanket. Despite the fact that she has lots of company in that area, she felt the situation was very unfair and was determined to be listed among the peers of the realm, one way or another."

Jillian took over. "Possibly determined enough to kill. If Devlin died on the way here, either beneath the wheels of the subway at the airport or at the hands of the two men who followed us around London, half of her problem would be solved. Colin could be dealt with more easily, given that he spends so much time abroad, where accidents are less readily investigated."

Several moments of silence followed this last statement, moments in which the two officers stared at Jillian with inscrutable expressions. Finally Albert nodded slowly, then spoke.

"Well, there's just one thing wrong with that. We *know* who has been following you, Miss Gibson."

Jillian stared into the man's dark eyes as her stomach tightened.

"Scotland Yard," Albert said. "I thought you looked familiar when we met you at the pub earlier today. And, it turns out, a picture of you had been faxed to us just this morning. It seems that the authorities are looking for you, in connection to some international financial swindle with your fiancé, Brett Turner."

"Oh, God." Jillian shook her head in total disbelief, then pulled herself together and tried to explain. "Look, I was engaged to marry that man, but the marriage never happened. He was arrested for embezzlement and fraud and who-knows-what-else before I left San Francisco. I did come into England using his last name, but that's a very long story, and we don't have time for it now. However, I had nothing to do with his crimes, and the FBI knows that."

As the two men gazed blankly at her, Jillian felt the warmth leave her face, then drain from her arms. Her hands began to tingle. She swayed and the room seemed to darken.

Warm fingers closed around hers, and Mirabell Sutton's voice rose over the ringing in Jillian's ears.

"Officers, I'm sure you'll find that Miss Gibson is telling you the truth, but really, all that has nothing to do with *this* situation. You haven't heard the entire story. Yesterday, Prudence St. Clair rang my husband and practically begged him to get down here today. She claimed that Devlin wanted to see him. But when we started to approach Devlin at the pub, that Sedgewicke fellow stopped us and said there'd been a mistake, and that we were to leave or be arrested for harassment."

Evan's eyes narrowed, as if trying to recall the scene in the pub. Before he could say another dismissive word, Jillian stepped forward.

"Look, everyone knows that the Sutton family played some particularly nasty tricks on the St. Clairs, both before and after Nigel's trial. If someone wanted to harm Devlin, how better to cover this up than to have Nigel in the vicinity when Devlin has another accident, this one fatal?"

Evan looked closely at her. Her heart beat several times before he nodded.

"All right," he said. "I'll go up there and check on this." He turned to Albert. "Why don't you notify Scotland Yard about Miss Gibson-Turner-St. Clair here while I'm gone? Perhaps the two of you can clear that matter up over the phone."

Jillian grabbed Evan's arm and tightened her features into her best I'm-the-oldest-sister, I-mean-business expression as she said, "I'm going with you."

Evan gazed down at her a minute, then shrugged. "Let's go."

Nigel insisted on coming, too, getting into the back of the small black police car. Jillian sat to Evan's left, watching him drive, silently urging speed as they started up the dark road alongside the river.

She was probably being silly, she told herself, overreacting, even. She hoped that was the case. But the tight knot in the center of her stomach told her otherwise. From the moment that Nigel had explained what he and his wife were doing in the village, she'd had the strongest sense of impending doom.

When they reached the small stone barrier overlooking the river, marking the final turn up the hill leading to Blodwell Hall, she released a small sigh of relief. She'd be able to warn Devlin now. He would probably laugh at her, of course. The entire family would probably have a great giggle. All except Pru, of course. The woman would most likely be a little miffed, and with—

Jillian's thoughts froze as she caught sight of twin beams shining out of the night ahead.

"Oh, no," she breathed.

"What?" Evan said.

Jillian and Nigel responded at the same time. "The brakes."

Both of them, she knew, were thinking about Lord St. Clair's close brush with death so many years ago. Descending this very hill.

"Don't be silly," Evan said as he stepped on the gas. "No one would be so daft as to—"

"As to repeat a trick that had been tried and failed before?" Nigel finished. "Only if one wanted to make it look like it was the work of a member of the same family that caused the first accident."

Jillian found she was barely breathing. The level cant of the beams ahead told her that the approaching car hadn't started down the hill yet. It was still several hundred yards away, though close enough for her to recognize the hulking shape of the Rolls-Royce.

The car the earl had been driving years ago had been a small sports model. Once this larger, heavier vehicle started down the steep decline, building up speed as it rolled unchecked, nothing would prevent it from flying into the river. Certainly not a little three-foot-high by two-foot-thick rock wall.

She was aware that Evan had jammed the accelerater to the floor, that he was trying to coax all possible speed from the little car, but the steep uphill grade was fighting against him. The headlights of the larger car began to point down. The two cars were closer now, but by the time the police vehicle reached the Rolls, it would be too late for the driver of the larger car to stop, if indeed the brakes had been tampered with.

A glance at Evan's frowning face revealed doubt and indecision. There was only one thing to do. Waiting until the other car was ten feet away, Jillian grabbed the steering wheel and jerked it to the right, sending her side of the car directly into the path of the Rolls.

The impact followed in seconds, throwing her head against Evan's broad shoulder. The sound of crunching metal and breaking glass all but drowned out the officer's angry "Bloody hell!"

Jillian didn't even look at him. Her eyes were on the the fender directly in front of her, watching it crumple like an empty beer can beneath the powerful bumper of the Rolls.

A moment later, the crunching stopped. She was aware that both cars were now sliding down the gravel driveway. There was nothing she could do but pray, placing all her faith in some unseen hand that might slow them, stop them.

It happened. All motion halted for a second. The cars slid another foot, then stopped moving completely.

"Get out, both of you."

Jillian tried to obey Evan's order, but her door wouldn't budge. Before she could say anything, strong hands were tugging on her right arm, pulling her over the gearshift and hand brake, and out the driver's side door.

Jillian looked up, surprised to find Nigel at her side. "It looks like both of them are all right," he said.

Turning so quickly that she grew dizzy, Jillian saw that two men had gotten out the passenger side of the other car, and were talking to Evan. When Nigel started toward them, Jillian forced her shaky legs to follow.

"You must be right, Evan," Devlin was saying. "When I realized how quickly your car was coming up the hill, I wondered what might be up, and I tried braking. Nothing happened. If you hadn't pulled that stunt, turning in front of me before we built up any more speed, I have a feeling that Colin and I would have become part of the Larson Group's planned river tour. You know, 'And over here we have the spot where the two St. Clair brothers met their tragic end.' "

"Well, you have this young lady to thank for that," Evan said. "Not only did she turn the wheel, but she was the one who insisted that you were in danger, bringing us up here in the first place."

As Evan finished, Devlin turned to Jillian. Her face was pale in the moonlight. A thousand words raced through his mind, words that thanked her, that asked how she'd guessed he was in danger, that begged her to return to him and help him believe.

But before he could even sort all this out, let alone say a word, Evan spoke again.

"Oh, and your old friend Nigel Sutton had a help in this, as well."

Those words stunned Devlin out of his thoughts. Turning to the man behind the officer, he stared at the familiar freckled face for a long minute, then slowly shook his head.

"Nigel? You helped save me?"

A ghost of the man's once boyish, jaunty grin creased his features as he replied, "Strange but true, old friend."

"How—"

"This isn't the time for explanations," Evan interrupted. "Tell me, whose idea was it that you take this particular car?"

He turned to Colin, who was holding a piece of white cloth to the left side of his head.

"Prudence," he replied.

"And when did you last see your wife?"

"Just before we left. Jerome Sedgewicke had arrived with Bradley Larson to discuss the sale of the house with my father."

"Well, then. I say we get ourselves up there and get this all sorted out. Everyone can walk, I see."

Devlin let Evan lead the way, then take charge when they reached the house, where the family, along with Larson and Sedgewicke, had gathered in his father's study.

Standing in the corner as Evan began his interrogation, Devlin watched Prudence and Jerome closely. They were good liars, yet more than one quick, sideways glance passed between them as Evan asked his questions.

Growing weary of listening to their protestations of innocence, Devlin looked at his brother. Colin was sitting in a chair, outside the main circle. The cut on the side of his head had stopped bleeding, but the mark was obvious, as was the pain in Colin's eyes, a pain that no doubt was the result of seeing Prudence clearly for the very first time.

Devlin knew just what his brother was feeling. He also knew that the last thing Colin wanted at this time was attention, especially from him.

Another person that shunned the limelight was Jillian. She'd moved to the far end of the room, to stand in front of the fire, her arms wrapped around herself. She looked so very alone, so very small and defenseless, and yet he knew the kind of strength that resided within that fragile frame—the strength that took on the job of mother when she was still a child, the strength to attempt salvaging what she could of her life in the face of Brett Turner's betrayal, the strength to walk away from a man who couldn't stop running, even when he wanted to.

Strong *and* smart.

A shiver ran down Jillian's arms, in spite of the fire dancing on the hearth before her as she listened to Evan inform everyone that a mechanic would examine the Rolls-Royce the next day, and that more questioning would follow those findings. She didn't realize that someone had come to stand next to her until a hand fell on her shoulder. She jumped, looked up and found Devlin gazing down at her.

"Are you all right?" he asked.

She stared up into the dark, fathomless depths of his eyes for a moment before replying.

"Yes. I bumped my head against Evan's shoulder, but it's just a little tender, no big deal. And you?"

One side of his mouth twitched. "I'm fine. I had the steering wheel to hold on to. Colin cracked his head against the side window, but other than a small gash, he appears to be fine."

"I'm sorry he got hurt," she said. "I didn't know what else to—"

"Don't apologize," he said with a shake of his head. "I want to thank you. Besides, if anyone has anything to be sorry—"

"Devlin, excuse me," Evan interrupted. "Your chauffeur just returned and has offered to take the three of us back to the village. There is a matter of a Scotland Yard inquiry regarding Miss Gibson here we have to see to, so we'll be going now."

Devlin's frowning eyes held Jillian's. Silence stretched between them until Jillian managed a smile. "It's a long story," she said simply before she turned to walk out the front door for the third time that day.

Jillian sat in the chair in the constables' office, as Albert Hornsby gripped the telephone receiver, on hold with Scotland Yard. She sighed as she blinked herself awake. She decided that this had been the longest day of her life. Much longer, even, than the day of her "almost wedding."

Only five days ago. It was almost funny. That day had begun with Brett's run-in with the law, and this one was ending with it. Full circle. In less than a week.

"Miss Gibson, Detective Crummins would like to speak with you."

Jillian took the receiver with little interest. She was too wounded in both body and soul to care what Scotland Yard was planning to do to her. Send her out of the country, if she was lucky. The only thing she wanted to do was go home.

"Miss Gibson," a scratchy male voice said, "we've just learned that Brett Turner has revealed where he transferred those funds. This has, of course, cleared you of any suspicion. I wanted to apologize personally if you have been inconvenienced in any manner by this situation."

Inconvenienced?

Jillian shook her head, said, "No, everything is fine," and handed the receiver back to Officer Hornsby. If she said another word, she was certain she would dissolve into hopeless, hysterical laughter. Or tears. Or perhaps both.

"Jillian?"

Mirabell's soft voice made Jillian turn toward the woman, sitting next to Nigel. The Suttons had been reunited at the station and insisted on staying with her until the matter with the Yard was settled.

"We're leaving for the airport, first thing tomorrow morning," Mirabell said. "We have a plane to catch to New Zealand. Can we drop you anywhere?"

"Actually," Jillian replied after a minute, "the airport will be perfect."

Chapter 16

The jet hummed loudly as it waited for the last passengers to board, covering Jillian's soft sigh as she sat up from stowing the blue backpack beneath the seat in front of her.

She glanced at the empty seat next to her, then closed her eyes and rested her head back.

She was tired. Way past tired, actually. But, she told herself, at least there had been no argument at the ticket desk when she'd asked to use her ticket to return on an earlier flight.

She'd even managed to pick up a few gifts for her gran and sisters in the duty-free shop. They weren't the special sort of things she'd hoped to find in the little out-of-the-way places she'd planned on visiting. But then, nothing had gone as planned on this trip. Besides, she had the feeling that they'd enjoy the story she had to tell better than any souvenirs she could have found, anyway.

Not that they were likely to believe a word of it, at least at first.

Her lips curved as she imagined Holly's surprise at

learning that, for once, *she* wasn't the one involved in an adventure. Quiet Emily would shudder at the scary parts, and Sarah would no doubt try to analyze it all.

And Gran would pull Jillian into her arms, and let her cry as long as she needed when she told her about the love she'd found, only to lose.

Sudden tears formed behind Jillian's eyelids. She held the moisture there, telling herself that it was all right to cry, but not now. Now she wanted the romantic part of her to take a back seat to the more practical side of her personality, which was somewhat better at keeping pain and disappointment at bay, until she'd managed to get herself home.

"Oh, there you are, love. Why didn't you wait for me?"

The familiar voice brought Jillian's eyes open and her head up. She turned to her left and stared as Devlin St. Clair lowered himself into the seat next to her. The blue eyes that met hers held none of the breezy humor that had echoed in his words. They were dark with doubt and uncertainty.

She closed her eyes, then opened them. When she found Devlin hadn't disappeared, she asked, "What are you doing here?"

"Returning to San Francisco. I have business to attend to."

Of course. How could she have forgotten? Nice that *he* had something waiting for him, other than memories.

"Aren't you at all curious?"

The click of his seat belt punctuated Devlin's question. Jillian frowned.

"About what?"

"About *what?* You've already forgotten Prudence and Sedgewicke and the car?"

No, she wanted to say, *I've just put those memories away with other, more painful ones for the moment.*

"Oh—of course," she said out loud. "What happened?"

"Well, first off, Colin managed to reach someone at the dig in Italy, and learn that his presence there had *not* been requested. Lie number one for Prudence. Then the mechanic from the village determined that the brake lines on the Rolls had indeed been cut, just as you and Nigel suggested. When that came out, Jerome and Prudence fell all over each other, blaming each other. You would have enjoyed the scene. It was like the end of a 'Murder, She Wrote,' with overtones of a 'Masterpiece Theatre' mystery."

Devlin's smile didn't reach his eyes. Jillian didn't bother to return it.

"I don't suppose Colin found this amusing," she said.

The curve disappeared from Devlin's lips. "No. He'd guessed that his marriage was in trouble, but he had no idea what a truly conniving witch he'd married." He paused as he frowned. "I can't help thinking that if I'd stayed around and played the role of big brother, rather than nipping out all those years ago, he might have been spared that particular mistake."

The plane began to move backward as he finished speaking. Jillian shrugged in response to his last statement, then turned to stare out the window at the tarmac. She wanted to tell him not to blame himself, but she knew better than to waste her breath. Devlin had spent half a lifetime feeling responsible for the past, letting it control him in one way or another. She had learned the hard way that he'd become comfortable with that. Far be it from her to try to change what he so obviously didn't want changed.

"Jillian. There's more to the story."

Devlin's words drew her attention back to his face.

The frown continued to ride over his eyes as his gaze held hers.

"I went to the village this morning, looking for you," he said softly. "After Mrs. Leeds told me you'd left for the airport, I followed, worrying all the way here that you'd fly off before I got the chance to thank you."

Jillian frowned. "You did—you thanked me last night."

"Not nearly enough. I wanted to say more." A frown dropped over his eyes. "In fact, the whole family wants to offer their gratitude."

Jillian thought about the people she'd met at Blodwell Hall, and had come to like in such a short time. She'd already put all of them in a dark, walled-off corner of her soul, along with the rest of the memories of the past six days of her life, thinking that she'd never learn how they fared. Now that she had the chance, she might as well satisfy her curiosity.

"How's Colin's head?" she asked.

The frown above Devlin's eyes eased but didn't disappear as he replied, "It still hurts. The village doctor came by, diagnosed a slight concussion and ordered him to stay in bed for a few days. But, I've a feeling he'll escape to one of his digs soon."

Jillian recalled the tight expression she'd seen on Colin's face the night before and the look of betrayal that had tightened his kind features.

"There is one person who isn't too happy with you, however," Devlin said.

Jillian pulled her thoughts from Colin to ask, "Who?"

"Bradley Larson. Because of you, he's not getting the house. I told him that the tenth Earl of Axeleigh was taking over."

The *tenth* earl? Jillian felt her heart take one hard thud, then stop completely as she recalled Devlin telling her that his father was the ninth earl.

She was aware that the jet had begun taxiing forward as she stared up into Devlin's dark eyes. Finally her heart began to beat again. She took a deep breath, then said, "You?"

Devlin nodded. "I got to thinking about the explanation I gave you about the English underdog mentality, finding glory when taking on impossible odds. I decided that the odds on my restoring the house without going bankrupt should keep me rushing into the fray, blood racing, for the rest of my life."

He paused. His eyes narrowed as they gazed into hers. "Someone recently reminded me that an important ingredient in bringing something back to life is believing in it. I figure if it can work with fairies, it might work with a crumbling old house and out-of-date way of life. However, I also seem to recall that the more people who share that belief, the better the chances, and..."

Again he paused as a crease formed between his tightly drawn eyebrows.

"And...I was hoping you could help me out with that."

The jet bounced slightly as it picked up speed. Jillian's heart did the same. She swallowed, telling her heart to settle down. She tried to keep her voice light as she spoke.

"I hope you aren't about to ask me to clap my hands."

Devlin's lips twitched ever so slightly as he shook his head. "No. But I *am* going to ask for one of them."

His eyes darkened as he reached into his breast pocket. Without taking his eyes from hers, he took her and and placed something small on her palm. His voice was very deep as he asked, "Will you marry me?"

Jillian couldn't do anything but stare into his eyes.

The idea was preposterous. Six days ago, her near-marriage to a liar and a thief had convinced her that her instincts regarding men were faulty. Now she was expected to listen to the little voice that was urging her to marry a man she hardly knew.

No, she thought. That wasn't true. She and Devlin knew each other very well, had been in sync almost from the moment they'd met. They were both equal parts romantic and pragmatist. So the question was, could she let go of all her fears, and believe in the power of fate and the feelings that had drawn the two of them together?

Jillian glanced down. A gold ring lay on her palm. Within the old-fashioned filigree setting, a diamond winked in the light.

"It's been in the family for centuries, a part of Blodwell Hall. As you and I should be."

Jillian looked up to see Devlin's frown tighten into a deep scowl above his eyes. She felt tears rise to hers. She didn't try to blink them back, though. She just nodded, then croaked, "Yes."

Devlin's frown disappeared. His midnight blue eyes held hers as he leaned toward her. His warm breath caressed her cheek as his lips drew near. Several moments after their lips met, the plane took off, but Jillian felt sure that she'd started to fly the second the kiss began.

A month later, Devlin and Jillian stood in the Victorian parlor of the Gibson house in San Francisco and exchanged their vows in front of both her family and his. When it came time for the bride and groom to leave on their honeymoon, if anyone wondered why, instead of the traditional rice, they'd been given sparkling glitter, fine enough to have been collected from the wings of butterflies, or perhaps fairies, to throw at the departing couple, they didn't ask.

* * * * *